The
Scar
Rule

HEIDI
VANDERBILT

BUCHANAN BOOKS

Buchanan Books
PO Box 535
Tryon, NC 28782
info@BuchananBooks.com

ISBN-13: 978-0-9995430-8-5 (paperback)
ISBN-13: 978-0-9995430-9-2 (ebook)

Library of Congress Control Number: 2019956591
Buchanan Books, Tryon, NC

This is a work of fiction. Names, characters, businesses, places, events and incidents are either the products of the author's imagination or used fictitiously. Any resemblance to actual persons, living or dead, events, or locales is purely coincidental.

DEDICATION

FOR MY SON

Jack Harris

ACKNOWLEDGEMENTS

I'm grateful to the owners and trainers who opened their farms and barns to me.

Thanks to Pamela Reband, Pamela Uschuk and William Pitt Root, Dan B. Dobbs, Kate Christensen, Steve Cox, Liz LaFarge, Joan Weimer, Donley Watt, Linda Griffith, Cynthia Knox, Franci McMahon, Annina Lavee, G. Davis Jandrey, Cornelia and Mel Carlson, Barbara Atwood, Jose Arizpe, and Jane See White.

The art community of Rancho Linda Vista in Oracle, AZ gave me a space to write when I needed it.

Sue Day, Jessica Harrison, and Diane Samsel and Hans Picard fed me, advised me, and put me up for long periods in their guest rooms. We are still friends. I love them.

Thanks to Molly Fisk for her skills as a life coach and her fantastic laugh.

FOSH, Friends of Sound Horses, encouraged me early in the project. Readers looking for more information about soring can visit their website: www.fosh.info.

I am beyond grateful to Brad Buchanan, publisher of Buchanan Books, for his insights, attention to detail, kindness, and courage. He's a dream to work with.

Special thanks to Bernard Fierro for being there.

To the late Pam Nelson: I wish you were still here.

I hope that I've thanked everyone who helped me with The Scar Rule. If I missed anyone, I'm sorry—and grateful for your help. All errors are mine alone.

The
Scar
Rule

PROLOGUE

A YARD-WIDE SWATH OF daffodils bloomed on each side of the circular driveway that led to the huge barn at Angel Hair Walkers, an hour south of Nashville, Tennessee. Driving in for the first time, Jared Frederick admired the welcoming effect of the windblown yellow flowers. He parked his truck at the open barn door and got out. A lanky man, hardly more than a boy, greeted him, hand extended.

"I'm Dale Thornton. This is my barn. Thanks for filling in for Sam."

"No problem. He's filled in for me a few times."

"Have you shod performance Tennessee walkers before?"

"No, sir. But if they wear shoes, I can shoe them."

Dale Thornton led the way into the barn, dark and chilly out of the sun. A child of about eight sat astride a saddle rack, pretending to ride.

"Charley," Dale said. "This is Jared. He's come to shoe Field Marshal."

The kid ignored the introduction.

I

Jared saw horses looking out at him from their stalls. Only one stood in the aisle near the door. Cross ties were attached to each side of its halter. At first glance, the horse looked huge then Jared realized it was standing on massive, stacked shoes.

"Him," Dale said, gesturing at the animal's feet. "He only needs a trim and a reset."

Jared nodded, understanding that Dale wanted him to remove the shoes, shorten and shape the hooves, then replace the old shoes rather than make new ones. It was common to alternate full shoeings with resets, and more economical than paying for a new set of shoes before needed.

He stepped in close to the horse's shoulder and bent to pick up its foot. He looked at the shoe, the complicated layers of wedges, and the metal strap holding it on in addition to nails. He could get the job done. When he set the hoof down, before moving to the other foot, he felt his palm tingle then start to burn. He looked at it. The skin was reddening.

"Where are your gloves?" The speaker was a tall young woman wearing jodhpurs and boots. He hadn't noticed her before.

"I don't use gloves, ma'am," Jared answered. He couldn't keep his attention off his burning hand.

"Dale," the woman said, "he's bare-handed."

"Sam didn't tell you to bring gloves?"

"I brought them," Jared said. "But he didn't say why I should. I never use them when I work. God this hurts."

"Eudora, get him some water."

Cold water helped for a second, but the burning spread up his thumb and between his fingers. "I can't stand it. I've got to leave and find a doc."

Charley dismounted from the saddle rack and came over to look. "My dad says go to the hospital for chemical burns."

"Chemical?" Jared asked.

"You should wear gloves," the kid said.

"I'll take you," Eudora said. "I just need to get my handbag."

"I'm sorry, ma'am. I can't wait." His hand screaming in pain, he ran over a stretch of daffodils on his way out.

At the hospital, Jared's hand was treated and bandaged, but for a long time, the pain wouldn't quit. The burn left a scar he carried through his life.

PART I

CHAPTER 1

BILLIE SNOW SLID to the ground, her back against the wall of the horse show office building. She pressed her forehead against her bent knees, weary from waiting. Her neck itched with dried sweat and her teeth felt gritty. When she reached into her pocket for her cell phone, she found an envelope folded double. Her bank statement. She'd cry but she was all cried out.

At home on the ranch, she had nine horses to feed, land taxes due, the electric bill, and car and ranch insurance. Pet insurance, too, for her dog, Gulliver, in case he got kicked by a horse, hit by a truck, snakebit. She paid the monthly charge for the pet insurance, too scared of what could happen to him if she didn't. If she was careful about spending, and if nothing went wrong with the ranch, her truck or the animals, there was just enough money to last to the end of the month. Then she'd need to buy more hay.

Billie had spent most of the day hanging flyers:

HORSES BOARDED — DEVOTED CARE

typed in large maroon letters over a photo of her gray gelding,

Starship, standing in front of the mountains north of the ranch. In the bottom left corner was her name, Billie Snow, with her phone number and email address in the right corner. She had hung the flyers in a dozen feed and tack stores in and around Tucson, at the local rodeo arenas, the auction lot, and finally she'd remembered the Rio del Oro showgrounds, which was almost a half hour from her place and always bustling with horses.

Over her head, an air conditioner groaned, dribbling water into the dirt. The office door, closed against the wind and late afternoon sun, finally opened. Two girls and two boys in polished boots, sleek breeches, and white shirts scuffed past her. She lifted her head to watch them and listened to their excited chatter as they passed.

"Wait!" Billie called. When they turned, she held out a flyer in her raised hand.

They looked at her, uncertain. She might be a panhandler, a beggar, or a crazed religious zealot about to proselytize salvation and the end of the world.

"What do you want?" asked one of the girls. Her blonde ponytail protruded beneath her bowler hat. Expensive-looking sunglasses covered most of her face above a pointy nose and cleft chin.

Billie could tell that there was almost no chance these kids would be helpful, but exhaustion drove her to at least try. "I'd like you to post this flyer for me. It's for my place. I board horses. I rehabilitate injuries, and I take care of sick horses." She was talking too fast, babbling like an infomercial. But she couldn't stop. "I do some rescue work too. And there's great trail riding at my place."

The girl said, "This is a gaited horse show for Tennessee walking horses. We are totally not into trail riding." She turned away, ponytail swinging.

"But wait!" Billie called, as if she were pitching hair dye on the Home Shopping Network.

The girl looked back at her as the kids moved away. "You won't get any takers during this show."

"So when's the next one?" she called.

"Check the board," the girl yelled back. "Duh!"

Billie felt thirsty, the kind of crazy thirst that came from hours in 105-degree heat with the humidity below ten percent. There was no moisture left in her body. She stood, feeling light-headed. At the far end of the office building, she spotted a refreshment stand with *SODAS* hand-printed on orange poster board taped to the side of a freezer. She pulled a dollar bill from her pocket and headed that way.

"You got water?" Billie asked the wizened man behind the white folding table.

He opened the freezer, rummaged, brought out a frosted plastic bottle, and handed it to her. "Dollar." It sounded like, *dolor,* Spanish for pain.

She handed him the bill.

"You ride here?" His accent was south of the border.

She shook her head. Between gulps of icy water, she showed him her flyers. "I'm putting these up," she said.

"There's boards inside the barns. But they won't let you inside unless you're one of them."

"One of who?"

"Them who shows these horses that are here at this show." He leaned closer. "They don't let you inside the barns when they're here with their horses. Not like other shows here where it's all open. There's some barns that people can't go into at those shows, but they're just roped off. These walking horse people close and lock the doors. I'm here for all the shows, selling food, selling drinks. This one . . ." He shook his head.

Billie looked over his shoulder to the nearest barn. If she hadn't been so focused on drumming up business, she would have noticed the closed doors and shuttered stall windows that ran the length of the buildings. There were other oddities too. Normally at a horse show, there were horses everywhere. Horses being walked, groomed, saddled, and ridden. But at this show, she didn't see any. And, except for three or four snazzily dressed riders lolling on chairs in lengthening patches of late afternoon shade, the place looked and felt deserted.

"So, why are the barns closed?" she asked him.

"Stuff they don't want you to see."

Stuff they didn't want her to see?

Fine. She had enough going on that she didn't need to dig into the secrets of these strangers. She had given that up when she left New York and investigative journalism. No more snooping for her. No more digs into the archaeology of human wickedness. Now her life was her ranch, her horses, and her pitiful, dwindling bank account.

At least that was what she tried to tell herself, but her fascination with secrets was ingrained—immediate, profound, professional. Secrets had paid her bills. For nearly a decade, her life revolved around secrets she exposed for the magazine *Frankly*. She'd even married Frank, its founder and editor. They had eaten secrets for breakfast, digested them for lunch, and regurgitated them at dinner. *Stuff they don't want you to see* tasted better than caviar. She forgot the flyers, forgot the bills. She was transported back to her old life, searching for secrets buried like ticks in flesh.

"What kind of stuff?" she asked.

Before he could answer, another couple of riders in their mid-teens wandered up on foot, wallets in hand. They reminded her of Mutt and Jeff as they ordered hot dogs and cheeseburgers, chips, corn on the cob, kraut, chili, french fries, onion rings, and an assortment of condiments. Billie's stomach growled so loudly the taller boy guffawed. She assembled a smile on her face and managed not to slap him.

"Hey," she said. "I'd like to get these posters up on the message boards in the barns."

She sensed him hesitate so briefly it was almost imperceptible.

"Give them to me, ma'am," the short boy said around the onion rings he'd stuffed into his mouth. "I'll put them up."

The wall she was running into made her all the more determined not to back off. "I can do it myself. Just tell me where to hang them."

"You can't go into the barns," the tall one said.

"I've never been to a show where I can't go into the barns."

"Well, you're at one now." He extended a mustardy hand. "I'll be happy to put those up for you, though, ma'am."

Billie handed the flyers to him. As she walked away, she felt eyes on her back, heard the kids' silence as they watched her. Once, she had written an article about an evangelical church with a charismatic leader, a church so guarded and selective it amounted to a cult. She had the same feeling now as she'd had back when she'd left the church's meeting house. Watched.

She should be heading home. It was almost time to feed the horses their supper. Of the nine she cared for, eight were her own and one she boarded for a client. Gulliver also needed to be let out of the house for a run before he got desperate.

Billie turned to see the boy with her flyers walk to the trash bin and throw them in.

He and his friend headed off between a row of barns whose entrances were decorated with embroidered banners. Folding chairs arranged in conversation groups on ersatz emerald mini-lawns matched the banners' colors—red, royal blue, kelly green, and gold. Card tables served as bars stocked with diet sodas, bottled water, and booze; but no one was hanging out.

The first rays of sunset turned the whitewashed barn walls shades of tangerine. Shadows striped the ground. Billie looked around, wondering where to go, what to look at, what to look for. Nothing, probably. Horse shows were horse shows. Maybe she was just inventing a story worth following. But, still, where were the horses? She had to at least look before she left. She moved in closer and worked her way down the row of barns farthest from the arena, buildings so quiet they seemed almost deserted, hoping no one would notice her.

The door to the last barn stood ajar. She stepped quickly inside, the step more a reflex than a considered choice, and stood still, listening, smelling. The building reeked of dry manure heated by the long day's sun. A tiny breeze pushed through the opened doors at each end, and she was grateful for it. After baking all day in the early summer sun, the temperature inside must have been close to 120 degrees.

She didn't hear anything that alarmed her, so she wandered down the aisle, making herself look relaxed, checking out the empty stalls on either side. Some had been raked bare, others left uncleaned, mounded with dried manure and strands of hay and straw. She counted twenty-five stalls to a side, fifty altogether.

At the far end of the barn, the stalls had been enclosed, walls built, and doors hung to make tack and storage rooms. In one, a gray metal bookcase stood empty except for stacks of old magazines and newspapers. A dinged-up Bakelite radio sat unplugged on a gray metal desk. Beside it, an alarm clock lay face down. A calendar two years out of date hung askew from a nail. She opened the door opposite the one she had come in and stepped from the sweltering building out into the evening's cooler air.

She prowled between the buildings, trying to see into the stalls, hoping to spot some horses. But the windows were shut tight with shutters closed over them, which was strange because in the heat all the doors and windows should have been left open to give horses and humans a breeze. It didn't make sense. Horse shows were public events, implied by the word *show*. All her life she'd gone to horse events every chance she got—shows and rodeos, gymkhanas, barrel races, team penning, and horse races. Billie had never encountered anything like this.

Halfway down the row, she stepped up to the double doors of the barn with vehicles parked outside. A huge photo portrait showed an elegant older woman standing between two men—one white-haired, with a goatee, dressed in a maroon riding suit; and a man in work clothes who held a brush and lead rope in his hands. Cautiously, Billie pulled the door open.

Inside, she smelled horse sweat, human sweat, and fresh manure. She heard a horse snort, hooves on dirt. Almost blinded in the dark aisle, she stood still, listening, waiting for her eyes to adjust. She heard some sort of engine, voices indistinct beneath the roar. Just as her eyes got used to the gloom, the door at the far end of the barn opened, and figures passed through it as horses and people left. The door closed, and the barn went dark again. She squeezed her eyes shut then opened them.

There was nothing to see, just an ordinary aisle in a barn like hundreds of barns in Arizona. This barn had wooden walls, stall doors scalloped by decades of horse teeth, wheelbarrows heaped with filthy straw parked at intervals, and shovels and mucking forks leaning against the plank walls nearby.

Thinking of her own hungry horses and uncomfortable dog, she turned to leave.

"Quit!" She heard a man's voice, annoyed, resigned. "Quit, damn you."

She crept toward his voice. A stall door stood open. His back to her, a man crouched, shirtless. His skin had the texture of parchment, thin and wrinkled under striped, threadbare overalls. Billie recognized him as the man in work clothes in the portrait outside.

He squatted beside a palomino filly, just a yearling, judging by her stumpy foal tail. The groom wore latex gloves covered in a glistening greenish gel he must have scooped from the tub beside him. One of the filly's lower legs was already covered in the stuff. As he tried to smear some on the other leg, she stamped and pulled away.

"QUIT!" He yanked on her lead rope. When he reached

toward her, she backed away, tossing her head, her eyes rimmed in white.

Billie couldn't stop herself. "Can I help?"

He twisted toward Billie and rose stiffly from his squat, his hand drawn back into a fist.

"Who are you?" he asked.

"I'm Billie Snow. Who are you?"

"Charley. I work for Dale Thornton. He's the trainer of the horses in this barn. He won't take kindly to you being in here."

Released from the man's grip, the filly backed into the far corner of the stall.

"Is something wrong with this horse?" Billie asked, keeping her voice neutral, curious, encouraging—a technique she had refined as a reporter.

"Ma'am, you better get yourself out of here before you get yourself into serious trouble."

The filly shook the smeared leg, tapped it on the ground, and snatched it up so it hung in the air.

"Why would being here get me in trouble?" Billie moved toward the filly and touched the backs of her fingers against the quivering neck.

Charley stepped between them. She sensed powerful muscles beneath his sagging skin. He was old but strong, his arms covered in keloid scars that disappeared into the gloves. He used his body to block her view of the horse and stepped toward her.

Billie spread her hands in a gesture of submission and backed out the stall door then down the barn aisle, careful not to stumble over anything, watching him as she went. Her heart slammed around in her throat like a caged lizard.

She didn't know what she'd just seen, but it felt as wrong as if she'd witnessed a murder. *Get out of here,* she told herself. *Go! NOW!*

But she forced herself to stand still, to count her breaths, to slow them. Finally she eased out through the barn door. She stood alone outside, her heart slamming into her throat, terrified, but of what? She glanced back toward the door but no one came after her.

Bracing herself against the wall with one hand, she stilled her breathing even more and listened intently. Maybe she should just keep on going now that she was outside. Maybe not. She had seen all kinds of horsemen during her life. Some blindly fell in love with what horses could do, unaware or uncritical of how they were trained. Others saw abuse everywhere and ran to the nearest phone to make senseless trouble. She was neither, but what she'd just seen made her horrified and angry.

The groom, she figured, had even more years with horses than she did. He would recognize that she was a horseman. He would know from the way she moved around the barn, in the stall, the way she looked at the animal, knowing with a glance its age, sex, conformation, and temperament. He would know by the way she modulated her voice to let him know her anger, while not further alarming the young horse, and by the way she had pressed the backs of her fingers against the filly's neck . . . he would know damned well that was a promise of some sort—to come back, to bring help.

Billie thought that Charley would probably report her, maybe right away. He could be on the phone this minute letting his boss know that some woman named Billie Snow had seen him messing with the filly in the barn and that the woman was steaming mad.

She glanced over her shoulder, looking into the dark, but she didn't see him. She went to her truck, opened the door, and got in. She slammed the door shut and sat there, her left arm hanging out the window, jiggling her keys in her hand before inserting them and starting the engine. It was an old Chevy Silverado single-axle one-ton, white and boxy. For a moment she just sat there, listening to the throaty rumble of the idling engine. She leaned back against the seat and tipped her head back. Then she straightened and put the truck into gear and headed out toward the highway.

As she drove, Billie tried to make sense of what had just happened. Before she reached the highway, she began to feel angry at Charley for scaring her.

At the next intersection, she wrenched the truck into a U-turn and headed back. She drove down the far side of the showgrounds, circling toward Charley's barn, and parked in the shadow of a huge dumpster filled with trash from the show. She got out, quietly shut the truck door, and slipped inside the barn.

Bare bulbs hung from the ceiling, throwing cones of light that flickered with moths. Charley was gone from the stall. The filly stood tied to the wall, sweat-drenched and trembling. Her front legs were covered in bandages, and Billie saw the glisten of plastic wrap below and above the fleece. The filly had tucked her hind legs far up under her, taking the weight off her front feet. The position screamed of agony.

Billie heard footsteps limping down the aisle and slid into the empty stall beside the filly's and crouched down.

Charley hobbled like his knees hurt, like he had a new pair in his future, like he might need some new feet too. He lurched into the stall, balancing himself with the crook of one arm hooked on the door jamb. He held a small bottle with a dropper. The filly pulled harder against her rope. He bent toward her front hoof, lifted the bandage with his index finger, and squirted something onto her leg. She squealed and reared, thrashing. Calmly he went to the other side and bent to do it again.

"Stop!" Billie didn't remember getting out of her crouch and stepping forward, but there she was, at the door to the filly's stall.

"You've got no business here!" Charley shouted, limping toward her.

"What's wrong with this horse?"

He grabbed her shoulder hard, pushing her back. She struggled against his grip, trying to pry his fingers off.

"You. Are. Trespassing." He squeezed harder. "Get on out of here or I'm calling the cops."

"I've already called them," she lied.

Reflexively, his eyes flicked past her. She wrenched out of his grip and spun to face him. They stood glaring at each other. Charley didn't look any surer about what to do next than Billie. Sweat she hadn't been aware of coursed down the middle of her back and under her arms, slicked her cheeks and her upper lip. When she wiped it away, her hand shook. When she tried to swallow, she couldn't. Her tongue wouldn't move. He shoved her again, forcing her down the barn aisle and outside. Then he bolted the double door in her face.

CHAPTER 2

IF BILLIE DIDN'T get going home she would be feeding her horses after dark. She'd be walking around on ground she couldn't see among spiders, scorpions, and rattlesnakes that might or might not give a warning buzz before striking. Even if they did warn her, there was no guarantee she'd jump the right way to escape. More important was the fact that she tried never to make her animals wait for their meals and that she checked each one several times a day to make sure they were all healthy.

She pulled her cell phone out of her hip pocket and made a call. It rang a long time, and she was about to hang up when he answered. "Doc here."

"It's me. Billie."

"Howdy, m'dear."

"I know it's late, Doc. I'm sorry. But can I talk to you about something?"

"Anything."

She heard wind through the phone, and cattle. He was outside somewhere, in the near dark.

"I can call back if this is a bad time," she said.

"Couldn't be much better, Billie. I'm waiting for the folks here to catch the bull I'm supposed to castrate."

He was almost laughing, but she heard the years in his voice. Somewhere in his seventies, he was still out on the range, working into the night.

"I'm at the showgrounds, Doc. I came out here to put up flyers for my place. And I saw a horse being hurt in one of the barns.

His voice turned serious. "How was it being hurt?"

"Something was put on her front legs—on the pastern, just above the hooves. Then they were wrapped in fleece bandages with plastic wrap under them. The groom left her tied to the wall. She was trying to pull away. He came back in with a dropper and squirted something more onto her legs, under the wraps."

"Were you at a Tennessee walking horse show?" Doc sounded incredulous.

"Yes."

"I'll be darned. I didn't think we had any of those gaited horse shows way out here. In the Southeast and Midwest, even in Oregon and California. But not here. What they're doing is illegal." A crescendo of lowing drowned out his voice. "It's called soring," he said when things quieted down.

"Soring? This horse wasn't just sore! This horse was in agony!"

"Soring's what they call burning a horse's legs to make it step higher, do a gait called the Big Lick. It's one of the cruelest practices in the world of horses. Illegal, inhumane. I'm sorry it's come here."

"What should I do?"

"Nothing you can do, Billie. Lots have tried." He told her about a federal law against it. There was even a reward being offered to try to get people on the inside of the industry to turn in their bosses. But so far nothing had come of it. And the law itself made no difference. "It's damn near useless," he said. "Almost never gets enforced, and what little enforcement is done doesn't amount to even a slap on the wrist."

Through her phone, Billie heard men shouting and the bellow of an irate bull.

"Gotta go, m'dear. They've found my patient."

Billie thought that Doc had hung up when she heard his voice again.

"Billie? Those folk are dangerous, no different from the mafia. It's organized crime, and people have died trying to stop them. You stay away, you hear?"

"I do, Doc. I hear you."

She was headed back toward the barn when the door opened and a tall, heavy man in dusty black pants turned up at the cuff and a sweat-stained white shirt stepped out. Billie realized he must be Dale Thornton, the trainer Charley worked for. He was a lot older and fatter than he looked in the photo, but the white hair and beard were the same. From his shirt pocket, he pulled a pack of cigarettes, tapped one through his beard into his lips, and lit it with a match he slid from between the cellophane and the box. He shook out the flame, wet the match end with his tongue, and slipped it into his pocket. His first drag burned almost halfway to the filter. He closed his eyes, held the smoke a long time, and exhaled long and slow through his nose. He took a second drag and held in the smoke.

The door opened again, and the woman from the photo stepped out and stood beside him. She too looked much older. With ruby-painted fingernails, she pinched a cigarette from his pack. He lit it for her, and they stood close together, pulling smoke deep into their lungs, holding it, easing it back into the air. Dale paused when he spotted Billie, as if trying to decide if he knew her, then nodded a casual greeting.

Billie watched them walk away. Ignoring the nagging tug to go home and feed her animals, she stuffed her hands in her jeans pockets and followed them.

At the arena turnstile, she handed five dollars to a girl dressed all in black. The girl stamped Billie's hand with something illegible and said around her tongue stud, "Thow this if you leaf and want to get bag in."

Scuffed wooden stairs led up to the bleachers. Billie climbed, wondering what acid green lipstick like the goth girl's tasted like—key lime pie?—and if it was true that a tongue stud enhanced oral sex. She sighed. Maybe she'd gotten old, but if she met a man with a tongue stud she'd run the other way.

The sky was almost black, with a vivid swath of orange at the horizon. Billie climbed the bleachers in the open-air arena. Luna moths and June bugs flickered through the vapor lights that illuminated the stands, hammering themselves against the fluorescent rods. A large mow of hay, stacked between the barns, glittered in the lights.

There were only a few dozen people scattered through the tiers of benches, sitting alone or in small clumps—boys and girls in tight dark riding pants and white shirts, sleeves rolled up to cool their forearms. They clutched paper cups of soda between their knees and smartphones in their hands, texting with their thumbs, giggling and sighing at their palms.

Organ music coming from somewhere Billie couldn't see swung into "East Side, West Side." She leaned forward, elbows on knees. The in-gate opened and the announcer's bass voice floated over the PA system.

"Ladies and gentlemen, this is class 104. Horses four years and older ridden by our outstanding junior riders!" When the applause died down, he announced, "Riders, let's have a flat walk, please. Do the flat walk!"

Billie counted as seven horses, already lathered with sweat, entered the ring. Massive, stacked black blocks attached to the bottoms of their hooves weighted their front feet. Chains circled their ankles.

She wanted to shout, "What the fuck is this? STOP!" but she kept her mouth shut and her hand over it. And watched.

She spotted the slender girl with the blond ponytail she had seen earlier. The kid rode well, quietly, poised, her long legs almost straight, her hands raised to waist height, her eyes looking forward. She smiled as if she were the happiest, proudest equestrienne on the planet. The horse beneath her roiled along the rail, his front hooves thrown fast and high, his hind feet reaching unnaturally far forward. He looked like a huge insect, a praying mantis.

Dale, the trainer, took up a spot on the railing a few feet down from where Billie sat, a walkie-talkie in his hand, cigarette hanging from the corner of his mouth.

"There you go, Sylvie," he spoke into the handset. "Come on, kid. Use your legs! Kick! Kick! Set your hands!" He seemed about to say something else when Charley, talking into a handset of his own, moved over next to him.

"Ride him, Bo!" Billie heard Charley say to a weedy teen. "Don't quit! Think blue ribbon!" He grinned at Dale. "We've got some hot kids here, don't we?"

Dale nodded toward Sylvie. "Wish I had a dozen more like her."

"Her brother's good too," Charley objected.

"Bo doesn't give a shit. I can't believe they're siblings. She's the one and you know it."

Sylvie guided her horse to the inside of Bo's and flew past him, catching the judge's eye. Bo quickly flashed his sister the finger as she pulled away from him, navigating her way through the other horses, keeping herself in front of the judge. Billie recognized the boy as the charmer who tossed her flyers.

The announcer asked for the running walk, and the horses moved around faster, laboring, foam dripping down their necks and flanks. A big chestnut mare ridden by a skinny girl in a bowler hat stopped suddenly, hopping a few strides on three legs. The rider looked down and cursed. The mare stood like a woman who had broken the heel off her high-heeled shoes. On the ground behind her lay the black stacked shoe she'd been wearing, still attached to part of her hoof. Billie gasped but no one else seemed concerned. Kids still texted. Adults continued their conversations as if nothing remarkable had happened. The announcer called for a veterinarian and farrier to come to the arena out-gate. The rider dismounted and led the hobbling mare out of the ring.

"And again, the flat walk, riders, please," the announcer asked, and the horses and riders resumed circling in front of the judge.

Billie scanned the young riders' faces. No one seemed upset or even concerned. It appeared to be normal that one of these horses would tear off part of its hoof, but in her entire life, Billie had never seen this happen.

Dale and Charley spoke into the handsets to coach their riders until the announcer asked for a halt and reverse.

As the riders got their horses to stop and turn around, lumbering and cumbersome in their huge shoes, Billie overheard Dale tell Charley, "I told Eudora the sand's so deep it'll pull the hair off the horse's legs."

Billie looked down at the arena. The sand was nothing exceptional as far as she could tell. Just normal arena footing. She couldn't imagine why it would remove hair, unless it had something to do with the stuff she'd seen Charley put on the filly's legs in the barn.

The announcer called for the flat walk in the new direction, then the running walk again. Flecks of white foamy sweat flew off the horses. When he called for the riders to line up, the horses stood panting, their sides heaving. They shifted their weight off their front legs onto splayed hind legs.

Sylvie won and, to the sound of flickering applause, spurred her horse into a victory lap. She and Bo dismounted at the out-gate and led their horses toward a truck parked under a vapor light.

Billie followed as they approached a sunburned man in khaki pants, a white shirt, and a wide-brimmed hat, lounging on the truck tailgate. He sipped on a can of Dr Pepper, his feet propped on a folding chair with a flimsy striped umbrella attached to its back. A sign propped against the truck fender read, *INSPECTOR: All horses, all classes.* She had never seen inspectors at horse shows and wondered why he was here, but by then a string of horses and riders had lined up behind Sylvie.

She watched Sylvie bend and unbuckle the chains wrapped around her horse's legs, preparing to show him to the inspector. Billie thought she spotted a trickle of blood running down the back of the pastern, over the bulb of the heel and into the dirt. Charley appeared beside Sylvie, bent to scoop a handful of sand, and tossed it against the horse's leg. The blood disappeared.

"Howdy," Charley boomed at the inspector. "Hotter 'n hotter ain't it?"

Billie listened to them chat as the man glanced at the horse's lower legs and feet.

"You headed to Tennessee for the Big Show come August?" Charley asked, his tone relaxed and friendly. "Dale's taking the whole barn so I'll be coming along too."

"Me too," Sylvie smiled.

The inspector nodded. "Yep, I'll be there. High point of my year. Wouldn't miss it." He lifted one front leg, examined it, and set it down. When he tried to lift the other, the horse pulled away. The inspector bent over for a closer look. He glanced up at Sylvie then at Charley, shook his head and straightened. As he reached for the clipboard on the truck's tailgate, Billie saw Charley's hand come out of his pocket, fingers extended, thumb folded under, like a magician doing a card trick. The inspector set the clipboard back down and reached out to shake the groom's hand.

"Always a pleasure to see you," Charley said. "Thanks for a job well done."

CHAPTER 3

NIGHT HAD FALLEN by the time Billie got home. She fed the horses under a thick blanket of stars, dropping flakes of hay on the ground and scoops of pellets into buckets hung on fences. Starship had his own corral, as did Hashtag, the only horse who boarded with her. The rescues she'd taken in who were now hers shared a pasture. Her small terrier, Gulliver, who viewed the world as an unruly place that could be barked into submission, ran in looping circles around her, yapping at invisible threats.

She filled the horses' water buckets and checked that the door to the feed shed was closed and latched. None of the horses would try to escape, but Hashtag unlatched the gate to her corral any chance she got and headed over to the feed shed to try to jimmy that door open. Once, she broke into the shed and devoured so much grain Billie had had to call Doc out to treat the mare before she foundered or colicked. Since then, Billie double-checked the chain on Hashtag's gate every night.

She climbed the hill to her casita on foot. The driveway was a tenth of a mile long and so steep that, when driving, she would put the truck into four-wheel drive. She paused to catch her breath where the driveway leveled before reaching the casita. No amount of climbing that hill seemed to make her fit enough to do it without gasping. The tiny adobe building had been built over a hundred years ago by her great grandfather for his hired hands. It was the only surviving structure on this old cattle ranch that had passed from generation to generation of Snows, ignored until Billie told her grandmother that she wanted it. When her grandparents died, she inherited it. She made a mental note to paint the front door—blue or red?—opened the door and stepped into the homey smell of hot, dry adobe.

She fed Gulliver in the kitchen then they settled onto the futon in the casita's one room. As Billie ran her fingertips up the little dog's muzzle, between his eyes, and down his neck, Gully sighed and rested his black chin on her thigh.

Eventually he hopped off the futon. Billie headed back to the kitchen and searched through the refrigerator. She found half of a veggie burrito that she had bought at a taco shop in Tucson a couple of days ago. It was wrapped in greasy paper and cradled in a white cardboard container. Nuked, it would do fine. She caught a glimpse of her reflection in the darkened kitchen window, lit by the bathroom lights. Her hair, dark brown, almost black, was rough cut above her ears, styled by herself with the horse clippers. Her latest buzz had taken it down to her scalp, but it had grown and was about two inches long all over now. She liked it.

She poured a water glass full of white wine and made her way back to the futon. On the end table nearby the answering machine light flashed. She ignored it, leaned against the futon pillows, swallowed a gulp of wine, shuddered, and downed most of the rest fast. Images from the day floated in front of everything she did. The groom. The filly. Her terror.

Billie rose and carried the almost empty wine glass into the bathroom and set it beside the sink.

She ran hot water into the claw-footed tub that had been her grandmother's, then her mother's. When it filled, she padded back to the fridge for the wine bottle then kicked off her jeans and dropped her T-shirt on the floor beside the tub. Grateful for this end to her day, she climbed into the tub and leaned back.

A horse whinnied in the barnyard—one sharp call. She recognized Starship's voice, higher than the other horses', as if he were still a foal and not a middle-aged gelding. When his horse friends left him behind in his corral and climbed the hill of their pasture without him, he objected with a series of plaintive don't-leave-me whinnies. But this one was different.

From the tub, Billie listened for what would come next so she'd know what he was talking about. He had a special call if he'd hurt himself and wanted her, another if Hashtag opened the gate and wandered away. When she didn't hear anything else from him, she poured more wine. She avoided the mirror, didn't want to be faced with the parallel scars on her upper thighs and the insides of her arms.

Something rattled in the barnyard. She grabbed her towel, looked out the bathroom window, and saw red taillights heading away from her place, down the road, toward the distant highway. That could be Sam and Josie Wilde, her neighbors up the valley, heading to the highway for an evening at DT's

Bar and Grill, or their son Ty on his way home after visiting them.

Gulliver was asleep, not barking at the disturbance, but Billie felt uneasy. She set the bottle and glass down, pulled on her soiled jeans and T-shirt, and wiggled her feet into her boots. Alerted to an outing, Gulliver raced to the door.

Using her cell phone's flashlight, she scuffed down the hill to check, slipping on loose gravel, watching as best she could for rattlers. Gulliver trotted beside her, wary of something. Near the bottom of the hill, staring into the dark, he growled, ears pricked. It could have been anything—a coyote, a white-tailed deer, a herd of javelinas, a cactus—anything at all.

They walked from corral to corral, checking on the horses. They all seemed fine, ghostly in the starlight, whuffling to her, hoping for a slice of apple or a carrot. Billie stopped in front of Starship's gate and whistled for him. Almost invisible in the dark, the gray horse moved in next to her. She scratched his withers, pressed her cheek against his, breathed into his breath.

How could anyone deliberately hurt these sweet, gentle creatures? She didn't mean the question literally. She knew better than most that people would do anything they wanted. She could consult any part of her being for reminders of that. But standing with her horse's head against hers, their breaths mingled, she asked it as an expression of outrage. Not "how could" but "how dare."

Without wanting or even meaning to, she started thinking about an article, using the same techniques she used for exposés for Frank. She asked the five *W* questions and *how:* Who was doing this? What was being done? Where was it happening—at the horse show here, but where else? When did it start, and why do it? And lastly how far did the problem reach? As she climbed back up the hill to her casita, the questions flopped around in her head.

Back in her kitchen, she rescued a moth from her wine and poured herself a little more. The tub had drained itself halfway while she was out, so she turned on the tap and added hot water. This time she tossed her clothes into the wicker basket she used as a hamper, and without thinking, stepped into the tub. Too hot. Much too hot. The burn started in her instep and spread up her leg. She pulled back out as fast as she could and turned on the cold water, but after a month of hundred-degree days, there wasn't any cold water in the pipes. She sat on the toilet to wait, looking at her reddened ankles and feet that still burned. Once, in some awful tabloid she had picked up at a supermarket, she'd read a story about two men captured by savages who boiled them alive. The description of their agonies had horrified her, but she couldn't stop reading. Now, a decade later, the story came surging back.

What if she couldn't have stepped out of the tub? What if her legs were being smeared with chemicals, wrapped to make the pain worse, to force the burn deeper? What if she then was tied to a wall and left to suffer?

She flicked the inside of her arm with her fingernail, hard, harder until the small sharp stings pulled her back from her imagining. *Stay present,* she ordered herself with each little flick. *Stay right here.* Between the nails of her thumb and index finger, she pinched soft skin then twisted.

Her wine glass sat on the floor beside the tub, just within her reach. She wanted to let go of the day, drink it away, until the sight of the tortured horse, the feel of Charley grabbing her shoulder, floated away. She wanted to take a pill, sleep a dozen hours, wake rested and solvent and sure that what she had seen today wasn't real. But her horses might need her tonight; she couldn't just let go. At least not all the way. She slid into the bathwater, tolerable now, until it lapped at the nape of her neck. Then she closed her eyes and relaxed.

After the bath, Billie played the messages on the answering machine: Bank of America, the insurance company, and a hang-up. She checked the caller ID and recognized her ex-husband Frank's number. Billie ran her tongue around the lip of the wine glass.

She chose old cotton pajama bottoms and a loose tank top from one of the baskets where she kept her clothes. She lay down on the futon and pulled a thin sheet over herself. Gulliver hopped onto the bed and nosed underneath the sheet to curl against her belly.

The phone wakened her. Two rings, a pause, three rings, a pause. She picked up on the next ring.

"It's late," she said.

"Not really." Frank's voice sounded lively, energetic. "Not even one yet here."

That made it almost ten Billie's time. "I thought it was later. I was asleep."

Gulliver had shoved deeper under the sheet, his chin now resting on her foot.

"What are you wearing, sweetheart?"

What was she wearing? She glanced down at her tank top and pajama bottoms. "Clothes."

"You went to bed in your clothes?"

"Frank," she sighed, "why are you calling?"

"I'm coming to Tucson for an editors' conference. I'd love to see you, Billie."

She felt the pull back toward him, his voice so familiar. She heard the way he used to talk to her when they made love, felt the way he had held her.

"Not a good idea," she said.

He didn't say anything. Her eyes closed and she listened to him breathe. They used to talk like this every night when they were married if either of them was away from home. After the divorce, they had hardly spoken at all, but then they had drifted back into the habit. He would call. If she were alone, she'd answer. Old friends, she told herself. Good old friends.

"Come back to work for me, sweetheart. You're the best writer I ever had. No one could go after the ugly stuff better than you. You won't spook again. You're tough as they come. And I've got this great lead . . ."

The tug she felt turned into a tidal wave of longing for her career, the thrill of getting a new assignment and starting to dig into the worst forms of cruelty—hours that turned to days and weeks when she would explore lives gone horribly wrong, would listen to stories told a myriad of ways to justify atrocities. With that longing came fury. Frank McMannis, her husband, editor, and boss, had pushed her deeper and deeper until, finally . . .

"No," she said. "I don't want to talk about it, think about it, remember any of it. No." She listened to the silence that followed, then to a subtle shift in his breathing. She still knew him so well that she knew what this meant. He was finished with her. For now . . .

"Good night, Billie." He hung up.

She replaced the receiver, turned on her side, and slipped her hand under the elastic waistband of her pajamas.

She woke in the morning to the taste of Frank. Not the taste of his body, although that remained as vivid today as when she'd left him. She had tried to erase it with other men in the same way she had cleansed the casita when she'd moved here, blasting it with air fresheners and scrubs, scented candles and incense, and burning cedar, sage, and sweetgrass. Despite her efforts, the little building kept its own flavor, especially pungent during monsoon season when every year the late summer rains freed the scents of those who had lived there before her: migrants and outlaws, ranch hands and fugitives. But summer had barely started. The rains wouldn't come for weeks.

The taste in her mouth was of her work back in New York, the career she'd once had, the metallic rain, the stench of gasoline on pavement, the scream of sirens.

She stretched, realized she'd been waiting for the screech owl who lived in the juniper outside her window and woke her each morning before dawn. She hadn't heard it this morning, or maybe she'd slept through it. She lay under the sheet, watched the sky turn opalescent then pink, felt the air in the room heat up, listened for something she couldn't hear.

She got up and, chilly in the thin pajamas, walked down the snaking driveway to the barnyard. Gulliver skittered around her, just beyond her footfall, almost tripping her then bounding away. She could feel Frank still with her, as though he'd preceded her down the hill, as if, when she reached the bottom, he'd be there, his iPad in one hand, cell phone pressed to his ear, telling her where to go, what to do, what to write about. "By Tuesday, by God!" he'd shout, and she would have her assignment and her deadline.

The horses nickered as she approached. She fed them thick flakes of alfalfa, all except Starship. He got a scoop of pellets—a quick nourishing meal. Billie leaned against the gate to his corral as he ate. Tire marks in the dirt—not hers—caught her eye, and she followed them a few steps. Someone had driven in, followed the fence line past the corrals, circled the barn, and then left. Those must have been the lights she'd seen from the casita. Sam and Josie or Ty might have driven in to check on something. UPS and FedEx left parcels for her neighbors in Billie's feed shed rather than drive the rutted mile to their place. But when that happened, Billie would call to alert them of a delivery, or if they checked first, they would call to let her know. People didn't just stop by out here. If her neighbors had driven into her barnyard, they would have told her.

She slipped a halter onto Starship's head, climbed the fence, and from there slid onto his smooth back. In no way did he resemble the starved creature he was that day she had seen him in a herd at the local auction, bones all of them, being whipped into the van of the kill buyer who had bought them to sell to slaughter in Mexico.

"How much?" Billie had asked him. The price he quoted her was for the horse by weight, as meat. "How much for the others too?" she had asked.

He had laughed at her, refused her check, and only when she paid with cash, plus extra for delivery, had he agreed to unload the eight breathing skeletons at her ranch. That had been three years ago. She'd planned to find homes for them all, but they were still with her, still eating her hay.

Starship carried her out the gate and down the road for a half mile while she followed the tire marks until they disappeared in a deep sand wash crisscrossed by the wheels of every rancher out here.

Feeling the soft morning air, breathing Starship's warm scent, Billie wanted to ride all day with no destination, safe from bills and money worries, her cell phone turned off. She wanted to ride until she was exhausted and hot and dying to go home, but she couldn't. Images of the horse show intruded along with the taillights she'd seen last night, the tire marks, and the filly's scream. She needed to figure out who had trespassed into her barnyard in the dark. Was it someone from the show? Charley, the man who threatened her? She turned Starship around, dread in her gut, and headed back home along the dirt road.

A faded blue pickup raced toward them, braked and skidded. Billie hadn't noticed it approach. Startled, she saw Sam and Josie gaping at her through their filthy windshield. Both had cigarettes between their lips and wore bandanas around their turkey necks. As the truck fishtailed, Starship spooked sideways and Billie fell, landing in a mound of dirt and sand. The reins pulled out of her hand, and her horse sidestepped away from her.

"Sorry!" Sam leapt out and stood over her, his hand stretched down, and pulled her to her feet. "Didn't see you."

"No problem, Sam. I didn't see you either."

She reached for Starship's reins, but he realized he was on his own, flagged his tail over his back, and snorted. He galloped, farting, for home and the hay pile. Gulliver chased him, yipping.

"Never thought much of a horse that wouldn't wait for its fallen rider," Josie said. She leaned her elbows on the open window and gnawed her home-rolled. More than once she had told Billie that she and Sam had run a pack outfit years ago and took high-paying dudes into the mountains for a week. "Where Wilde Meets Wild" had been their slogan, Wilde being their last names. To this day, they had a lot of opinions about things Billie did wrong. They enjoyed not mentioning them to her, which Billie appreciated, but she could tell when they were not saying something.

Billie's right forearm felt raw, so she knew she'd pulled the skin off it again. She had broken so many falls by putting out that arm that the skin there was puckered and white, and with each new injury, it got lumpier and whiter when it healed.

"You're bleeding," Sam said.

"Bit your lip," Josie added. She gave Billie the bandana from around her neck.

Billie pressed it to her mouth, feeling to see if she had knocked out a tooth. Everything seemed to be in place. But the reek of cigarette smoke on the fabric made her hand the bandana back.

"We're late for work," Sam said. They owned an equipment rental place several exits to the west on the highway. "You plannin' on livin' or you want I should get a backhoe and bury you?"

"I'll be fine." Billie ran her tongue over the swelling on her lip.

"You want a lift to your house?" Josie asked.

That sounded good, but Billie didn't want to admit it, or to crowd onto the bench seat of their truck, her knees crammed against the overflowing ashtray, to listen to a lecture on their glory days as horsemen up in the Grand Tetons. She shook her head no.

"Guess I'll go catch my pony."

Sam climbed back into the pickup, leaned across the seat, and rolled down the crank window. "Out here," he said, "most of us wear denim and leather when we ride."

They drove off before Billie realized he was referring to her pajamas. Then she noticed the bottoms had ripped open from knee to hip, showing a lot of scraped leg.

She hobbled after Starship. Whenever she got close to catching him, he trotted off until he was out of reach then dropped his head to lip up whatever bits of weeds he found. Her leg was throbbing before he quit playing games and let her catch him and return him to his corral. When she climbed up the hill to the casita, every step hurt. In the kitchen, she sadly ripped what was left of her favorite pajamas into rags and jammed them under the sink.

The shower stung her scrapes. But when she looked in the bathroom mirror, she didn't think she had added any new scars to the old ones. Today's dings would heal up and not leave any stories behind. She pulled on shorts—careful not to rub the scrapes on her leg—and a lilac sleeveless top that showed off her bruised and ropy arms. After slapping a Band-Aid on her peeled elbow, she grabbed the baseball cap with her ranch logo on it—a silhouette of Gulliver leading Starship, reins in his mouth. Very cute.

CHAPTER 4

A HUNDRED AND FIFTY years ago, the Depot Feed Store had been a stop on the Butterfield stagecoach route. The adobe building had sheltered travelers waiting to be picked up and transported west to San Diego or east to El Paso. Tickets sold from behind an iron grille were passed from ticket agent to passenger over a mesquite counter. The dirt floors had been covered with coarsely woven rugs and horse blankets worn to tatters by filthy boots. Not much had been done to spruce up the Depot since then. Over the years the roof had thickened, layer being added to layer of whatever was available to keep things from blowing off—tiles and shingles, tar paper and tin, and finally, in the last twenty years, tires from cars and trucks heaved up and arranged in rows by size. A half-moon of dirt swept to the edge of a wobbly porch whose splintered stairs sagged under piles of buckets, metal horse troughs, and exhausted potted saplings.

Billie parked beside a silver dually one-ton Dodge truck, a monster with two tires in front and four behind, loaded with bales of alfalfa and Bermuda hay. She imagined she could smell the clean of that brand new dually, see the salesman's fingerprints still on the side mirrors. The truck wasn't even dusty. She glanced around, looking for its owner. But all she saw in the yard was the Depot's trio of antique red gasoline pumps.

She opened her own pockmarked truck's door to let Gulliver out, propping it with her foot it so it wouldn't swing shut as the terrier leapt down. She climbed out after him, slammed the door, and left the Chevy unlocked. With its single headlight and missing tailgate, no one would try to steal it anyway.

Inside the old adobe, the iron grill hung in its original place, and what remained of the rugs were nailed to the walls for decoration, along with feed sack covers, antique spurs, and twisted amber curls of flypaper.

"Hot 'nuf for yeh?" the owner, Ty Wilde, son of her neighbors, asked.

Billie was too tired for the tattered cowboy routine. She knew that Ty had graduated magna cum laude from the University of Arizona with a degree in equine studies. She had found his diploma in the Depot bathroom a couple of years before, framed and under glass, tucked into a stack of catalogs advertising chickens and their accoutrements. She hadn't told him she'd seen it, but she knew damn well that Cow Patty wasn't his native tongue.

One night last year at DT's Bar and Grill out on the highway, he had asked her if she'd care to join him. He hadn't specified where or for what, but she sensed he didn't want to be alone. She had perched beside him on a barstool and hooked her thumbs around her wine glass stem while he expounded on an elaborate conspiracy theory about chemtrails and jihad.

"You're kidding, right?" she had asked when he wound down.

He stared into his mug of Tombstone Double IPA. "Maybe. You never know."

"Never know what?"

"I thought you'd be interested."

"I was interested, just not persuaded."

"Not persuaded by me?"

She felt wary, as if she had to be careful or she'd hurt his feelings. "I don't believe the government is spraying me with chemicals, Ty. And if they are, I don't think I can do anything about it, so I'm not going to worry about it."

"Ah." He had looked for a while longer at the dregs of his beer while she tried unsuccessfully to think of something to say that would change the subject. Then he reached into his shirt pocket and placed a ten-dollar bill on the counter, smoothing it with the side of his hand. "Okay." He stood and, tucking his shirttail into his belt, gave her shoulder an awkward pat. "Well, I'm off to see my folks. Hope to see you around."

DT had lumbered down the bar toward the money and pocketed it while pouring Billie another white wine.

"He strike out?" the old man asked her.

She hadn't answered.

Now in the Depot, sniffing along every aisle, Gulliver toured Ty's store, tail wagging. Ty leaned against the counter, a pencil balanced on top of his ear, an order pad folded back to a blank page in front of him.

"Can I help you, Billie?" he asked.

"I need some Equine Senior feed."

"Gotcha." He never referred to their drink that night. "One? Two?"

"One." At twenty-five dollars for each sack of grain, a single fifty-pound bag was all she could afford. It wouldn't last long, a day or two if she was careful about doling it out. All the horses she rescued at the auction had gained weight, but Starship was middle-aged and couldn't maintain his weight on hay alone. She needed to supplement his diet.

"Nothing else?" Ty asked.

Billie shook her head no, thinking of the long list of things she really did need, oats and fly spray especially. Hashtag had already torn her fly mask, and Billie didn't want to tell the owner her mare needed a new one. Running up someone's board bill pretty much guaranteed that the boarder would be taken away and business lost. She would replace the mask herself when she could.

While Ty went to the storage shed to get the sack of senior feed, and Gulliver nosed through a bin of shrink-wrapped trotters, Billie wandered toward the bulletin board at the back of the store to check on the flyers she had put up yesterday. Maybe they would all be gone by now, signaling a rush on her services. And maybe when she got home later, the answering machine would be filled with requests to board horses, dozens of horses, hundreds at her place. They'd ask what she charged and pay her double. Sure.

At least someone was looking at them. The man was just a bit taller than Billie, maybe five foot eight or nine. He was stocky with curly hair streaked with gray that once might have been red. Afternoon stubble speckled his jaw. His shirt looked clean, and he had rolled the cuffs above his elbows. She could tell he needed reading glasses by the way he leaned away from the board and squinted.

"That's my flyer," Billie said.

He turned to look at her.

"I board horses."

"Devoted care," he read aloud. "Sounds pretty nice."

"It *is* nice," she said. *Inane,* she thought. *I'm an idiot.*

"What do you charge?"

Billie quelled an urge to offer him a deal.

"Is that all?" he asked. "Back home board runs two, three times as much."

"I could charge you more."

He laughed.

"Where's home?" she asked.

"Tennessee. But I live here now. I bought a place, other side of the highway." He offered his hand. "My name's Richard Collier."

Billie's hand felt like it was being undressed and taken to bed. She put it in her pocket as Ty hefted the bag of Equine Senior feed onto the counter and slapped open his receipt pad.

"This is your new neighbor, Billie," Ty said. "In a distant sense. He's south of the freeway, you're north." He folded the pad's top sheets underneath and pulled the pencil stub from behind his ear and licked the tip.

"I could use some dog food too," Billie said, even though she didn't need any and wouldn't for another week and shouldn't be running up the bill. It was out of her mouth before she could stop herself. It kept her from leaving.

"Is that your little dog I saw in here?" Richard asked.

"Gulliver," Billie said.

The screen door banged hard behind her, and Billie felt Ty's attention slide past her and get stuck on something.

"Dad?"

She turned to see the blonde girl she had watched riding in the show, dressed today in a blingy pink T-shirt and shorts as small as pot holders. She had long tan legs and slender feet in cheap rubber flip flops. On her, they looked like props for a *Vogue* magazine shoot. Ty's eyes were big and bright. Sylvie, Billie remembered the girl's name from somewhere deep. Yeah, she had won at the horse show. Billie noticed that Richard's eyes were silvery blue.

"You almost done, Dad? I want to get . . . home." Sylvie hesitated before she said *home*. She looked from her father to Billie. "Oh," she said as if Billie were a pool of barf on the floor.

"My daughter, Sylvie," Richard introduced her. "This is our neighbor across the highway, Syl. I'm sorry. I missed your name." He looked at Billie as if she were the most interesting item on a long and complicated menu.

"Billie Snow. I saw you ride at the show, Sylvie, and win."

"I saw you, too." Sylvie's lips parted in a smile. She had pretty, smooth, young teeth. "So you got those flyers up someplace. Here, right?"

"Right." Billie wondered where Sylvie's obnoxious brother was.

"Da-ad?"

"Okay, Sylvie. Going!"

He unfolded a thick pad of bills from a roll and set them on the counter. He headed for the door, his hand on the back of his daughter's blonde head. When he looked back, Billie was staring at him.

"What kind of dog food you want?" Ty asked, looking out the door, watching the slim tanned legs topped by the tiny tight shorts.

"Never mind," Billie said. "I'll get it later."

She made out a check for the bag of Equine Senior and hoisted it from the counter onto her shoulder.

"You didn't use to be able to do that," Ty said.

"I bet there was a time when you couldn't either."

"I've been lifting sacks since I was a little kid, Billie. You came to it late."

"But I'm good at it."

Outside, she flipped the sack over the truck side. In a shimmering heat haze, she watched the dust plume raised by Richard's dually on the dirt road headed south.

Gulliver took his time peeing on the gas pumps, sniffing first, circling, sniffing again. A thick coating of white dust settled onto Billie while she waited for him to finish. She licked her parched lips and opened the truck door for the dog to jump in.

"Billie?" Ty seemed to waver in the heat beside her, almost a mirage.

"Yeah?"

"You went to that walking horse show?"

"Yeah. By accident. I was at the showgrounds. I'd never seen one of those shows before."

"I heard it was coming here, but I didn't believe it."

Billie pulled herself into the truck. The cracked leather seat seared the backs of her legs. She settled her feet on the pedals. "Why not?"

"Whatever we have wrong here with horses—and there's plenty," Ty said, "at least it isn't that."

"Isn't what?" She wondered if he knew what went on at walking horse shows or if he was talking about something else.

He pushed the Chevy's door closed for her, so it latched easily and quietly. Then he hung on the open window by his fingertips, stretching onto his heels then pulling himself back up close. He was as long and supple as the bamboo growing in Billie's barnyard.

"Didn't you see?" he asked her.

"See what?"

"What they do to those horses? C'mon Billie Snow, you're the first person who'd notice and start hollering about it."

"Yes, I saw. I even called Doc to ask him about it. But I still don't understand. Why do they do it?"

"Well, Google it. I bet you'll find a ton of stuff on it. My point is, we never had them—the walking horse folks, the Big Lickers—here before this." He stood up, his head above the window so his voice floated down to her. "What are they doing here, Billie? That's what I wonder. Why have they come? What have we got way out here in the desert that they want?"

CHAPTER 5

BILLIE STOOD AT her kitchen window, looking out over summer-dry grazing land. In the distance, half-starved cattle struggled to survive for another month or six weeks on brittle love grass and withered cactus. When the rains finally came, the land would green up almost instantly. The desert would look as lush as Kentucky for a couple of months and be soft on the eyes.

She finished making a nopalito salad for dinner and carried it to the futon to eat. She couldn't get Ty's questions out of her mind. Earlier, as she fed the horses, her eyes ran over their legs. She remembered what she'd seen Charley do to the filly tied in her stall. Each of his movements, the sound of his voice as he scolded her, ordered her to quit trying to escape. The way he had seemed indifferent to her pain, annoyed when she struggled to save herself. But Billie had also seen him stroke her neck when he was done. And she was sure she'd heard him say, "I'm sorry, baby . . ."

She awoke hours later from an unintended sleep. She got up and made a cup of coffee, drank it gazing out the kitchen window, trying to shake off the dream that had been part of her life since childhood, strangling her sleep. It wasn't apnea; she'd been tested, eagerly hoping for a cure, a mask to wear at night that would solve the problem. Every time the dream came, she woke shuddering with horror and bolted from the futon to stand at the window, grasping the sill. From his spot under the sheet, Gulliver watched her. Outside, a falling star caught the edge of Billie's vision, arcing to the north. She closed her eyes, exhaled, and opened them to see a thick splash of stars sprawled across the sky.

At last she knew what had been bothering her, what she had to do. She opened the door with Gulliver at her heels and jogged down the driveway to the barnyard, starlight all she needed to see her way. The horses nickered, hoping she would give them treats. Not even the low light affected her ability to line up and back the truck to the trailer. A lifetime spent hauling horses made every step as familiar as brushing her teeth. She set the brake, got out of the truck, winched the trailer tongue onto the hitch, coupled them, and slipped on the safety chains and emergency brake wire. She tossed the trailer's wheel chocks into the toolbox, whistled her dog up onto the seat, and they took off.

Gulliver stood on the ripped bench seat beside her, his paws on the dashboard, alert for any nocturnal excitements—the flight of a nightjar, a bat, cattle on the road, jackrabbits—that he might spot through the windshield. As the truck chattered down the ribbed dirt road toward the highway, the mug of coffee Billie had in the cupholder at her knee sloshed onto her leg. The empty trailer, jolted by every ridge and hole in the road, rattled behind. Years of dirt roads had jarred its welds loose. Gulliver pushed off from the dashboard and planted his forepaws on the passenger side door, peered out that window, then curled against Billie's thigh, licked the drying coffee, and sighed himself to sleep.

At the interstate, they joined the nightly convoy of big rigs headed to California, driving into the headlights of other rigs driving east. Billie turned on NPR and listened to Dave Brubeck for a while. Gulliver stirred then settled.

The road to the Rio del Oro showgrounds was narrow, winding, unlit, and deserted except for Billie. She needed to be finished and out of there before dawn, when people would begin moving about and she would be spotted. She wanted to get in and out while it was dark and the trainers and grooms were asleep. The dashboard clock read 2:17, so she had about two hours before daylight. She pulled into the showgrounds and parked behind the barns, between a huge pile of dry, old manure and a row of dumpsters. Certain the rattle of the trailer would bring someone to investigate, she sat with the window down, listening for voices, footsteps, the sound of a door closing. But except for a couple of whinnies, she heard no one.

She pulled the keys from the ignition before opening the door so the alarm wouldn't sound. It did anyway, warning beeps so loud she was sure it would summon security. Panicking, she fumbled with the steering wheel controls and discovered that she had left the parking light wand cocked on. She twisted it off: silence. Her heart made its own racket while she waited to see if anyone would show up to find out who she was and what she was doing there in the middle of the night.

After a few minutes, satisfied that no one had been disturbed, she whistled softly for Gulliver and headed for the filly's barn. A few blue lights outside fried bugs, making loud zapping sounds, but the arena and barns were dark, lit only by an occasional dim bulb.

The barn doors were locked, but the shutters on the filly's stall window stood ajar, and when she checked, they were unlatched. She climbed in over the sill and dropped into hay that reeked of something she couldn't identify that made her eyes water. Behind her, Gulliver scratched on the outside wall and whined.

"Okay. Up!" she whispered and he jumped onto the sill and from there down into the stall with her. Instead of startling, the filly seemed frozen in place.

Billie waited for her eyes to get accustomed to the darkness, deeper than the starry night outside. She heard banging and what she thought were moans. Feeling her way along the wall, she went to see what was wrong. In the other stalls, horses stood tied, their heads only inches from the walls, their hooves beating against the wood. A few who weren't tied lay stretched out in filthy bedding.

She unlocked the big doors at the end of the building then entered the stalls, untied each horse, and left the doors open.

The horses didn't move. But at least now they could.

She returned to the filly's stall. Billie could just make out the fleece bandages that wound up her legs to her knees. Billie knelt beside her and struggled with the Velcro closure at the top of one of the wraps, finally getting it to open. As fast as she could, she unwound the bandage then the plastic wrap that covered the horse's lower legs. Something thick and slimy filled Billie's palm. Flesh had pulled off with the wraps. Appalled, she scrubbed her hands against her jeans. The filly tried to pull away from her. Billie didn't know what to do—keep unwinding and pull off more of her skin or stop and let the chemicals stay on her legs. Billie stopped. Since she didn't know what to do, she would do nothing more. The lead rope, pulled taut by the filly's efforts to get away, was knotted so tightly Billie couldn't undo it, so she grabbed the filly's halter and led her down the aisle, shushing as the filly nickered to her barn mates.

"Hush," Billie whispered.

Lame on both front feet, the young horse stayed close to her, obedient.

Billie expected to be stopped, but no one came. No one shouted at her, no one grabbed her.

She loaded the filly into the trailer, amazed by how easily the baby stepped up and walked into the dark metal box. Billie closed the trailer door, got into the truck with Gulliver, and drove out of the Rio del Oro showgrounds a horse thief.

It was nearly dawn when Billie pulled into her barnyard. The sky was turning ashy, but the barnyard was still dark. She didn't want to unload the filly, asking her to step into an unfamiliar place on her painful legs, so she left her loose in the trailer so she could move around as she wanted. Billie hung a hay bag stuffed with alfalfa and a bucket full of clean water from the trailer wall. Exuberant whinnies greeted them, and the filly called back.

Billie climbed onto the haymow. Alfalfa stalks stabbed her hands and the backs of her legs as she sat. Gulliver curled up in her lap. She fell asleep with her feet dangling, leaning against a bale, listening as the horses settled down. She slept until the sun pierced the eastern sky. Gulliver still dozed on her lap, stirring only when a coyote—skinny, lame, and mangy—trotted across the barnyard and passed beneath their perch. The little dog whined, and the coyote glanced up to see who had made that sound, then trotted on about his business.

As the searing sun split the horizon, Billie pulled out her phone and called.

"Doc," he answered, already awake.

"It's Billie."

"What can I do for you?"

The glare of the sun spreading across the flat grazing land to the east felt Saharan. "I went to the show again last night," Billie said. "I saw that filly I told you about."

He didn't say anything.

"I went into her stall, and I undid her bandages."

She paused, waiting. Still he didn't say anything.

"I tried to take them off but her skin came off too."

Silence.

"Wads of it," Billie said. "In my hand."

He sighed. "Nothing I can do about that, Billie. That horse's owner would have to call me."

"Why would her skin come off like that?" She stepped up on the bumper of her horse trailer and looked in at the filly through the bars, waiting for Doc to answer. "I think I can see holes so deep her tendons show, Doc. Maybe I'm imagining it?"

"The chemicals they use cause terrible burns," Doc said. "They're supposed to be put on so that the burning isn't visible and you can't see that the horse is being hurt. Scars build up over time but that takes months to develop. What you're describing sounds like someone did it wrong, used too much."

"If the filly's owner did call you," Billie asked, watching the filly shift her weight and lower her muzzle to her damaged leg. "What would you tell her to do?"

"Listen to me, Billie. You can't do a damned thing for this horse. She's not yours, and if you try to interfere, you're going to get yourself hurt."

"But what would help her, if I were able to help her?" Billie asked. "Say I bought her or something."

"By God, you are the dumbest girl I ever met. Do you have any idea what it takes to get this stuff off a horse's legs?"

"No."

"Weeks and weeks of working to get it off, to get it out of their skin. It's not just lying on top; it's gone way in deep. Once a chemical gets its teeth into flesh, it can devour everything—muscle, tendons, even bone. But if you do get that filly, give me a call and I'll come look at her."

"Come now."

While she waited, Billie drove the trailer into the shade of the hay barn where the filly would catch a breeze until Doc got there. Then she fed the other horses. The bag of Equine Senior was almost gone already.

By eight the heat had climbed to ninety. In another couple of hours, it would reach ninety-five then climb higher. Billie loaded hundred-pound hay bales into the wheeled cart, pushing it from corral to corral, cutting the bright yellow baling twine with her pocketknife, separating the thick flakes from the bales and throwing armloads over the fences into the feeders on the other side.

In the feed shed, she scooped the dwindling senior feed into buckets for Starship and Hashtag. Grabbing one bucket handle in each hand, she pushed open the door with her hip and stepped out into a morning turning white with heat.

Fingers dug into her shoulder. "Set them down."

CHAPTER 6

BILLIE SLOWLY BENT her knees until the bucket bottoms rested on the ground then she released her grip on the handles. As she rose, Charley turned her to face him. He still wore the same threadbare overalls he'd had on when she'd first seen him hurting the filly, and the hand digging into her shoulder was the same hand she'd seen two days ago covered in a latex glove, smearing chemicals on the filly's legs. Incensed, she twisted her head and sank her teeth into his hand, biting down hard on a fleshless, bony knuckle. His other hand balled into a fist and he swung wildly, socking her in the side of her mouth and breaking her hold. Billie's head snapped back then forward. Pain shot down her neck. She tried to bite him again.

He slapped her hard across the face. This time the pain in her neck made her scream. He let her go.

"Much as I'd like to just leave you here to deal with the trouble you're making," he said, "we need to talk. You're going to get me killed. And yourself."

"Fuck you." Billie reached for her neck.

Charley pushed her ahead of him to the open feed shed door. She tried to grab the jamb, but he pried off her fingers and shoved her inside then stepped up behind her and closed the door. He looked around then pushed her onto a stool.

"Now sit still and listen." He leaned against the wall beside her, both of them panting. "Don't you have an air conditioner?" he asked. "Some water?"

Billie wanted some too. Badly. Slowly, keeping her eyes on him, she crouched and reached under the table to the door of the mini fridge she kept there. He shoved her aside, reached in, and brought out two icy bottles. He handed her one and wrenched the cap off the other. He took a couple of swallows then waited, his chest heaving, before taking more. Watching him from the stool, she drank hers.

When he finished, he screwed the cap back onto the bottle, pulled the bottom of his T-shirt out of his overalls, and wiped it all over before setting it in the trash. *He's going to kill me,* she thought. *That's why he's getting rid of his fingerprints.* She glanced around the familiar shed, looking for a way out that didn't exist.

"Where's my horse?" he asked.

Neither of them moved. She thought about what would happen when he found the horse in the trailer, which he almost certainly would. Flies drugged with heat stumbled across feed that had spilled on the floor, climbed the window screens, and landed on her hands, arms, neck, lips, and eyes. And on his.

Gulliver scratched at the door. Charley opened it, and the dog trotted in to flop on the floor, panting. Charley's eyes returned to the little fridge under the table, and Billie knew he was still thirsty. She bent down, got two more bottles, looked at them, and put one back. She opened the other, poured some water into a bowl for Gulliver, and slowly drank the rest, expecting Charley to shove her aside, to force his way to the refrigerator and take another bottle.

Instead, he reached into his pocket. She tensed, not knowing if he was after a gun, but his hand reappeared holding a leather billfold. He flipped it open with his thumb and held it toward her. She glimpsed a card behind cracked plastic.

"What's that?" she asked.

He snapped the case closed. "I'm working with the Department of Agriculture," he said.

"And I'm Annie Oakley." She didn't want him to know how badly her neck hurt, how much she wanted to escape back to the casita and lie on her futon with a bag of frozen corn under her head.

"We're on the same side, Billie."

"No, we're not. I saw you with that filly."

"You mean the one you stole? I can get you prosecuted for that," he said.

"Really? You're going to call the cops and say you can identify her by what you did to her legs? No one's going to try to get her back and we both know it."

He sighed as if exhaustion had overcome him and pressed the heel of his hand to his forehead.

"I've worked for Dale's family since I was a kid. I learned the tricks from them. I've been doing it all my life."

"How in hell can you stand yourself?"

"I can't," he said so softly she almost didn't hear him. He shifted his weight, and she recoiled, but he just extended his hand toward Gulliver then bent to scratch him. "I can't stand the things I've done all my life."

Gulliver rolled onto his back, inviting further rubs, but Charley straightened up.

"I had thought that I could just call the 800 number," he said, "and collect the reward the Humane Society is offering. Ten thousand dollars! I'd just name some names. It was going to be my way out of this life."

Billie massaged her neck.

"They said my word wasn't enough."

"Imagine that."

"I've been taking pictures and videos most of this past year. I've got enough now. I can turn them in and apply for the reward."

"I got news, Charley. Ten thousand won't get you much in the way of a fresh start."

"It's ten thousand per conviction. I can give them a lot of other people besides Eudora and Dale. I can take them all the way to the top."

"Who's at the top?" she asked.

He shook his head. He wasn't going to tell her. "That's going to be my money, not yours. I want it to get started with my own farm."

"You shouldn't be allowed anywhere near a horse for the rest of your life."

"Horses are all I know."

She thought she heard a swarm of bees outside, but the sound grew until it became more like a train headed for them. She and Charley peered out the shed window. Branches slapped against each other. Dirt swirled upward into a dust

devil and roared toward them. Gulliver whined as it passed
the shed, lifting objects in its path—a currycomb and brushes,
a light plastic chair—then dropped them. In a minute it was
over, the devil diminishing as it reached the bamboo grove
by a horse trough. The air returned to its summer stillness.

"How could you do that to the filly?"

"It wasn't supposed to happen." He rubbed his palms along
his overalls. "I've cooked horses' legs all my life and never had
that happen. You want heat and pain, not damage."

Billie wondered if the irony of what he'd said had occurred
to him. "Could someone else have messed with what was in
the bottle?" she asked. "Could it have been tampered with?"

"I've been gathering information for months, doing it the
way the Ag folks want it done . . ." He faded out, thinking.
"Maybe someone could have done that."

"But why?" she asked.

He started to say something but stopped. Blinked. Swallowed. Wiped a mustache of sweat that had beaded his upper
lip. His hand shook. He stuffed it deep into the pockets of
his overalls.

"You're going to turn in your bosses? Is that it?" Billie
prompted. "Would that have made someone . . . ?"

He reached into the bib pocket of his overalls and pulled out
a red flash drive. "I want you to take this. Everything's in here—
the photos, the video, recordings. I don't think . . . I think I've
been found out. Take this."

"You're setting me up. I have no idea what's really in there."

"I'm not. I need to get rid of this, in case . . ."

Billie turned away from him, glimpsing herself in the mirror
of the medicine cabinet, its glass spotted with years of her

own fingerprints along its edges, prints that were stained with iodine, greasy with ointments. The face that looked back at her was flushed from the heat, bruises forming at her mouth and on her cheek where Charley had hit her. And her neck still hurt.

"You won't help me?"

"You've spent your life torturing horses. Now you want to make a killing from turning in your pals. No, I won't help you."

He wiped his forehead with the back of his hand then slipped the flash drive back into his overalls.

"You'll have to destroy that filly," he said.

"What do you mean?"

"She's suffering. That filly can't make it. You'd do her a kindness to put her out of her misery."

"Did you say 'kindness'?"

"If you try to save her, she'll just suffer more."

"Get out! I don't give a shit about you."

"Listen, tonight Dale and I pack up and go back to his new farm in Sonoita. I'm offering you a chance to find out what really goes on in a Big Lick barn. Behind the scenes where no one else has gone. I checked up on you, and with your background as a reporter, that's got to appeal to you. A chance to write about this? Right up your alley."

He took a lopsided step toward the door. Gulliver wagged his tail.

"I don't suppose you'd give a lame old man a lift down the road to his truck, would you? I parked on the far side of that wash and hiked in when it was a lot cooler than it is now."

"You trespass, you beat me up, you threaten me, and now you want a lift?"

He looked at her, asking, not pleading. "Angel Hair Walkers is the name of the place. Take the left fork toward Rain Valley, go a couple miles. You'll find the sign."

"Get out of here. GO! Think of that filly while you're roasting out in the desert."

He nodded and left, limping across the shimmering barnyard and out onto the road.

A few minutes later, feeling guilty, Billie followed in the truck with Gulliver. Two bottles of water jiggled on the seat beside her. She drove to the wash and beyond, but didn't find Charley. When she got out to look for his tracks, all she saw were the maze of daily tire crossings left by ranchers on their way to check livestock.

CHAPTER 7

JUST AFTER NOON Doc's truck bounced over the washboard road and parked in front of the barn. He slid out, holding his left arm close to his body, in a sling, his face tight and gray.

"It's nothing," he said, his voice breathless from pain. "That bull just wanted to keep his balls. Understandable, but I got 'em. Then he got me back. Busted my collar bone. Not serious. Hurts like hell though."

"And you're working today?"

"You sound like my daughter, Billie."

"I do?"

"Molly and I couldn't have kids. But I imagine if we'd had a daughter she'd have been a lot like you."

Billie looked away, confused by his compliment.

"Maybe you're lucky you didn't have kids," she said. "I can't have any. I used to wish I could . . . But I can't and that's that."

"I'm sorry to hear that."

Billie shrugged. She wanted him to say more to her, tell her what he liked about her, what made him feel she could belong to him, even remotely. It had to do with what she did rather than who she was, she was sure. Still, she wanted him to explain the goodness he seemed to see in her.

"What do you want me to look at?" he asked.

Grateful to move on, Billie pointed. "Behind the barn." Her voice sounded high and childish to her, the words coming too fast.

They scuffed their way around the barn, Billie adjusting her stride so Doc could keep pace with her. The last time he'd been out he had hiked around the corrals like a young man. Today, aged by exhaustion and his broken collarbone, he seemed old.

"She's still in the trailer," Billie explained as they approached. "I parked it in the shade."

Doc glanced at her but didn't say anything as Billie unlatched the groom door at the front of the trailer and half stepped, half pulled herself inside.

The little horse stood with her head down, her eyes half-closed. She didn't startle when Billie appeared or flinch as Billie clipped a lead rope to her halter. Billie thought she looked like she hurt too much to move.

Billie leaned down to give Doc a hand as he negotiated the high step up into the narrow trailer door. Having his arm in a sling made his balance uncertain, but in no way diminished the power of a lifetime of physical work with big animals.

"You shouldn't go climbing into trailers with injured animals," he told her. "Way to get yourself hurt."

"She won't hurt us, Doc. She can't even move."

"I can see that."

Slowly, in the cramped metal horse trailer, he examined the filly, first with his eyes, then with his one good hand, his fingers light and careful over her burned legs.

"The man I got her from says she needs to be put down." Tears surprised her. Quickly she wiped her eyes.

"Who'd you get her from?" Doc asked.

"A guy named Charley."

Billie figured that Doc knew she wasn't telling him the whole truth but had decided not to press it. Knowing what had really happened wouldn't change his diagnosis or prognosis of the horse.

"I've been doing this for fifty years," he said, turning to Billie. "And I've treated horses burned by fires and hurt by stupidity. And I read about this soring stuff, but I've never seen it for myself. Until now."

Looking back at the filly, he said, "She'll be scarred, Billie, but she could recover."

"Really?"

He picked up the filly's hoof. "Oh, those sons of bitches."

"What?"

"See this?" With the index finger of his damaged arm, he pointed at the bottom of her hoof cradled in his good hand. The filly squealed and tried to pull away from him. While Billie leaned against her shoulder, gently stroking her neck, murmuring reassurances, Doc explained that someone had rasped her hooves until they bled then cut into the laminae, the tender quick. "Their next move would have been to stick something up in her hoof—a screw or something like that— then nail on shoes so it wouldn't be seen. Good thing you got her when you did."

Doc released her leg, and Billie winced as the filly set it gingerly on the ground then tentatively eased some weight onto it to relieve her other foot.

"I won't have anything to do with these people," Doc said. "They maim their horses for a rayon show ribbon."

"I was thinking I should write an article about it," Billie said.

He placed his stethoscope against the filly's heart. "You won't be the first."

There had been articles about soring for decades, he told her, watching the second hand of his Timex. "Pulse is seventy-eight," he reported. "An elevated pulse means pain."

He placed the head of his stethoscope against the filly's flank, listened, moved it lower, listened again. "Diminished gut sounds," he said, sliding around to her rump on her other side. Before he placed the stethoscope on her right flank, he said, "A couple of years ago a national veterinarians' association wrote a white paper calling for the end of soring." Looking at Billie over the horse's back, he shook his head. "It didn't do any good. Nothing stops these people."

Billie felt sweat running between her shoulder blades and down her back. She wiped her forehead with her palm, pushing damp hair up her forehead, then wiped her upper lip on the inside of her shirt. It was cooler in the trailer than out, but it had to be over a hundred degrees.

Doc looped the stethoscope around his neck and looked in the filly's eyes and mouth. He stroked the side of her face.

"Poor girl," he said. "You didn't deserve this."

Billie backed out through the groom door on the side of the trailer, followed by Doc. "Want some water?" she asked. "I've got some in the feed shed."

The walk back was even slower than the one to the trailer, and Doc's fatigue was palpable. Billie shortened her stride to stay close beside him in case he needed her. In the shed, he accepted the icy bottle, and they leaned against the side of the building to drink, grateful for the bit of shade.

"Did you know there's been a movement back east to get soring stopped?" Doc asked. "It's had some success, so it's harder now for Big Lickers to get away with what they do. The inspections are a little tougher, the fines are a little bigger."

"So, that's good?"

"As far as it goes, but it doesn't go nearly far enough. I hope you decide to write that article, Billie. I don't think it'll stop them, m'dear, but it could help some."

Billie fetched two more bottles of water, handed him one. "Do you think that's why they've shown up here? In Arizona?"

"I don't know about that. If you ask me, you should stay away from this whole thing. But if you do decide to pursue it, well, that might be a worthy effort." He looked around. "Where's your little dog?"

"Up at the casita."

Doc nodded and finished most of his second bottle of water before screwing the top back on.

"Doc, what will it take to fix the filly?"

"Luck. Plus a lot of time and some money, Billie. And a lot of pain for her. Some might say it'd be a kindness to put her down."

"Let's try to save her."

As they walked back to the barn, Doc outlined a course of treatment. Medicines, salves, months of specially made shoes and pads to protect her damaged feet until they could grow out and she could again walk without pain. Billie wanted to ask how much it would cost, but what difference would the answer really make? Money aside, what was the best thing for the horse? Try to save her or euthanize her? As Doc talked, her mind wandered into the world of grotesque abuse the horse had suffered. Her article might make a difference to the horses suffering in darkened barns. Or maybe it would just help this one horse here, standing in misery in her trailer. If Billie could sell it, she'd have money for vet care. She couldn't wait to start.

"How widespread is it?" she asked Doc.

He blinked at her, uncertain. "How widespread is what?"

"How widespread is soring?"

"It's done to show horses and horses that might show. Thousands and thousands of them over the years. It's a multi-million dollar business."

"Well," Billie said, "that has to stop."

Doc started to laugh, first a slight chuckle, then a big deep rumble. "You're really something!" he gasped, holding his arm tightly against his body to stop it from moving with his laughter. "Oh my, dear. You are right. It has to stop. It won't, but it has to."

He loaded Billie up with medicines for the filly and started to write her bill, leaning against the side of his truck.

"What's her name?" he asked.

Until this second Billie hadn't thought about a name.

"Hope," she said. It would do for now.

When Doc drove off, he took with him a good chunk of her remaining money.

She started to imagine what she'd write. Not the details— she didn't know them yet. She didn't know who was involved, beyond Charley and Dale and Eudora and Sylvie, if you could count a kid. She didn't know the extent of the problem. She couldn't even fully define the crimes being committed. But the structure of the piece, its rhythm and form, she already knew.

CHAPTER 8

BILLIE STRETCHED OUT on a hay bale under the Milky Way, searching the sky for shooting stars. Alfalfa stems prickled her shoulder blades. She wriggled to avoid them, but each time they just got stuck someplace else—in the small of her back, the back of her neck, the backs of her knees.

She lay there anyway, waiting for the perfect star. Then she would go up to the casita and write. Somewhere in the words she would find a way to feed her animals, find a way to stay on her ranch.

She should have taken Charley's thumb drive, should have given him a lift, should have thought of what he could do for her instead of just getting angry.

I bolted like a spooked horse instead of staying to figure it out, reason it out, fight it out, she thought. *I'll never learn.*

She closed her eyes. Night sounds filled her mind. The horses lipped hay off the ground, a sound like water flowing over rocks. She heard them shift their weight, sigh, shuffle, snort. A screech owl started its predawn call. When she opened her eyes to look for it, the star she had been waiting

71

for arced directly over her, a streak that shrank to a soft astral sizzle then disappeared.

Gulliver lay on his back on her stomach, all four feet in the air. She played her fingers over his belly—single notes, chords. When she sat up, he leapt off and shook himself.

As she hiked back up the hill to the house, Gulliver trotting beside her, Frank's voice played in her head. *Come back,* he said. *Work for me again. Pick your project or take on mine.*

She let herself into the casita and settled cross-legged on the futon. She could have reached for her computer, but she had a favorite pen, a fine-point steel-bodied ballpoint, and a notebook whose pages sagged beneath the pen's pressure.

Where to start? She had a pile of worries—about her writing, about what her life would be if she went back to writing. Would she solve the problem of income at the cost of this life she had chosen? By making money to feed the horses, would she have to leave them, even lose them? If she agreed to write for Frank, she would have to leave, if not right away, then after a while.

She looked out the kitchen window over the barnyard, into the barely lightening sky, and started to outline the article. "The Plight of the Tennessee Walking Horse" by Arabella Snow. Arabella! A name branded onto her by her parents, who named her for fame. "No one will be able to forget it," her mother had told her. "It's the name of a heroine, a star." Billie wrote under it as a way to save her private world from what became the high profile, high danger life of Arabella Snow, journalist. It had worked for a while, but her nickname had eventually gotten out. It hadn't been a big deal to her at the time, but it did allow curious people—like Charley—to find

Arabella the journalist by Googling Billie. *The former journalist,* she corrected herself.

Once, she was interviewed about the exposés she wrote. *Is it true?* The desiccated wispy-haired interviewer had squinted at her, his feigned disbelief representing that of his viewers. *Is it true, Ms. Snow, that some parents actually sell their children into slavery?* Billie had seen this exact same expression on other interviewers on other shows, had heard the same incredulity in his tone in myriad interviews with other guests. *Low-fat corn oil?* he had asked in exactly the same way. *You found a python in your baggage?*

She set the notebook on the futon beside her. That old life had been so urban. Exciting. Well-paid. She could have bought tractor-trailers stacked with bales of Bermuda grass and alfalfa hay. Tons of oats, Equine Senior, vitamins, and supplements. She could have paid for veterinary ultrasounds, radiographs, surgeries . . . whatever the horses needed.

The sky turned pearly grey then coral. She stood and went to the kitchen window to look out, searching the land that stretched for miles before her, looking for just one lone ranch-er out riding fence, or dust from a truck on its way to check the dirt tanks where the cattle drank and the miles of pipe that carried water to them. She saw a spiral of vultures riding the day's first thermals, searching too.

While the air was still crisp and the coffee had filled her with energy, she hiked back down the hill to check on the horses. The filly stood with her head lowered, shifting her weight, trying to ease the pain in her legs. Billie injected her with the medicine Doc had left then moved her to a shady stall under the hay barn roof. She had not eaten her hay from last night. Billie scooped oats into a feed bucket to tempt her, but she ignored them too, her eyes small with misery.

Billie chewed the inside of her cheek, wondering what she should do. Charley had suggested she go to the farm where he worked. Maybe that would lead her straight to her next exposé. Charley might be a gift horse, and who was she to look him in the mouth? If she got a job there, she'd get paid while she researched by the people she was investigating. Was that ethical? Why not?

The sun rose as she drove, blinding her as she headed east over the mountains into a valley bisected by a crisp blue stream. The road dipped from mountain pass to river's edge, and she followed it, her windows rolled down. The stream's banks were furred with cattails and bamboo. She knew the valley, not a half hour from her own place. She had driven through it a few times, just for the scenery.

The humped black shapes of cattle freckled the pale pastures. Ranch land stretched as far as she could see. No power lines, no pavement, no houses. Just miles of land that looked as it had for generations. She passed a couple of cowhands riding the edge of the road, a blue heeler dog trotting behind them. She raised her hand in a small salute. They nodded in return.

Billie turned off at a ranch sign featuring a walking horse strutting over the words: *Angel Hair Walkers.* She stopped the truck to look at it, incongruous in the midst of a cattle ranch. On the sign, the horse's right front leg was lifted almost as high as its muzzle, while its hind feet stretched way under its belly in what she now knew was the classic Big Lick pose. A stride that couldn't be come by naturally, that only happened through pain. Of course the sign didn't show the leg chains.

She restarted the Silverado. The driveway curved between thick white eucalyptus trunks. Through a mist of sprinklers, she peered at a Spanish hacienda. Raked and graveled paths led to benches placed invitingly against the building's stucco walls. Red clay tiles created a graceful, Mediterranean-style roof.

The circular drive was crowded with parked cars. She wedged her truck into a slot between a royal blue Mercedes and a white Chevy Tahoe. She parked and got out, breathing the aromas of baked earth and watered grass. She heard the creek behind her, and when she turned to look, she saw a stand of trees and grasses, dusty but thriving. Two coyotes trotted out, one silvery red, the other dark, fringed in black. They saw her, stopped, and faded back into the scrub. A raven fluttered to the spot where they disappeared, landed hopping, pecked at the ground, and took off toward the whitewashed building.

White walls, green grass, red roof, blackbirds. Billie wished she could stand there, listening to running water, smelling moist earth, and looking at the ranch house forever. But the rapidly rising heat mobilized her.

A sign reading *Office* was screwed into the wall to the right of a massive, carved oak door. She decided that the sign meant she didn't need to knock or ring, so she opened the door and stepped from the heat into a room so cold icicles could hang from the curtain rods. Heavy green drapes blocked the sun. One mustard-colored wall was covered with ribbons presumably won by the horses of this farm. Multicolored streamers fell from blue and red and gold rosettes. Championship ribbons, all of them. Photographs slathered another wall. A mahogany drop-leaf table held silver trophies, overflow from the collection lined up on shelves behind an ornate wooden desk. Eudora, the older woman Billie had seen at the show talking to Dale, sat behind it.

"Yes?" she asked.

"I'm looking for a job."

"Didn't I meet you last weekend?" she asked. "At the show?"

Billie stuffed her hands in her jeans pockets, ducked her head, tried to look embarrassed, and said, "Right. I'm Billie Snow. I met a guy at the show named Charley. He offered me a job."

"*Charley* offered you a job?" Eudora sounded incredulous. "*I'm* the owner. My name is Eudora Thornton. I decide who gets hired." Eudora drummed the end of a ballpoint pen against the glowing wood of the desktop. "What kind of job are you looking for?"

Billie felt as if a stuck door just opened a crack.

"I've got my own place with my own horses and I board some, but I'm struggling." Frank had taught her the finer points of successful lying. *Tell as much of the truth as you can. The truth sounds like truth, and you're less likely to forget what you said.*

"I need more business," Billie said. "Or I need a job. I was putting up flyers at the showgrounds when I met Charley. We got to talking, and he said I could come ask for work here. I really need it."

Eudora settled back and her chair squealed.

"What can you do?" Eudora asked.

"For a start, I could fix that squeak. A few squirts of WD-40 would do it," Billie said.

"I'll call maintenance for that," Eudora said. "What else?"

"I can do anything with horses. I can ride, school, exercise. I can start colts, handle foals . . ."

"Will you muck?"

"You bet!" She hoped Eudora would figure that Billie's enthusiasm for this menial job had to do with the hourly wage, but she was thinking: I'm in! Not far in, but this was how every piece of research started, with a small widening of the view.

"I'll do whatever you need done," Billie said.

"You can start right away?"

"You bet," Billie grinned.

"Good." Eudora nodded. "All right, I'll show you around."

She stood up, stylish in a white silk blouse and tailored skirt. Her high heels clicked as she led Billie under a shady archway into a courtyard with whitewashed barns on three sides. Hitching rails lined each wall, interspersed with more benches. The center of the courtyard had been raked into a pattern of swirled white pebbles. The place practically glittered. Through an archway in the farthest barn, Billie saw a dirt exercise track, and beyond the track, desert stretching to serrated mountains.

"Wow!" Billie said and meant it.

"Nice, isn't it?" Eudora asked.

"Beyond nice."

Eudora took Billie through the massive door into the first barn on the left and then into a small storage room. She handed Billie a mucking fork and showed her the wheeled cart she should fill.

"Empty it on the manure pile outside. I'll show you." She led the way to the back of the building, to a mound of manure, soiled hay, and straw. "There's a pile behind each barn, for convenience. You won't have to walk far, no matter where you're working." She showed Billie where the bedding was stored in its own shed adjacent to the building, bales of straw and bags of wood shavings stacked neatly.

Inside the barn, she opened a door. "Tack room. Any questions?"

You bet, Billie thought. Where was everyone? Where were the owners of the cars and trucks she'd seen parked outside? Where were the horses she had seen at the show? The animals in this barn weren't standing on stacked shoes. They looked like any other horses.

"Just muck this broodmare barn today. We'll see how it goes. Come see me when you're finished."

The horses looked well-cared for. Their weight was good, their coats shone, their eyes were soft and friendly.

After Eudora disappeared, Billie settled into the rhythm of stall cleaning. Each horse she tied to a ring in the wall farthest from the door. She left the stall door open, the cart outside, and with the fork, she removed the bedding the horse had soiled during the past day. She closed the stall door behind her and wheeled the cart out to the manure pile, dumped it, and returned to the barn. She loaded a bale of straw and a bag of shavings, wheeled them to the stall and spread them out on the floor, fluffing with the rake. She checked to be certain each horse had water in its bucket that hung from the wall beside the door. Then she removed the halter and let the horse loose. It was simple work that she had done all her life. Different details in different barns, but the swing of the fork into bedding, the heft and lift, the twist to dump it into the wheelbarrow were the same everywhere, every time.

She worked down one side of the aisle, ten stalls, and started up the other side cleaning each stall with its broodmare shaded and cool under ceiling fans in the thick-walled barn.

A stall at the end of the row had drapes pulled across it. Billie glanced around to be certain she was still alone, and pulled the drapes aside, finding a closed door. She tried the handle and opened the door into a big room. Harnesses hung from hooks on the walls. A table held medical instruments. In the middle of the space, parallel iron poles created a chute in which a chestnut mare had been tied. A solid gate closed off the front of the chute. Its back gate stood open. The mare wore a set of breeding hobbles—straps around her hind legs to keep her from kicking the stallion during breeding. She turned her head and looked at Billie, her eyes wide. It was dangerous to leave a twelve-hundred-pound animal, capable of explosive thrashing, tied and alone. The breeding hobbles indicated a nearby stallion, ready to mount her. But there was no other horse in there and no stallions in this building that Billie had noticed.

She crossed the floor to look at the table beside the stocks. It was laid out with surgical implements—latex gloves, cotton balls, gauze pads, Betadine, bandages, and scalpels. Quickly, she took a picture with her cell phone.

Sweat ran off the mare, and when Billie touched her the horse trembled, her heart slamming against her chest. Billie didn't know what was going to happen in there, but she was almost as scared as the horse. If she got caught . . . The whole setup gave her the creeps.

As she wondered if she could lead the horse out, the door to the room opened.

"What are you doing in here?" Eudora asked, her tone guarded.

"Just looking around."

"Not in here you don't."

"I wanted to familiarize myself with—"

"Private. Get back to work." She stood with her back to the door, holding it open for Billie to leave.

With a firm click, Eudora shut the door as Billie pushed her way back through the curtains, fighting a moment of claustrophobic panic.

Billie grabbed the muck cart handle and a manure fork and headed for the next stall. To calm herself as she worked, she hummed a song she sang to her own horses when she cleaned their stalls.

"Tom Paxton?"

She spun around.

Richard Collier stood in the middle of the aisle, grinning. "I saw your truck outside. Eudora says you're working here?"

"As of about an hour ago. Mucking."

"That's honest work."

Billie wondered what he would think if he knew her motive for getting this job.

I have got to get myself to quit grinning, she thought. Pleasure had erased her fear, and Richard was grinning back at her, making her grin more. He had nice teeth, she noticed, even and not too white.

"My kids take lessons here," he said.

Billie tried to stop smiling, but the effort made her blush. He held her eyes as she colored. *I might as well take off my clothes and lie on my back right here,* she thought. That thought gave the blush an extra dimension. She ripped her gaze away from his face, but she glanced at his belt buckle, at the way his shirt tucked into the tops of his pants.

"How about dinner?" he asked.

"Now?"

"I think it's a little early, don't you?"

Oh, God, she thought, *just kill me dead.*

"How about tomorrow evening? Around seven at my place, after we get the horses fed?"

She nodded. "I'll need directions though."

Richard pulled a pad from his hip pocket and propped it against the lid of a wooden grooming box. Using a pencil pulled from the same pocket, he leaned forward to write. The muscles along his outer thigh tensed. When he handed the paper to her, he caught her looking and grinned. "See you at seven then."

He walked past her, headed toward the office. Billie pushed the almost full cart down the aisle, out the door, and bounced it over to the manure pile where she dumped it. When she returned, she spotted him standing beside the office door, talking on his cell phone.

She was humming the Tom Paxton song when she heard the heavy thud of hooves approaching.

Through the far arch, Eudora's husband Dale led a blue roan stallion that towered over him. White lather coated the horse's neck. Foam sprayed from the corners of his mouth, dripped down the long shanks of a wicked-looking bit, and dotted his chest. Each foreleg was circled in chains, and he wore stacks on his hooves like the ones she had seen at the show. With each stride, he placed one hind foot directly in front of the other, as if walking a tight rope.

Dale saw her and stopped. The horse tucked his hind feet tightly under his belly and rocked back on his haunches.

"What are you doing here?" he demanded.

"I just started work here," Billie said.

Dale glanced past her toward the office, as if hoping Eudora would appear to explain why she had been hired.

"What's wrong with your horse?" she asked him.

"I take it you don't know anything about these animals. Dom!" he called.

A groom appeared from the barn opposite the one Billie had been mucking, rags stuffed in his pockets. Dale handed him the reins. Dom pulled. The horse lifted one massive, burdened hoof, swung it outward, dropped it to the ground with a shudder that ran all the way up his shoulder, and then lifted the other leg.

"More juice," Dale Thornton said. "*Comprende?*"

"Sure, Boss."

Dale stepped toward Billie, forcing her to step backward. Heat from the wall burned through her shirt. She smelled cigarettes, cologne, and sweat. "Get back to work," he said.

He followed the groom and horse into the opposite barn.

Billie leaned against the hot wall, her heart as jittery as a trapped lizard. From the driveway she heard truck and car doors, people laughing and calling to each other. She licked her dust-coated lips, waited. Her T-shirt chafed her neck. Her scalp felt singed. She pushed off from the wall and followed him.

The barn she entered was darker than the one she had been cleaning. The windows to the outside were closed, like the ones she'd seen at the show. Two commercial floor fans roared at either end of the aisle, moving the air. She paused to let her eyes adjust. Movement at the far end drew her attention, and she walked toward it, squelching the inner voice that ordered her to turn around and get out of there fast.

Stalls gave way to open areas where horses stood tied from either side in cross ties so they couldn't move. Dom bent forward, using an eyedropper to drizzle something on the stallion's lower legs. Then he wrapped plastic around and around in quick expert gestures before adding fleece wraps on top of that. The horse tried to rear but the cross ties held him in place. He sank onto his haunches as far as he could, lifting one front foot then the other, then the first again.

Billie backed away, bumped into the wall. She wanted to stop what she was seeing, to scream, accuse, demand, and run.

Through the wall behind her, Billie felt a thump, then another. Dom, absorbed with his dropper and the horse tied beside the stallion, maybe deafened by the fans' roaring, didn't react. Billie turned to look into the stall behind her where the noise came from. Blood ran from a horse's nose. Dale raised a baseball bat, aiming.

"What are you doing?" she yelled. "STOP!"

Billie lunged forward and grabbed his wrist across the stall divider. He wrenched away and wheeled around to see who he was fighting.

"You are *fired!*"

"What the fuck are you doing?"

"Defending myself. That horse is vicious."

Billie looked past him to the horse. Her eyes traveled down from its bleeding nostrils to its bandaged legs.

"Get out of here!" Dale ordered. "Don't come back!"

She left the muck cart where it was and bolted out of her stall and down the barn aisle, dodging piles of manure awaiting removal. Blinded by the sunlight outdoors, she tripped over a pitchfork and fell hard onto her hands, scrambled back to her feet, and ran across the lawn to her truck.

CHAPTER 9

RIVING HOME, BILLIE was tormented by images of Dale and Eudora's farm, the sored horse he led, the strange room with its medical instruments. When she got out of the truck, her legs felt spongy. She remembered fear like this from her childhood, helpless terror. She made it into the feed shed, slumped to the floor and closed her eyes, forcing herself to breathe deeply and slowly, to count back from three hundred by sevens, to steady herself until her heart slowed and she felt stronger.

She still had a lot to do to bed down the horses, but it would stay light until 8:30, so there was time to head up into the mountains, change the scenery, get away from the ranch. Get away from everything.

She checked on Hope in her stall inside the hay barn. The filly looked miserable but was standing in the shade where she would be okay until Billie returned. She had hay in her feeder and bales and bales within reach, if she wanted to stretch out her neck beyond the corral panels. The stacked bales threw a little more shade onto her, blocking the late afternoon sun.

Billie silenced her phone before tucking it into her pocket. Only a few years ago, phones were in living rooms. Everywhere else, you were on your own. That's what Billie needed now, to be on her own.

She caught Starship and, with only the halter he wore on his head—no bridle or bit—his lead rope for a rein, she got on him bareback. Then she leaned down and slipped off her shoes, tied the laces together, and hung them around her neck. She could put them on if she absolutely had to, if she fell off.

Gulliver trotted at Starship's heels, down the road and out across the parched mesa. Sere grasses tickled the bottoms of Billie's bare feet. She tried to catch the stalks between her toes as Starship walked.

When she came to a barbed wire fence, she turned north along the dirt two-track utility access road and climbed a series of lumpy hills until, at the highest one, she pulled up to enjoy the view. The mesa stretched south. She could just barely make out trucks and cars traveling along the interstate. Beyond it, the Whetstone Mountains jutted up into an almost white, parched sky.

They walked on, Gulliver panting as he trotted. Billie was relieved when they finally descended into a narrow canyon that led to a big metal stock tank filled with water for the cattle. The water was greenish, thick with a sort of wide-leafed desert seaweed and algae, but it was cool and wet.

She dismounted, landing barefoot in soft sand, picked up her dog, and set him into the drinker. As he paddled, she splashed water over his head until she knew he had cooled off. In the deep sand beside the trough, Starship lowered himself to his knees then his side. Grunting, he flipped to his back. From one side to the other he rolled, scratching. When he was satisfied, he rolled onto his belly, stretched his forelegs in front of himself, and lurched to his feet. With her hand, Billie brushed him to get off some of the sand. She tossed her tied sneakers over his neck and hopped up so her belly lay across his back. For a moment, she lay there, feet hanging off one side, head and arms dangling off the other, feeling her back muscles stretch. For just this moment, she was not Billie Snow, owner of a struggling horse ranch, a failure at that as well as so much else. Hanging in this perilous position across this horse she had saved from slaughter and nursed to health, she was exactly who she should be and where she should be. Then she swung her leg over Starship's back and sat up.

Through low-hanging branches they climbed, through patches of shade populated with cattle that didn't bother to move at their approach, continuing to lay peacefully while flies swarmed over them. They wore the brand of the rancher who leased this land from the state: a mountain circled by a crescent moon, old brands burned deeply into their skin, long ago healed.

Starship's hair prickled against her bare legs. She felt free and happy to be out in the countryside with her horse and dog, wearing whatever she pleased, shoeless in cactus country, riding.

A couple of miles farther on, at an old campsite—its fire ring trashed with shot-up beer cans and broken glass—she turned Starship toward a mountain that rose forbiddingly before them, onto a nearly invisible trail. Wrapping her hands into his mane, she asked him to climb.

It had taken her two years of exploring to find the start of this trail then to follow it through undergrowth so densely woven that she had had to return with loppers to trim it, hiding her work in case someone else discovered it. This was her favorite spot on earth, where she was always, truly alone.

Starship lunged through the trees, bounding up and up. Billie gripped his sides with her calves and clung to his mane. Branches lashed her face while her knees and shins cracked against jutting rocks. When a huge boulder blocked their path, Starship stopped abruptly. She nearly flew over his head but wound up sitting on his neck. She wriggled back until she was once again where she should be then they started up again.

The trail ended in a cliff at the edge of a canyon. A series of thin waterfalls dribbled down the mountain face opposite, hidden to anyone not standing exactly where Billie stood. Waterfalls she hadn't known existed until she had found them one day last summer. They fed a deep pool beaten out of the rock face, smooth-sided from eons of watery concussion. The waterfall was intermittent, running hard and fast during the monsoon and the winter storms, and the rest of the year, like now, barely trickling.

She got off, dropped the cotton lead rope she had been using as a rein, and let Starship find his own way down to the small pebbly beach. He pawed the water then lumbered in for a swim. Gulliver bounded after him.

After a quick glance around to reassure herself she truly was alone, Billie stripped off her shorts and top, considered leaving on her underwear, then pulled off her panties and bra, wrapped her phone in her shirt, and eased herself into the water. With her horse and dog, she swam, cooling off, sloughing bit by bit the jagged fear of her day at the walking horse stable.

Sitting wet and naked on a rock with Gulliver flopped beside her while Starship grazed the sparse gray grasses, Doc's warning played over and over in her head . . . *be careful* . . . *don't* . . . She thought of the way her horse had rolled earlier in the sand. The way, before rising, he had turned onto his stomach, front legs extended. It was the most natural pose for him, one she had seen thousands of times. But now it was superimposed on the memory of the horses she had seen at the show and at the farm.

She looked at Starship's lower legs, his pasterns, trying to imagine pouring acid on them, tying him so he couldn't move, muzzling him so he couldn't tear off the wraps, couldn't help himself, ignoring his anguish, leaving him to writhe.

She sank deeper into her own body. The sound of the waterfall, bird calls . . .

She dozed. Just for a minute, at least that's what it felt like. She opened her eyes, listening. A faint rustling had disturbed her sleep, a sound like wind through dry grass, crumbling leaves, like air leaving a punctured tire. When she didn't hear it again, she sat up, looked around. The rattle grew louder. Adrenaline froze her. Only her eyes moved, looking into the brush, trying to see the snake. She looked left then right. Nothing. The sound faded, but whenever she moved, it grew louder. She knew the snake could see her, but she couldn't see it even though it was close enough that her every movement alarmed it. She tried not even to breathe.

Gulliver stood up from his nap and stretched. The rattling exploded from a clump of grass about five feet away. Startled, the little dog looked into the brush. Billie still couldn't see the snake, but it had to be where Gulliver was looking, probably too far for it to strike her. She inched away, sharp pebbles digging into her palms, and got to her feet.

Since moving back to Arizona, she had expected fangs to sink into her, to pump their venom. She expected one day to become a statistic: "This year seventeen people were bitten by rattlesnakes," Channel Five on Your Side would summarize. Channel 13-Live Local Late-breaking would photograph the damage, the necrotic tissue, the sloughing, her eventual survival. Today could be the day that she would finally get snakebit. While naked. Her leg would swell grotesquely. She would have to ride for help swollen and bare-assed, and she would pass out in front of astonished cowboys.

Gulliver looked again into the brush then trotted away. Knowing that he'd found a safe way out, Billie followed him. She quickly dressed and cautiously retraced her steps to the pool to get Starship.

They wound their way back through the dense mesquite bosque, dodging prickly pear, and cholla that grew between the trees, and came out the other side into a darkness so intense that, for a moment, Billie thought that night had fallen, that she had stayed too long dozing and awakened at dusk. She felt a raindrop, then another and suddenly more. In seconds, she was shivering. Starship snorted and pawed, getting ready to lie down and roll to dry himself. As suddenly as it started, the rain stopped. Clouds skimmed from west to east and, in the distance, Billie saw a single, jagged lightning bolt.

She used a rock to stand on and climbed onto Starship's back. When she snapped her fingers to invite Gulliver aboard, the terrier jumped up in front of her, his butt against her stomach, paws straddling the gray horse's withers and neck. They started on the long ride home. Billie wondered if she *had* dawdled too long, if she would get back before it was dark or if she would have to feed and water the horses under the night sky using her cell phone as a flashlight.

At the crest of a hill, she reined in and sat. Legs dangling, she ran her toes over Starship's elbows and watched the sky, fascinated by the first summer clouds. Not yet formed into monsoon's anvil-shaped thunderheads, these were high, dense, flat, and blackened. They covered the mesa and the valley between the mountain ranges. Syncopated lightning bolts shot from them, and horizontal bolts leapt from cloud to cloud.

At her urging, Starship skittered down the side of the hill, his hooves sliding on scree. They turned into the sandy wash that led to the ranch. The air smelled of ozone and creosote, that special desert rain smell Billie loved, which had been released by even the few drops that fell. Gulliver lifted his muzzle and sniffed. Billie breathed deeply, sampling the air. She smelled Starship's sweat rising from his body beneath her. Gulliver sniffed again, then Billie smelled it too.

Something burning. Something on fire. One of the lightning strikes must have caught a dry burro weed bush or a parched mesquite tree. She looked for smoke but couldn't see any.

The wash wound between deep cliffs pocked with tiny caves. A white owl flew from one of the holes, swooping in front of them before soaring into the treetops. Starship froze and started to spook, but Billie kicked his sides with her bare heels, and he leapt forward to pick up an exquisitely soft trot, perfect for bareback rides. He moved beneath her with a fluid rhythm, no jarring, so smooth that she didn't even tighten her legs to grip. She rode loosely balanced, perfectly comfortable.

Deer and javelina had made a thread-thin trail out of the wash, up between the cliffs. She grabbed Starship's mane in one hand and wrapped her other around Gulliver to hold him to her. With a dozen scrabbling strides, Starship bounded up the cliff's edge to the flat mesa floor and gave a little buck to celebrate. Billie nearly came off, nearly dropped Gulliver, and as she struggled to regain her balance, she dug her heels into Starship's sides causing him to break into a canter. She struggled to keep hold of her dog, regain her balance on the horse's sweat-slick back, and eventually to slow him.

Finally, they stopped atop a small rise, horse and human panting. As she sat trying to catch her breath, she saw smoke coming from somewhere near her ranch. She wondered if the fire would block her way home. She couldn't tell if it was big or small.

As they got closer, it seemed to shift position. One minute it appeared to be coming from Sam and Josie's place, so Billie wondered if their tool shed was burning, or—far worse— their house. But as she trotted around a big barrel cactus, the smoke seemed to come from the hill between Sam and Josie's ranch and Billie's. Brushfire flames could shoot across the countryside in seconds, leaping from bush to tree to grass where they could fan out into unstoppable walls of flame. But this was a steady plume, bending like a thick snake in the hot evening wind.

The wash dipped through a stand of huge cottonwood trees then opened onto the dirt road that first passed Sam and

Josie's house then continued on to Billie's barnyard. And there she saw that the fire was in her barnyard. Hugging Gulliver tight to her stomach she squeezed Starship's sides. He immediately broke into a fast canter that shifted up to a gallop in a single stride. In minutes they were racing down the driveway toward the barn, toward the fire truck. Her ranch sign lay in the dirt, clipped by the truck's ladder as it drove underneath. It must have made a hideous metal-on-metal shriek when it hit and could have severed an arm or even killed someone when it fell. Four men and a woman sprayed her hay with high-pressure water. The barn was still standing. She thought of the horses, all of them luckily turned out in corrals and pastures, away from the fire. She vaulted off, landed running, dropped Gulliver to the ground, and spotted Sam's pickup parked on the far side of the barnyard from the fire. Sam stood beside it, waving her over.

She raced to him. "What happened?"

"Your hay caught fire. Lucky there wasn't more or it'd burn for days. It's mostly out by now. But the hay you had is all gone."

What would it cost to replace? Maybe Ty would give her credit. She saw embers under the metal roof, glowing between the metal poles.

She couldn't take it all in. Something felt wrong, but she didn't know what. Everything, she realized. Everything was wrong.

"What about the horses, Billie?" Sam asked.

"They're turned out. They aren't here in the barnyard," she said.

Then she remembered Hope in her stall, surrounded by the hay bales that were shading her.

"Oh my God," she said it so softly she hardly heard it herself. "There's a horse in there!"

She spoke in a soft, flat voice, unable to scream. Powerless. Helpless, she made herself move, made herself run toward the embers.

"Don't touch anything!" Sam yelled. "It's hot!"

It gave off a terrible heat, and when Billie got close, an even more terrible smell.

"I've got to get her out!"

Sam grabbed her arm. She twisted away. He grabbed her around the waist, held her, his arms strong and old, sharp and thin as wires that seem to cut her as she fought him.

"You can't do anything, Billie," Ty shouted at her. She wondered what he was doing here then remembered he volunteered as fire marshal. "That horse is dead."

She couldn't take her eyes off the stall. Couldn't stop seeing it burn when she wasn't here to help, Hope trapped where she had left her.

"Did the lightning cause it?" Billie asked.

"We'll check with the weather service if there were any strikes here. They keep a record. I doubt it though. Dad and Mom didn't notice anything." He waved a hand toward the stall. "It doesn't look to me like an accelerant was used."

"My horse died in there!" Tears streaked her face. "She tried to escape, Ty. She died trying to escape." Her voice rose to a wail.

Ty walked to the stall and looked in. "Nah," he said.

"LOOK AT HER!" Billie knew she was hysterical, out of control.

"It's got nothing to do with her running. It's the fire makes them look like that. It dries the water from their muscles, pulls them short, makes 'em look like they ran. Same with people who die in fires. We'll check her throat and nostrils to be sure, but smoke's what probably killed her," he said. "You can take comfort in that."

When Ty and the rest of the fire crew left, Billie dragged herself to the casita, Gulliver trudging beside her. She wanted a drink. Several.

Images of the fire swarmed over her like hornets. She paced the tiny casita. Gulliver watched her from the futon, his chin on his paws. She opened the door, stuck her head out into a swarm of moths and bugs, beetles, and gnats. She slammed it shut, pulled her cell phone from her hip pocket, and just stared at it. She stood at the table in front of her computer and let her fingers jitter across the keyboard. She looked out the window, checking for flames.

She perched on the edge of the futon and set her laptop on her knees. When the Google page loaded, she typed in *soring*, waited a few seconds, watching her hand tremble, as the little blue circle spun on the screen, searching.

The page loaded with a string of small photos. She clicked on each in succession, opening views of horses' scarred legs; huge shoes weighted with dozens of nails; champions staggering around the arena at some show in Tennessee, blue ribbons in their bridles. The same things she had seen at the show down the road at Rio del Oro.

Beneath the photographs were dozens of pages of articles and posts on this topic. How, if soring was so well-known and well-documented, could it even exist? Why wasn't it being prevented?

Billie glanced at the by-line on the first article and saw it was by a former senator. He wrote about introducing the Horse Protection Act in 1970 to stop soring and lamented that, decades later, owners and trainers continued the despicable practice. He ended by calling on citizens to stop going to walking horse shows and to boycott the companies that support them.

Beneath the article, she read comments from people who agreed with the senator, and others who defended the rights of individuals to treat their animals any way they wanted, damn the government and animal rights meddlers.

Billie shut the laptop, and sat staring at the window frame, its old wood rotten in places, nailed up decades ago. Dust furred the upper strip. The butted joints were pocked by termite-chewed areas, miniature battlefields. She needed an exterminator.

The sill, worn clean of paint, was littered with pens, Chap-Stick, pennies, a pottery shard she had found in the barnyard when she was moving in, and a rusted shoeing nail. She sighed. Anything for a diversion.

Soring. The word was a euphemism for torture. It conjured aching muscles, bruises, even anger—*I'm sore at you.* The word must have been chosen to hide the practice rather than revealing or defining it.

She closed her eyes, trying to imagine the world these horses and owners lived in, beyond the world of barns and shows to the community that supported them, flouting the laws that prohibited their every action.

Only one trainer had ever gone to jail—not for long, but that first jail sentence indicated that the world of unparalleled and unquestioned freedom could be shrinking. Whistle-blowers who once complained ineffectually now had some clout. Things would feel tighter, Billie imagined, claustrophobic.

Who were the people being squeezed by this?

She made herself a cup of coffee and turned back to the Mac. She loved research, following a twig that turned into a branch, a limb, a tree, a forest. When she straightened her back, it was two hours later. Gulliver scratched at the door, wanting to go out. She was late feeding the horses.

She didn't know the name of the forest, but she had identified some of the trees. Dale. Eudora. Richard? Maybe Richard.

Finding his name on a list of trainers and owners who had been cited for soring violations, she felt sick with disappointment and anger. How could she have found him attractive? How could she have flirted with a man who would do something like this? Even though she hadn't known, shouldn't she have sensed something?

She shut the computer. She was finished with him. Done. Luckily things hadn't gone any further than just a little flirting.

She hiked down the hill in the dark to feed and check on the horses. It was hours since Ty had buried Hope but the smell lingered in the stagnant night air. He must have brought Billie some hay from the Depot because she found a dozen bales of alfalfa under a tarp beside the feed shed. She should call and thank him, but she needed to get away. She couldn't stay on the ranch another second. She climbed into the truck, Gulliver jumped into her lap, and they headed out. Her truck tires chattered over the washboard road, their rhythm accented by some loose metal banging beneath the motor.

As she drove, she worried. If she locked the casita door, anyone who wanted to get in could open a window. She hadn't closed them so that air from the swamp cooler could circulate and cool the space. And if she had closed them, they had no locks anyway. If she had shut and latched the gate to the barnyard, anyone who wanted to get in could just go around it. The fence on either side was a drift fence that petered out in a few yards. Living so far out in the country, she never thought of intruders, at least, not until this week. People rarely came down the road to visit, and most of them were her sparse clients wanting to visit their boarded horses. They called ahead. Solitude was its own protection.

She wondered who had been there. What sick son of a bitch had set the fire? And had he, or she, known the filly would die in it?

CHAPTER 10

IT LOOKED LIKE a big night at DT's Bar and Grill. The parking lot—a desert field flattened by decades of trucks and trailers—was full of randomly parked vehicles. She opened the glove box and got a rawhide bone for Gulliver, poured him a bowl of water, and set them on the passenger side floor. She cracked the windows and turned off the engine, got out, decided it was too hot to leave Gully in the truck, got back in, and turned on the air conditioner. She left the truck running and nearly ran to the bar.

When she pulled open the heavy Mexican door, she was clobbered with noise: laughter, shouting, glasses set down hard, and the Gipsy Kings playing too loudly through the speakers. She smelled booze and sweat, perfume, cheese pizza, vomit, disinfectant, and sawdust. People were nearby. Lots and lots of them around her. Close.

A ripple of silence spread when she entered, as if she were a pebble thrown into the sea of chatter. Heads came up, faces turned to her, staring. It immobilized her.

From behind, she felt arms tighten around her, Josie

embracing her. Sam stood beside his wife, his arms outstretched to gather Billie in as soon as Josie let go.

"Tough luck, kid," he said.

"We're all scared of fire out here," Josie added. "Every damn one of us. Every damn year I hold my breath in case it's us. We all do."

As Josie talked, they led Billie to their table, tucked in the far corner. As they sat, Billie noticed that the room had again filled with talk and the faces had turned away from her. She sat on an overturned barrel with a chair back added to it, and DT himself—all three hundred and fifty pounds of his bearded, bug-eyed self—appeared beside her to take her order.

"On us," Sam told her.

Billie thanked him. "White wine."

Josie pointed to the empty glass in front of her. "Me too. Fill me up."

DT finished scribbling and thumped Billie's upper arm with a huge, rubbery fist. "Hear you had a close call, pardner."

"I lost a horse." Tears flooded her eyes, but she refused to let herself blink so they wouldn't fall.

"But you didn't lose your herd, kid. Didn't lose your house. Not," he gestured to Josie and Sam, "their house."

Sam bolted the rest of his drink. "Didn't lose the valley," he added. "Gin 'n lime, DT. Okay?"

"Or the mountain," Josie added.

"Or the mesa grasslands and the cattle grazing there," said DT. "Back a dozen years ago, fire took out the whole east face of that range down south." He grabbed a glass of wine from the tray of a passing waiter dressed like a prospector.

"This gal needs it first," he told the startled man. "Fire up at her place today."

Billie said thank you a few more times then downed the wine in a couple of gulps, as if it were water and she was shipwrecked.

Another glass appeared in DT's paw, and he set it in front of her. From the corner of her eye, she noticed a thin body dragging up a chair toward their table, and Ty sat down with them. "Hey, Mom, Dad." He turned to Billie, pointed at her glass. "You might want to sip this one."

Billie glared at him and bolted the first half, then eased up. The wine, she noticed happily, had got hold of her joints. Her elbows felt relaxed. Her ankles, knees, even the nape of her neck felt juicy and limber.

"I sure appreciate you coming out with the backhoe," she said, careful to enunciate.

Ty cocked back his chair, sitting slantwise with one lengthy ankle hooked around the lowest rung. The other foot pushed back, piston-like, so he could rock. *We could be sitting on a Southern porch,* Billie thought. *Not hunching over cable spool tables in an ocean of sawdust.*

She raised her hand to ask for another glass before she had finished this one. Among the weathered faces of cowmen and repairmen drinking, talking, playing cards, and shooting pool at the tables along the far wall, she spotted Richard, clean as stainless steel, perched on a stool at the bar. Loose from booze, she waved to him. He cocked his head at her, half smiled and stood.

In one of those weird conversational lulls all bars are given to, she heard the wind shriek through the loosed window frames. She glanced outside and saw branches blown horizontal. Dirt pinged against the door and windows, and each new person who arrived was more disheveled than the last.

"Join you?" Richard stood between Josie and Ty, across the table from Billie. The question was directed at Ty, not her.

"Sure," Josie scooted her chair over.

Richard caught Billie's eye as he sat. He smiled without moving his lips, just a tightening at the corner of his eyes, unnoticeable to anyone but her. He leaned forward, reached across the table and shook her hand.

"I heard about your fire," Richard said. "Anything I can do to help—"

"We already helped her," Ty said.

Richard nodded. "Well, maybe down the road, then." He caught DT's attention with a wave and pointed a circle around the table. "Another round."

DT disappeared behind the bar for the drinks. Billie's palms were numb, her hips liquid, verging on molten. She wondered if anyone could tell.

"I'm thinking we should take you home," Josie whispered in her ear. "You're on your way to being drunk."

Nope, Billie thought. *Not going home now, not ever. Not drunk, either.* This seemed witty enough to say aloud. Then she realized just how much she didn't want to go home, didn't want to pass the barn, the burned hay, the trailer with its memories of the filly. She didn't want to crawl into bed with that fresh in her mind.

DT set down their glasses. Billie grabbed at hers with both hands, circled its base, rested her chin on its lip.

"You're pretty bombed, honey," Josie said.

"I don't think so." Billie spoke on an exhale, heard herself slur. "Oops. Gulliver will have to drive me home." She turned to Richard. "My dog is a designated driver."

Josie exchanged a look with Sam. Billie lifted her chin from her glass and wiggled back into her chair. She straightened her shoulders, took a deep breath, ready to pick a fight.

She leaned across the table toward Richard, a slight wave of vertigo putting a sharp edge on her anger. "Would you like to know about the horse who burned to death at my place?" she asked him.

The table fell totally quiet. Billie heard voices from other tables, laughter, calls for the waiter. But their table was hushed. She watched Richard register what she had said. His eyes flicked side to side, as if checking for ways out. She felt a regrettable pang of attraction to his stocky body, curly hair, a tug of sympathy and recognition that he felt trapped because he wanted her.

"Okay, tell me," he said, wary, resigned, unsure why she had focused on him.

Well, Billie thought, *he's going to find out.*

Images from her Google search rose before her. Images of Hope in her stall the night Billie first saw her, images from the show.

"Billie," Josie laid a warning hand on her forearm.

Billie pulled away, balled her hand into a fist. "She was a walking horse filly," she said to Richard. "Just a baby. A year-ling. I got her at your show."

"I don't have a show," he sounded defensive to her, relieved.

"The walking horse show," she clarified. "Last weekend. At the showgrounds. That show that you were at." She was aware that her grammar was flawed and her *s*'s sounded extra sibilant.

"Okay? So?"

"Okay?" she asked. "'Okay'? You know what that means."

"I'm sure I don't." His voice was low, clear, and angry.

"You're a liar," she said.

"And you're drunk."

Billie considered this and decided he was probably right. She was drunk. But not drunk enough. She was still seeing Hope's burned body. She was still thirsty. She grabbed Josie's glass and drained it.

"Hey!"

"Sorry, Josie. Thought it was mine. I'll buy you another."

Sam leaned across his wife. "Billie you've had a horrible day. We're all sympathetic. How about calling it quits while we're still friends? Josie and I'll drive you home."

Billie liked the way Josie's wine had her feeling, like Peter Pan flying over London. She wasn't ready to leave DT's. DT himself stood with a couple of beer mugs in his hands, looking at her. Billie noticed that her vision was extra sharp. She saw everything.

"You are part of that world," she told Richard.

"Excuse me?" he asked.

"The world of gaited horses that go to shows," she explained. "Like that little filly. Just a baby! You know what?" She stood up to draw attention to herself then realized she already had everyone's attention. The whole big room was thick with listening.

A few years ago, she'd gone to a boxing match with Frank, when they were still married. He was doing a feature on the featherweight champion, a fine-boned muscly man with freckled skin who was pretty enough to model for GQ and bright and outspoken enough to be interviewed for *Frankly*. "The Allure of Blood Sports" was the title Frank had planned for the piece. It never ran; Billie forgot why. Maybe the guy had lost a fight, got his aquiline nose smashed, or maybe something else had happened. Whatever. Standing up in DT's, she remembered that she loved the feel of ringside, the flecks of sweat, the thuds of gloves on flesh, the deep grunts. She loved the way men looked at each other before attacking. She loved the way she felt before she fought.

"You," she pointed at Richard, "are part of that *whole world* that tortures horses. I've been reading up on it. Burning their legs with acid and wrapping them in chains!" She was playing to the room. She spoke loudly so everyone would hear her and was pleased at the gasp that followed her accusation.

Josie buried her face in her hands. Billie ignored her.

"Here now, Billie," Sam handed her a big glass of something. "Try this."

Billie drank, not liking the taste. Maybe it was gin, which she didn't like, but hey, it was still a drink. Richard stood up, said something to Sam, and walked away.

CHAPTER 11

BILLIE WOKE AT home with a don't-lift-your-head-if-you-want-to-live hangover that brought with it a huge thirst, nausea, and a sticky shroud of guilt.

She lay on her stomach on the futon and tried to reconstruct what had happened between then and now. She couldn't come up with much. Who had she insulted? How had she gotten home? Where was her truck? If it was here, at home, had she driven it, and if she had driven it, had she hit anything or anyone?

She licked her cracked, parched lips. She could tell that her breath stank.

Where was Gulliver? She sat up fast, saw him watching her from the end of the futon, and quickly lay down again to wait for the room to stop whirling.

When she was able to open her eyes again, she saw the light on the answering machine blinking. Then her cell phone beeped to tell her she had a message. Hashtag's owner, Kristine. "Heard you had a fire out there! Call me!"

Gulliver, now tucked up under her arm, licked her chin.

Billie decided that she probably hadn't killed anyone or she would have woken up in jail, not on her scruffy futon with her dog beside her and her head dividing into wedges. The one time she was jailed, she'd been arrested for assault. Frank sent her to a loft in Tribeca to interview a family accused of molesting their foster children. She went to use the bathroom and mistakenly entered a bedroom where the foster mother was in bed with one of the kids. Billie lost it. The foster father called the cops. The cops called Frank, who bailed her out and got the charges dropped.

She'd written a good article.

She drifted away again.

She heard people talking nearby. She wanted them to be quiet, so she ignored them. Someone said her name. She tried to ignore them some more. But they were insistent, repeating themselves, "Wake up, Billie! Wake up!"

She really didn't want to. She knew that as soon as she connected with their voices, opened her eyes, she would feel a billion times worse than she already did. Which was very damn bad.

She heard Josie and a man, probably Sam. She decided to stay safely behind her eyelids, in the dark, but Josie said, "Honey, wake up. You're scaring Gulliver."

Bright, scalding light, divided into sharp spikes of color, snatched at her temples. Gulliver sat on the bed beside her, staring at her. His paw rested on her forearm. Josie stood beside the bed, looking blurry.

"I bet your head hurts," Josie seemed to scream. "You've got to have an epic hangover."

Billie wanted to throw up. Instead, she faded out.

She woke later, feeling like shit. The horses were hungry. She could cope no matter how badly she felt. She had fed with the flu and injuries; she could feed with a hangover. At least she was alone.

She was disappointed not to find her truck outside the casita. That meant someone had driven her home, got her into the house, and put her to bed. She hoped it was Josie, but Billie wasn't up to calling her yet to find out and maybe thank her. She trudged down the hill to the barnyard, each step sending shards of glass through her eyeballs. The truck was parked beside the hay barn. Billie found the keys under the floor mat with a note:

I think I understand how you feel. I'd like a chance to explain and defend myself. When I call you later, please don't hang up on me. Richard.

Billie considered lying down on a hay bale and going back to sleep. But Starship banged his feeder against the fence and whinnied. The pain of that noise propelled her through her morning chores.

She and Gulliver got back to the casita a little after eleven, much later than usual, but at least the horses were all fed and watered. Billie poured herself a glass of ice water and sipped it. Halfway through, she swallowed a couple of Advil, promising herself two more in a couple of hours. She'd worry about liver damage later. She just wanted the pain to ease. She turned off the house phone and switched her cell to vibrate. When it went off a little before noon, its motion felt like an assault.

"What?" she groaned.

"This is Richard. How are you feeling?"

"Fine," Billie said. "How are you?"

"Fine." He didn't say anything else. Then, "Did you find my note?"

"Yes."

"Well . . . ?"

She didn't answer.

"You still up for dinner like we'd planned?" he asked. "Say at seven? That'll give us both time to get our horses fed."

Absolutely not, she thought, but before she could stop herself, she asked, "What can I bring?"

"Could you pick up some milk for the kids? That way I won't have to go out for anything."

Milk for the kids? Was that a dig at her drinking? What about a bottle of wine for the adults?

She hung up and noticed that the light on the answering machine signaled three messages waiting. She played them.

She was into her overdraft protection.

She hadn't paid her Visa bill.

The charitable donation she had promised to make to a horse rescue in Colorado was past the date she had promised it by.

She shut her eyes.

Later, when Billie returned to the barnyard to feed, she crawled up the haymow and dragged three bales onto the truck bed. She drove around the barnyard and fed each horse, throwing huge flakes of hay over the fences into the feeders. Each twist of her body, each grunting effort, made her feel like she was going to pass out or be sick. She promised herself she would never get drunk again. While she fed, Gulliver waited in the passenger seat, one paw on the dashboard, braced.

When Billie had finished feeding, she climbed into the truck, turned on the air conditioning, pulled Gulliver onto her lap, and cried.

"Can I help?"

Gulliver looked at Ty leaning against the truck door next to him and wagged his tail.

"I'm fine," Billie said

"I can see that."

She hadn't even heard him drive in. She wiped her eyes with the heels of her palms.

"How about I give you a lift up the hill to my folks' and make us some dinner?"

"I've got a date. I've got to get dressed."

"Oh." He stepped away from the truck. "Well."

Her head still hurt. Her stomach still felt churned up. "I'm never drinking again," she said.

Ty turned back to his truck. "Might not be a bad idea. Have a nice night."

She thought there was an edge to his tone, maybe irony, or sarcasm.

For a few moments, she sat in her truck while memories ganged up on her. She was putting up roadblocks as fast as she could, but the images were sliding around them. The light she saw as she rode home on Starship. The flames. Hope dead in her stall, her legs pulled tight as if she were running. The smell.

CHAPTER 12

BILLIE SHOWERED AND dressed in a pair of navy shorts and a fitted white T-shirt. Her buzzed hair dried fast and in spikes, and she wished she'd remembered to use conditioner. Instead, she squirted hand lotion onto her palm, rubbed her hands together and finger-combed it through her hair. Not great but better.

There was no time for makeup, but she grabbed a tube of tinted lip gloss and swiped it over her lips.

She quickly rubbed cream on her arms and legs and found her flip-flops under the futon. Sunglasses hid her puffy eyes. She was still full of resolve and righteous anger, still ready to fight. But she wondered about his house, his horses, his kids. Him. She gave Gulliver a bowl of water and a beef-basted chew, stuck a steno pad into her handbag, made sure she had some pens and her cell phone, and headed out.

She almost forgot the milk and had to double back to the Depot, hoping Ty would have some in the cooler. She paid the kid, who worked there in the evenings, for the milk and a dozen eggs with dung and feathers still stuck on.

She slid out of the truck at Richard's, suddenly aware of the wet spot on her thighs where she'd held the bottle as she drove. Richard came out to greet her, wearing faded jeans and a softly worn denim shirt with the sleeves rolled up.

"Unpasteurized." She held out the milk. "Might be organic. Who knows? Came from a cow I know down the street."

"I'm glad you came." He took the bottle from her, his fingers grazing hers.

The door swung open, and Billie saw Sylvie with a teenage boy behind her, taller than his sister, but younger by a couple of years—the boy Billie had watched ride at the horse show. "My daughter Sylvie you've already met. And this is Bo, my son."

Billie smiled and said hi to them.

"Put this in the fridge, will you, Syl?" Richard asked.

Sylvie reached for the bottle and read the label. "It's from the feed store," she said. "Tuberculosis."

Billie felt her smile tighten.

"You're a total bitch," Bo said. "I like this kind of milk the best, with cream on the top."

"Whatever." Sylvie swanned her way up the porch steps and into the house, letting the screen door slam.

"I got you some eggs too." Billie reached back into her truck and handed them to Bo.

He opened the carton and looked inside. "All different colors," he said. "Those really are the best kind." Then he sang a snatch of the old Beastie Boys song "Egg Man."

"Shut up, Bo," his sister yelled from the house. "You sound like a cow in heat."

He grinned at Billie.

"Come in," Richard said.

Inside the house, log walls were whitewashed from the baseboards up to the vaulted ceiling. The plank floor gleamed, and the chairs and sofa were made from driftwood laced together with rawhide.

Billie felt as if she had known each cow whose hide stretched over a pillow.

"Did you kill and skin these?" It was out of her mouth before she even knew she was going to say it.

He blinked at her. "They came with the house. I bought it furnished a couple of months ago."

So this wasn't really his taste yet. She was relieved. The house felt like the architectural equivalent of a frozen dinner.

As if sensing her disappointment, he said, "I have added a few things. Mostly practical stuff to the barn and pastures. But that's mine." He pointed toward a small Navajo rug that hung on the wall, woven in earth tones with deep red arrows arced in flight above a forest of stylized pine trees.

She ran her fingers over the tightly woven wool. "It's gorgeous!"

"I bought it when I was about Sylvie's age. I had no idea about its history. I just thought it was pretty." He showed her to a glass-fronted cabinet. "I found these just lying around here. Mostly from the corrals near the barn."

Pottery shards, a couple of arrowheads, a mano, and part of what had been an axe blade lay on a shelf.

"I'm learning about the tribes who left these behind," he said. "Their lives, how they hunted and farmed, what they ate. It's fascinating."

"Did this interest you in Tennessee?"

"Not so much. It's all new to me here."

His enthusiasm made her grin.

Richard offered her a glass of wine, which she accepted with more gratitude than she hoped showed. He grabbed a Dos Equis from the fridge door, opened it, and perched on a stool, elbows on the counter. The kids had disappeared out the kitchen door. Billie heard them laughing.

"Before we eat, we need to talk," Richard said.

Billie settled onto a stool that faced him. "Okay."

He slid his fingers around the beer can's lip, staring at the tracks he made in the condensation, watching small droplets roll to the bottom.

"You were right about me," he said. "Don't look surprised. You did your research and you found out about me. I've sored horses."

"I'm surprised you admit it."

"I don't have a choice, do I? I grew up in Tennessee. My family raised walking horses and fox trotters and spotted saddle horses. We trained and showed them. That was how my folks made a living."

"How could you . . . ?"

He raised his hand asking her to wait.

"Listen to me. Soring started in the 1950s. Horses who walked big started to win big. If that's what it took . . . So my folks learned how to do it, to win."

He looked at her, his eyes troubled and serious.

"They taught me how to do it, and I did it. Thought nothing of it. We all did it. It never meant anything. We all got caught from time to time. We'd get a ticket and that was all. No fine. No punishment, certainly no jail time. Getting caught was just another rite of passage. Once you'd been written up, you were a real trainer."

He looked at her to see if she understood. Billie wished she could pull out her pad and take notes, because as he talked, she saw everything he said in quotations in her article. She was mentally underlining for emphasis, restructuring for clarity.

"And?" she prompted.

"I married another trainer, Mary Lou, the mother of the kids. We ran a really topflight barn. Won a lot. Had wealthy clients. Sylvie was born. Then Bo. They grew up in that world too."

"I saw them ride at the show."

"Right," he said. "Sylvie loves Big Lick horses, and she's a gifted rider. She's got a big future in this business."

Billie rocked back off the stool and stood. "You taught her to hurt horses?"

Hearing the anger in her voice, Richard looked down at his hands on the counter. "We did, me and my wife. We taught her—and Bo—everything they'd need to know to become successful."

Billie finished her wine and set the glass on the counter, trembling. "You son of a bitch."

He looked up at her. "I know. I know. But then I quit."

He'd quit? Billie had a dozen questions for him, maybe a hundred. While she was deciding where to start she heard, "Daddy?"

The little girl standing in the doorway held a toy horse in one hand and a toy horse trailer in the other. Billie recognized her as one of several children who had come out to the ranch on a kindergarten class trip in May. Billie remembered her as the star of that visit. While the other kids had chased each other around, climbed the haymow, and pretended to be disgusted by manure, this kid had stood at a corral gate, her elbows on the railing, and discussed Billie's horses with her, asking their names and whether or not they were trained to ride.

"Alice Dean, this is Billie Snow. She lives nearby."

"I know," the child said.

"You came out to my ranch with your class, right?" Billie asked. "We talked about my horses."

"You have a gray horse named Star Wars."

"Starship. Yes, he's mine."

Alice Dean grinned, a smile like her father's but missing her front teeth.

"Why are you here?" She spoke with her father's accent. The *why* pronounced *wha*. "Daddy?" Alice Dean tugged at her father's jeans. "Foamy won't load. I need help."

Richard dropped to his knees beside her. "Show me what you've been doing with him."

Alice Dean repeated her movements. The plastic horse twisted to the side at the trailer door.

"Maybe you're asking too much too soon," Richard said. "Have you let him just stand at the back of the trailer to get used to it?"

"I want him in NOW. Git UP!" She flicked Foamy's haunch with her fingernail, but he still wouldn't load.

"Think about what I suggested." Richard rose smoothly.

"When can I ride, Daddy?" Alice Dean asked. "Now?"

"Honey, it's late!"

"I want to ride now. Please?"

Richard gave Billie an *I'm helpless* look and opened the patio door. "BO!" he called. "Bo!"

The boy appeared, ribby and wet in his bathing suit. "What?"

"Get your sister up on Morning Glory, okay?"

"But, Dad—"

"Just do it, okay? You can swim more later."

"It'll be *dark*."

"The pool has lights, Bo. Take your sister to the barn, okay? Where's Sylvie?"

"She already went to the barn. Can't Alice Dean . . . ?"

"She's too little to go by herself. You take her. Now."

Alice Dean left her toys on the kitchen floor and took her brother's hand, smiling.

Richard turned to Billie and said, "At least I can make one of my children happy."

She wondered what he meant by that, if he was talking about the little tussle she had just witnessed between him and Bo or if he was referring to something bigger.

After they left, Richard started getting food out of the fridge and cabinets. Hamburger, rolls, pickles, mayo, onions, and lettuce. Billie watched without offering to help.

"You quit?" she prompted him.

He looked startled, as if he'd forgotten what they were talking about. Then he got himself another beer and poured her more wine.

"She made me," he said.

"Your wife?"

"No, Alice Dean."

"Alice Dean? How?"

"Just by being born, I guess. She came late. We didn't think we'd have any more kids. Alice Dean was a surprise. One day after she came, I was thinking about how I'd introduce her into the family business, how I'd tell her why her pony pranced and why she was winning blue ribbons. I couldn't do it." He shook his head. "I just couldn't do it."

"Even though you had done it with your other kids."

"Right. I don't know what changed in me. Maybe it was just getting older. I don't know, but I didn't want this baby to be any part of that world. So I quit."

"Just like that?"

He barked a laugh "Not quite. My wife was furious. My parents felt betrayed. My kids hated me. Sylvie still hates me. I don't know what to do about her. She still rides sore horses. I won't let her sore mine, so she rides for other people. I don't know that it would be worth it to really fight with her about it. She's nearly an adult, so she can do what she wants." Billie started to say something, but Richard kept on talking. "Bo hates horses and horse shows, so he's mostly glad I gave it up."

"You don't show at all anymore?" Billie asked.

"I only show sound horses now. By 'sound' I mean horses that haven't been sored. I can't undo what I did, but I can live my life differently from now on. That's why I'm here in Arizona. I left the scene back east, left all of it. It wasn't easy…"

He moved closer. Billie could smell the warm cotton of his shirt, a tantalizing hint of clean skin. He took a big breath and visibly forced himself to relax.

"You really don't do it anymore?" she asked.

"My barn and pastures are filled with animals I train to compete…" He made quotation marks with his index fingers. "'In compliance with federal animal cruelty laws.' Unlike just about everyone else in this business, I'm not watching for the

USDA inspectors to catch me with sored horses. I don't need to worry if I'm in compliance with the scar rule, because my horses don't have scars."

"What's the scar rule? I see it mentioned as a reason for disqualifying a horse at a show: scar rule violation."

"Haven't you looked that up yet? It's the rule that spells out what scars are *not* permitted on a show horse's legs. The rule that dictates what can and what can't be done to them. Of course, since I don't sore, I don't win. No wins, no customers. No income. No marriage. Mary Lou's born and bred into that world, as I was. She couldn't leave it behind—leave her folks, her brothers and sisters, her grandparents. They're all there, all involved with these horses. It's her life. And when I left it, I betrayed her. All of them."

"Dad?" Sylvie's appearance in the doorway seemed to startle her father. She had a pink cell phone pressed to her ear and a huge T-shirt over bare legs, dripping water.

"Sylvie, hi."

"Dad, I'm talking to Dale. I'm going to ride for him in the show next week, okay?" Her voice vibrated with excitement. "So can Bo take my rides on our horses?"

"You have to ask him yourself."

"I will, but I wanted to clear it with you first. Please, Daddy?"

"It's up to you." Billie heard the disapproval in his tone, but it seemed to wash over his daughter.

"Great!" She disappeared back out the door, leaving wet footprints behind.

"Sylvie is going to be the top junior rider in the country," Richard said.

"She is?"

"Now that she's riding for Dale."

Bo appeared at the door.

"Where's your sister?" Richard asked.

"I led her around for a bit. Now she's putting her bridle away and playing with her toy ponies."

"Don't just leave her alone!"

"Jeez, Dad. You and mom left me and Sylvie alone plenty."

Richard sighed. "Still. Go to her."

"In a moment," Bo said. "I want to get my fiddle first and take it out there."

"Really?" Billie asked. "You play?"

Richard answered for him. "He does. He's actually quite good."

"I'd like to hear you," she said.

Bo shrugged and picked up a violin Billie hadn't noticed propped on a chair in the corner.

"Sylvie wants you to take her rides," Richard told him as Bo started to leave.

"I know. I saw her. It's not like we have a chance anyway," Bo mumbled.

"Do the best you can, Bo. That's all I ask."

"Sylvie's going to beat me on Dale's horse."

"She's a better rider. She'd beat you anyway."

"Sad," Bo said. "Want to come watch me get whopped by my talented sister next weekend?" he asked Billie.

"Sure," she said. "I'd love to."

She and Richard ate silently, sitting on stools pulled to the kitchen window that overlooked the swimming pool. Red-tailed hawks hunted in cottonwoods that screened the pool from the barn. Billie was relieved he didn't need to talk anymore, and she didn't need to entertain him or answer him. When they had finished eating, he cleared the dishes, refusing her feeble offer to help. He carried everything to the sink, filled it with water and soaked the plates. Then he poured her another glass of wine and opened a third beer for himself.

Billie filled her mouth and swallowed.

His shirt mesmerized her, teal-colored cotton tucked loosely into jeans so it bloused at the waist. The button-down collar was unbuttoned, exposing a triangle of rusty curls flecked with grey. She could so easily have reached up to adjust that collar, to brush that hair with the backs of her fingers. She focused on the short whiskers he had missed when he shaved, the edge of his jaw softened by middle age.

He ran his index finger down her forearm and circled her wrist with his hand. She closed her eyes. He leaned forward and kissed her, pressing his lips harder against hers. Then he pulled away. "Is this all right?" he asked.

"Yes."

"You want me to stop?"

"No."

He stopped kissing her when the phone rang but let it go to voice mail. Billie heard a woman's deep Southern accent. "We need to talk, Richard."

Billie pulled away, watching him as he listened.

"I've got tickets for the kids' trip home, and I want you to arrange for them to be picked up at the airport. Beau Pa's in the hospital getting his pacemaker adjusted, so I don't think I can get to the airport to pick them up myself. You can call Hacker's Hacks . . ." She left a phone number for him to call. "So you call me, hear? By tomorrow noon."

Richard sighed when she hung up. "The kids' mother," he said.

"I thought you were divorced."

"I never said that."

"You're right. It's just what I thought."

"I will be divorced. We're separated, obviously," he said softly, his fingers hot little branding irons on her forearm. "She's in Tennessee. I'm here. We'll probably get divorced."

Billie pulled her arm away. "Probably? Separated? I'm heading home."

"Wait! Don't you want to see the barn? Meet the horses?"

"Maybe some other time."

He sighed. "Well, suit yourself."

Three children, she thought as she finished her drink. *Separated but not divorced. God, I'm an idiot.* All she needed in her bed was a married father of three with a history of torturing horses.

"I've got a lot of work to do at home." Billie slung her bag on her shoulder, fished out the keys to her truck, and headed for the door.

Richard caught her wrist in his hand, pressing the keys into her palm, and turned her to him. His hands massaged her shoulders, her neck. He kissed her forehead.

"We're looking for a venue for the next horse show," he said. "How about if we have it at your place?"

Billie shrugged although she was seeing images of trucks and trailers pulling into her barnyard, unloading potential customers who might want to board their horses with her.

"You'd get an admission fee percentage," Richard said. "And a use fee per horse. It could add up. Think about it."

She didn't need to think for more than a minute.

"Sure," Billie said. "But I mean this. No soring."

He kissed her lips, opening the door for her to leave. "No soring."

CHAPTER 13

BILLIE DROVE HOME from Richard's without turning
on the truck's air conditioning, just rolled down the
windows and let the night air blow over her. She had
had enough to drink that she was grateful to be on dirt roads,
nowhere near the highway. She noticed that she was driving
pretty well though.

In the casita, she poured another glass of wine, folded
herself onto the futon, looking out the window at the sky.
Gulliver curled up on her lap. A full moon slipped from
behind the clouds. Her fingertips beat a soft tattoo on Gulliver's back, soothing him.

She ignored the blinking red light on the answering machine. Unpaid bills again, or something else she didn't want
to deal with. If it was Richard, he could wait until tomorrow.
If it was Frank, he'd probably ask where she had been when
he'd called, which was none of his business anymore. Still,
she wanted to hear his voice, even if they argued. Talking to
him made her feel tethered, even if it shouldn't.

She almost reached over to push the play button but held

off. *Breathe,* she told herself, *just breathe.* In her lap, Gulliver sighed. She ran her fingertips over his back until he yawned and curled tighter, falling asleep. Billie leaned over and kissed the top of his head.

Was this a hopeless situation with Richard that she had better quit before it got worse, or could it work? Three children! She liked Alice Dean and Bo. Sylvie not so much. But did it matter? The girl was almost out on her own, as her father had said. So Billie's opinion of her—and hers of Billie—didn't really matter. Since he already had three children, most likely Richard wouldn't want more, if things got that far between them. Maybe they wouldn't even need to discuss it. She had been pregnant once when she and Frank were married, but she miscarried. Frank was as sad as she when it happened, but the sadness clung to Billie long after it became the past for him.

To distract herself from the impulse to call him, she reached for a bag hanging over the back of the futon's black metal frame and pulled out a smaller bag that held a ball of variegated yarn. A circular knitting needle hung from the yarn with a half-knitted sock attached. Settling back against the pillows, she wrapped the yarn around her left index finger and with her right hand, slid the stitches toward the needle's point, ready to be knit.

She had been working on this sock for six years. Frank had bought the yarn when they were on vacation in Maine and had asked her to knit him a pair.

"I've never made socks," Billie had told him.

"You can knit anything."

"Sweaters," she'd said. "Scarves. Hats. Mittens."

"So, make mittens for feet."

She didn't tell him that socks were the last thing she wanted to make. The thin yarn, the complicated shaping, those tiny needles felt too fussy, too domesticated. She knit with worsted and bulky yarn. Things that she could start one day and finish the next, things she barely had to think about, let alone concentrate on.

They split up before she had mastered the first heel and divorced at the instep.

I should have thrown this damn project away, she thought, cupping it in her hand.

Instead, the day the divorce was final, she had ripped out the stitches, re-wound the ball, and started over. This time she made the leg differently, in a knit 2, purl 2 ribbing, not the stockinette stitch the pattern had called for. She had thought the ribbing would help the sock stay up on whoever's leg she eventually gave it to. She had struggled again through turning the heel and headed into the long, dull foot. She knit sporadically, with stitchless months interspersed with intense bursts of attention to those fine needles. First in New York, then on the plane to Arizona, she imagined the man who'd wear the socks when they were done. Each time her mind wandered away from the fantasy mate, and she saw Frank.

"You ever going to finish my socks?" he still asked her once in a while.

Sometimes she thought she would finish them. She imagined surprising him with them one birthday. A slim box in a padded envelope, no note. He would open it, startled by his feelings as he looked at the familiar yarn he had chosen, made into the socks he had asked for.

But most of the time Billie hated him and his feet. She hated him for the way he had pushed her, using her past to hook her to crimes he wanted her to write about, crimes against children who were suffering as she had.

Frank's "You can do it" gradually morphed into "You've got to do it. You can save these kids. You have to."

The exposés she wrote for him made her career, and won her awards.

Then one night, beside a warehouse in a garbage strewn street, she stood frozen, notebook in hand, while a man held a pistol to the head of a toddler. "Leave!" he'd screamed at her. "I'll shoot!"

She ran to their apartment, threw her notebook on the kitchen counter, packed her suitcase, and flew home to Arizona.

Frank had apologized over and over, but she never returned. Eventually she forgave him enough to let in bits of fondness, bits of yearning, which she sometimes regretted.

Her fingers, thickened and coarse from years of ranch work, snagged on the yarn and needles for another few rows.

She held up the sock to check on her progress then slipped her own foot through the ribbing, down the leg, past the heel and out through the needles. It was too big for her. It bagged around her ankle and flopped over her arch.

She pulled her foot out and set the sock and yarn on the pillow beside her. Then she lay back, pulled the sleeping Gulliver against her chest, and closed her eyes.

When she woke, she found the knitting tucked under her chin. When she stretched, her joints squeaked and popped. Gulliver lay frog-like, awake, his chin on his paws, tail wagging an invitation. *Get up. Get going. Open that bag of kibble!*

She was pouring cream into her coffee—wondering about Richard, the kids, their mother, their horses—when she heard Starship bang his feeder. She opened the door and yelled, "Coming!"

He banged it again.

On her walk down the hill to feed the herd, Billie wondered how Richard could justify allowing Sylvie to ride sored horses, to compete for a trainer like Dale—especially now that it was not only illegal, but the laws were starting to be enforced. Hadn't it occurred to him that if Sylvie were caught, she could be prosecuted? Ethics and morals aside, the kid might go to jail.

She was wondering if the horse in that last stall at Dale's was a mess of burned flesh and stacked pads when she reached the barnyard and Gulliver started to bark. It took her a second to register that something was wrong. Starship stood at his feeder, lifting it away from the fence then letting it go, the way he did every morning and evening at mealtimes. The horses in the corral beside him looked fine too, peering at her, waiting for her to serve them breakfast.

But when Gulliver's sharp barks became frenetic and he dashed away around the barn, Billie followed him.

Hashtag stood with both forelegs stuck through the twisted wire fence. Billie hoped she would stay that way until she could find wire cutters and get her out.

"Steady, girl!" Billie called, backing toward the feed shed where she kept her tools.

Hashtag stood still for a moment then she thrashed, heaving herself up and back, trying to break free. Sweat drenched her shoulders and flanks, and her eyes went white with panic.

Billy returned and approached with the cutters, speaking soothingly while the mare struggled, the wires tightening around her forelegs. Pain and fear made her pull even harder. The wires cut deeper. Blood spurted from the leg closest to Billie.

"Easy, girl," Billie cooed. "Oh, God, easy." She tried to angle her way in close enough to grab a wire and cut, but each time she approached, Hashtag struggled harder.

Billie retreated far enough that the mare stopped struggling and pulled her cell phone from her pocket. When Doc answered, she didn't even introduce herself, just started talking. "Cutting her leg . . . can't get close . . . What should I do?"

Hashtag tried to rear, fell over in a horrifying slow-motion contortion distorted by her entangled legs. One of the strands of wire snapped as she kicked and wrapped itself around her face.

"Do you have a horse blanket nearby?" Doc asked. "No? Some cloth? Take off your shirt then. Approach her from behind her head so you don't get kicked, and be careful. If she swings her head and hits you, she could kill you. There's a rhythm to her movements, you see it? Thrash-rest. Thrash-rest. Get that shirt over her eyes while she rests. She'll hold still when she can't see. That'll get you time to cut her loose, but be quick."

"Don't hang up, Doc!" Billie crammed the phone back into her pocket and pulled her T-shirt over her head. It didn't look big enough to cover both of the horse's eyes, so Billie sliced it up the front with the wire cutters. Hashtag seemed to struggle forever this time, banging her head against the ground, pawing, kicking, with each movement pulling herself tighter and tighter into the web of fencing. The minute she finally lay flat, exhausted, Billie lunged, knelt on her neck, wrapped the shirt over her eyes, and tied it in a knot under her jaw. She jumped away, afraid the thrashing would start again. But the blindfolded horse lay still. Moving fast, Billie cut the wire, untangling it as she went, and carefully lifted the barbs from torn flesh, freeing her.

Billie heard a distant voice. Doc, she realized, still on the phone, talking in her pocket.

"She's squirting blood from her leg," she told him. "She's still lying down. I've cleared the wire away from her so she can get up."

"Leave the blindfold on. It's why she's staying down and quiet. Now press on the wound until the bleeding stops. Press hard. And don't get kicked."

Billie grabbed Hashtag's spurting foreleg and pressed into the blood with her thumbs while the horse lay quietly on her side, panting, soaked in sweat and blood.

"When it stops squirting . . ." Doc's voice crackled. "I'm getting out of range, Billie, so I'll try to get this said . . . When you can, roll up some cotton into a ball and stick it into the wound to keep pressure on. Bandage over that to hold it in place. That'll stop the bleed . . . She'll be fine . . ."

"Can you come?" Billie asked, but the call had ended.

She waited, counting one-one thousand, two-one thousand until she reached sixty. When she lifted her thumbs the bleeding had stopped. She had nothing to bandage with, so she took off her bra, cut it as she had her T-shirt and used that. Finally, she pulled the shirt from the horse's eyes. Blinking, Hashtag lay still then struggled to her feet, testing herself for pain. Once she was on her feet, Billie led her, limping, to a small pen near Starship. Then she fed them breakfast.

What would Doc tell her to do now, if she could reach him? Antibiotics, she knew, a tetanus booster and pain medicine. Billie got them from the refrigerator in the feed shed and gave the antibiotic and tetanus booster injections, one on each side of the neck. She sprinkled powdered pain medicine over a scoop of oats and fed her that. At least the horse had an appetite.

The sun was way up, scorching. Billie ran out of hay before she ran out of horses and headed back to the barn. She swung the hay hook into a bale that looked like it would easily slide away from the others and into the truck bed, but it wouldn't budge. She tugged and struggled until she gave up and climbed onto the mow to find the bale she wanted tied to another bale. She cut the twine and both bales skidded past her onto the ground. They were too heavy for her to lift into the truck. She'd have to cut the twine and lift each prickly, slippery flake, one at a time. From the corner of her eye, she watched Hashtag try, then succeed, to pull off her bandage.

Billie sank to her knees beside the searing truck bed and wept, half expecting someone to appear, Ty or Richard or Sam or Josie, or some stranger out in the middle of the desert. Someone who would say, "You always feed your horses naked?" and "Do you cry every day?"

She would scream, "YES! Every single fucking day! I cry because I am hurt and tired and broke, and my horses are hurt, and it's so fucking hot, and there are flies and rattlesnakes everywhere, and the baby horse burned to death, and the others are hungry, and I have to buy more hay, and I don't have any fucking money!"

But no one showed up and soon—very soon—it was too hot to cry anymore. So she loaded a different bale into the truck and fed the last few horses. She whistled up Gulliver, and this time she drove up the hill to the casita. She really needed to call Kristine back to return her messages, and now she would have to call her to report the injury.

Doc phoned just after noon. "How's the horse?"

She told him what she had done to care for her. "Can you come see her?"

He said, "You did fine. Nothing more I can do now except wait and see how she is in a day or two."

Billie felt bereft, abandoned, like a child left alone outside a new school. Even the realization that she wouldn't have another monster vet bill to pay for a ranch call and treatment didn't fill that hollow.

CHAPTER 14

O N THE EVENING of the horse show at her place,
Billie climbed into the hayloft and sat on the edge,
bare legs dangling out into the steamy, nearly still
air. Maybe she should have worn jeans instead of shorts, but
in the pre-monsoon humidity, she appreciated every little puff
of breeze on her skin. Shorts and sandals felt a whole world
better than jeans and boots in the heat. Hay stuck to her
sweaty palms as she fiddled with the unfinished rope halter
she had retrieved from the mess on the casita floor to finish
tying. Gulliver lay beside her, pressed against her thigh, his
paws over the sill too. The sun hung high in the western sky,
a fireball more than an hour from setting. On the horizon, a
few thick white clouds piled up into columns sparse and high
enough that Billie was certain they would stay dry at least for
the next day or two.

From this perch, she watched her barnyard fill. Trucks pulling horse trailers drove in through the gate and parked haphazardly on three sides of the big rectangular corral designated as
the arena. Earlier, she had set up an area for the inspector to

check each horse, marked with fifty-five-gallon water drums and posted with a cardboard sign: *INSPECTION.* It looked pretty iffy to her, but the people who drove in seemed to know what it was for, and they parked away from it.

She watched the drivers and passengers get out of their trucks, stretch, and get to work setting up. They unrolled carpets of fake grass, unfolded chairs and tables, and unloaded coolers from their vehicles. A white cargo van pulled into the arena, stopped, and a hefty woman in a spangled green dress emerged lugging first an electronic organ then a bench and a pot of geraniums. Within minutes, waltzes filled the air.

Starship and Hashtag leaned against the fence of their corrals, craning their necks to see as much as possible. As horses were unloaded they whinnied. Billie's whinnied back. A line formed as people waited for the caterer's truck to park and get set up, and soon Billie smelled fried meat and onions.

The inspector ran a yellow tape around the water drums Billie had put up. To one side he placed a table with a clipboard, pens, and a chair. Beside them, he set an ice chest. In the middle of the roped-off area, he put two orange cones on the ground. Immediately, a line of horses and their grooms formed, calling greetings to him, joking. One after another, the inspector examined the horses' lower legs and hooves, observed them walking a figure eight around the cones, and released them to compete.

"Hey!" Richard appeared below her, his head tipped back. "You going to come down and join us?"

"I didn't know you were here yet." She slid back from the edge of the hay, tucked Gulliver under her arm, and climbed down the ladder, enjoying the feel of Richard's eyes on her as she descended.

"Hold up." When she was near the bottom, he placed one hand on her waist, and with the fingers of his other hand, he peeled something off the back of her thigh. "Foliage." He reached around to show her the bit of hay, almost embracing her. She couldn't keep from leaning slightly into him, her body asking him to close his arms around her.

It was hotter on the ground without the breeze she had felt up on the mow. She set Gulliver down to race off to play with the other dogs.

"Where are the kids?" Billie asked, hoping it was just her and Richard for the evening.

"Sylvie's getting her horse ready for her classes later tonight," he said. "Alice Dean is at the trailer with her. And Bo is working on your arena lights. Where do you want them? On those posts there?"

They moved out to where they could give Bo some help. He set portable lights around the arena and attached them to a generator. In the early sunset glare, Billie switched them on, and she and Richard struggled to see if they were working or not.

"Hey, Billie! What's going on here?"

"Horse show, Josie. Stick around."

Josie was dressed in her outfitters clothes, real denim jeans and a snap-shut Western shirt with a bandana at her roadmap of a neck. It made Billie hot just looking at her, and knowing that she wore a cotton undershirt too made Billie feel even hotter. Josie had explained that the undershirt worked as a personal swamp cooler—sweat into it, and as the sweat dried, it cooled the wearer. Billie had tried it and never felt any benefit.

Josie marched over to take a look at the inspector checking horses. She rocked back and forth on the worn heels of her boots, squatted down to get a closer look at what the inspector saw, then returned to Billie. "Thanks, but this ain't my kind of thing. I'm more of a rodeo and gymkhana kind of gal. Rocky trails in the mountains, ya know? Inspections not needed."

Billie felt as if she should explain, tell her this was a show for sound horses, but that felt like asking for a kind of fight she didn't want.

As the three of them stood there in awkward silence, the announcer's voice welcomed the exhibitors to the show, thanked Billie for her hospitality in hosting it, and read an invocation. Everyone stood, hands on heart, for the Pledge of Allegiance. The national anthem, sung by the organist in a ripe mezzo-soprano voice, ended in cheers.

When the announcer called the first class, horses streamed into the ring, took up positions along the rail and waited to be told what to do. The riders wore tight pants in black, brown, red, olive green, and tan, with matching coats and bowler hats. It looked like a photograph from a much earlier time, maybe from the 1930s.

"Flat walk," the announcer said. "Riders, please show us the flat walk."

"I'm leaving." Billie watched as Josie turned and headed back toward her truck. Even over the announcer's voice, Billie heard her slam the door.

As the sun set and shadows lengthened, the temperature dropped, a breeze ruffled the horses' manes, and the lights

Bo had installed came on in the arena. Class after class was judged, applauded, and exited, ribbons fluttering from the horses' bridles. Horse after horse passed through inspection, and as she watched, Billie imagined that this little show here at her place might actually be the future of all walking horse shows: sound horses, happy people.

Good slogan, she thought, and pulled her notebook from her pocket to write it down.

"You taking notes?" Dale stood close behind her, his mouth close to her ear, his tone sarcastic.

She hadn't seen, heard or felt his approach. The tone of his voice flooded her with the adrenaline of danger.

She held out the notebook so he could read what she had written down for himself, and she also recited: "'Sound horses, happy people.' It makes a good slogan." She nodded at a blue ribbon clipped to the trainer's breast pocket. "You won."

"More to come," he said.

"I guess you'd know."

"You're pretty rude," he said.

"You're pretty crooked." She said it before she knew she was going to.

He brought his face so close to her she smelled hamburger on his breath. His eyes drilled hers, searching, threatening. He stepped forward, to force her backward. She shoved him hard in the chest.

He stumbled, caught himself. "Oh lady, you have no idea, do you? No idea at all. Well, you will." He turned and walked stiffly away.

She made it to the feed shed and turned on the lights, inside and out. Flies and moths gathered instantly, creating fluttering pillars of bug life that thickened by the second. They battered the windows and crawled on the walls: June bugs, kissing bugs, walking sticks, and praying mantises. She leaned against the side of the building in a dark, bugless spot and tried to stop shaking. Her mouth tasted like she'd chewed aspirin and hadn't spat it out. Her skin felt clammy. She couldn't breathe.

When that first breath finally came, she realized that Dale was busy talking animatedly to Richard by the arena in-gate, not paying any attention to her. Alice Dean was with them, playing at her father's feet. Billie shoved herself off the wall and, wobbly legged, drifted back toward the trailers, looking for Dale's rig.

Just as she found it, Dale's groom Dom backed out of the trailer on hands and knees, patting the floor as he went, as if he had dropped something. He rose to his feet, gave the trailer a final searching look, and sprawled onto a lounge chair. A match flared. Slowly he lifted a joint to his lips and inhaled, the tip glowed. He held the smoke in his lungs, stretched his arm to watch the ember fade, and then put the joint back between his lips for another toke.

Billie pulled out her cell phone and started a lively conversation with dead air, chatting about her board rates as if to a customer. Pretending to be distracted by her conversation, she drifted over to the trailer and plopped onto its fender. The groom looked up sleepily. Billie gestured at the air for emphasis.

"No, I charge more than that," she said. "And I add on a service charge for . . ."

She slid off the fender and wandered toward the back of the trailer, talking. Most of the trailer stalls had horses in them, but the one Dom had been searching was empty. She leaned against the trailer fender outside that stall, bracing herself with her free hand behind her. As she babbled on, her fingers explored the stall floor, searching where she had seen him looking. She touched something small and long and round under sodden sawdust, closed her fingers around it and slid it out of the muck just as Dom appeared in front of her.

"I know! I know!" she said to the phone, hoping he thought she was as oblivious as she was pretending to be.

He snapped his fingers to get her attention then waved her off the trailer. She stood, mouthed *sorry*, and walked away. When she looked for them, Richard and Dale were still talking.

She considered what she had found, a small syringe with a short slender needle, maybe 27 gauge, maybe even smaller, still in its guard. She held the syringe up to the light and saw that there was still some fluid in it. In the feed shed, she stored the syringe in a baggie on the refrigerator shelf beside other medicines.

She closed and locked the door when she left. As she stepped outside, a blurry movement, something dark at the edge of the shed wall, drew her attention. Maybe just a guy peeing where he shouldn't. But he turned without hitching his pants, looked both ways as if worried he'd be seen, and limped away. She couldn't see his face, but she had watched him limp away from that same building when they were in it the day he had grabbed her shoulder, the day he had asked her to work with him and she had said no. She recognized his shape and gait.

Charley.

She followed him around the shed's corner. As if he felt her behind him, he stopped and turned. Their eyes met.

"What?" Billie asked.

Keeping his hands low, his gestures small, he waved her away.

"What?" she almost pleaded.

"Nothing," he whispered so she could barely hear him. Then he turned and walked toward Dale's rig.

She watched as, at the trailer, Sylvie checked her horse's girth then mounted in a smooth arc. Like a ballerina waiting in the wings to go onstage—not in the full exaltation of performance but with a kind of inner preparation—an unconscious rehearsal of what was coming animated her body. Her back straightened, her shoulders dropped and squared, her neck elongated.

Charley walked alongside as Sylvie lined up her horse with the rest of her class, then he ran a rag over the stallion's face and legs and over Sylvie's boots, wiping away the minute amount of dust that might have settled during her short ride from the trailer.

Richard and Dale and Alice Dean were still there, next to the arena rails near the in-gate, the men still talking. Richard absently bent down and scooped up Alice Dean. Straddling his hip, she ran her toy horse trailer across his shoulders, up the back of his head.

When Billie approached, father and daughter smiled at her.

"So what do you think of the show, Billie?" Richard asked.

She looked around. Her barnyard was full of people who had paid to be there. The horses looked well cared for and, as Richard had promised, they were in flat shoes and not wearing chains. The arena had bloomed with riders and music. She heard laughter and applause.

But she wasn't going to make it easy for them. "There are horses in leg wraps in one of the trailers," she said, looking at Dale. "Why do they need leg wraps if they're sound?"

"Which trailer?" Richard asked.

Billie pointed toward Dale's red truck. "Dale's leg wraps look like the wraps trainers sore under," she said.

"Everyone here tonight promised not to fix their horses," said Richard. "Like Groucho Marx said, sometimes a bandage is just a bandage."

She turned from them as the next class was called and Sylvie seemed to float into the arena on her stallion along with eight other riders. Sylvie steered her horse to the rail and stopped behind her brother. Bo looked like an illustration from the pages of "The Legend of Sleepy Hollow," skinny in a black suit, slumped in the saddle as if barely alive. Billie watched the first few minutes of the class, certain that Sylvie had won. The blue roan stallion she rode for Dale moved out with more animation than the other horses, lifting his feet higher and faster.

When she turned away, Dale had left Richard leaning on the rail, watching his kids. She saw Charley waiting for the class to end, ready to lead Sylvie's horse back to the empty stall in Dale's trailer.

She eased over next to him. "Charley."

"Stay away from me."

"You were at my feed shed."

"I left you something. Now go."

"What did you leave me?"

"Shush! Get away from me," he said. "You'll really get me killed this time."

Wondering what he meant by that, Billie turned back to her feed shed. She pulled the door shut behind her and hit the light switch. Moths collided with each other. She batted them away from her face and started to search. She found nothing on the tabletops, grimy with spilled horse feed and mouse turds. Nothing was out of place on the shelves or the window ledges. She felt around the metal garbage cans that held oats and grains. Nothing. She looked through the wastebasket. Nothing. At last she found it, taped to the underside of the corkboard where she collected receipts from the stores, spearing them with push pins. The red flash drive he had tried to give her before now lay in her palm.

She tucked it into her bra to look at later, turned off the light, and went back outside. Applause from the spectators rolled over her. She heard Sylvie's name called. The winner.

CHAPTER 15

WHERE TRAILERS HAD been parked around the barnyard the night before, mounds of garbage cans and black trash bags waited in the early morning sunlight to be picked up. Billie's face was slick with sweat that wasn't drying. She glanced at the sky and found a single lonely cloud peeking above the mountain. Soon—today or tomorrow most likely—the rains would start. Until then, clouds would form, dissipate, re-form. The temperature would rise and with it humidity until the high Sonoran Desert felt like a Manhattan street in August.

At the far end of the arena, she saw Richard wipe his face on the back of his forearm. He had driven over before dawn to help her clean up from the show. She'd made iced coffee for them both, and they had started work just as the sun rose.

She tossed another garbage bag into the bed of the Silverado then started to tie off another one that was still in a garbage can. A couple of syringes like the one she had found in the bedding of Dale's trailer last night lay in it, near the top. She removed them, wrapped them in her blue bandana, and carried them the length of the arena to Richard. He smiled as she approached, sweet and slow, reminding her of the moment last night with his hand on her waist, his fingers on her leg. The way his arms almost had closed around her.

She held out the cloth. "What are these?"

He looked. "Syringes?"

"What are they for?"

"Giving shots, Billie. Duh?" He grinned, playing, teasing.

"Damn it, Richard. I know that. What kind of shots? Why would horses get shots last night?"

"I have no idea. Maybe they were vaccinations."

"Here? At a horse show?"

"I don't know what they're for." He turned away from her, back to the mountain of black plastic trash bags he had stacked, ready to be picked up. "Let's just get things cleaned up before it gets any hotter, okay?"

She carried the syringes to the feed shed, lay them on the table, and got back to work, checking each bag.

"What are you looking for?" Richard asked when she got close to him.

"I don't know. Stuff. More needles. Or...I don't know... what's this?" She held a nearly empty jar toward him. "Ginger?"

His eyes dropped, as if he needed to keep track of his hands. "That helps with tail set."

Billie knew exactly what he was talking about. Smearing ginger into and around a horse's anus burned the tender flesh and made him hold his tail high.

"It's illegal to ginger a horse," she said.

"Doesn't mean it doesn't happen, Billie."

She thought back to when she was a kid running barrels on her pony at local gymkhanas while her parents watched. She thought back to when she had read every novel she could find about kids who loved horses, showed horses, cared for horses, wanted horses, galloped bareback on wild horses across the prairie, and saved horses from abuse. She had read these books while tucked into the forks of tree trunks and in the back seat of her parents' truck. She had read them under covers, in the bathtub, in class, and in line. The literary world of horses, not far at all from the actual world she really did live in, was about ideals. She had learned right and wrong more thoroughly from the pages of *Black Beauty* than from watching her father school a horse or from riding that horse herself. She never lost the excitement she had felt when she read those books, never quit being involved in the story and in the lives of the horses, imaginary or not. She admired the heroes and heroines. She wanted to be them. All these years later, she still felt that way. She wondered if Richard's kids were readers.

Outside the shed, she dragged a heavy bag to the truck and heaved it in.

"Hey, Richard, how's Charley?"

"He's okay. I think his asthma's been bothering him."

"I saw him here last night."

"Well, he works for Dale and those guys. Want me to ask Sylvie about him? She'd know." He unholstered his phone and called her. "Syl, did Charley come here to Billie's with you guys last night?" he asked. "Yeah," he told Billie. "How's he doing?" He listened for a moment before thanking her and hanging up. "She says he's feeling fine now."

They worked for another half hour, until the backs of their shirts were drenched. Billie smelled her own sweat and deodorant. Her face and scalp itched with grit, but at last the barnyard looked as if nothing had happened last night—no show, no horses, no trucks and trailers.

She offered Richard a drink, but he declined in favor of going home to swim with his kids.

As he backed his truck out, mounded with trash bound for the dump, he leaned out the window. "Dinner again soon?"

"Sure," She grinned. "Absolutely."

After he drove away, she did a final patrol of the barnyard and arena, scuffing through soft dirt, kicking up dust as she went. She didn't find much more, just a handful of paper hot dog boats, discarded in a heap beside a garbage can. She dragged the can back to its usual place behind the feed shed and opened a garbage bag to throw in the trash. Inside the can, she found plastic film, the same stuff used to wrap the legs of horses being sored.

She pulled it out and looked deeper into the bag but didn't find anything else. She laid it on the table, next to the syringes and needles, and stood staring at it, wondering what those things were really about. The show here had only flat shod horses. No Big Lick horses. No chained legs, no platform shoes, no burning flesh. No sored horses. Richard had promised. Just sound walkers showing their natural gaits.

Right?

Gulliver raked the back of her calf with his paw, a rare rudeness, panting. She shouldn't have kept him out so long in the heat.

She opened the refrigerator where she stored medicines

and bottles of water, and poured one over Gully, making sure she wet under his chin, behind his ears, his armpits and belly. She turned on the table fan and directed it toward him. In a few minutes, he seemed better. Billie reached back into the fridge for more cool water and saw a piece of paper she hadn't noticed before, folded small and placed beneath some dark brown vials of homeopathic arnica she kept on hand for injuries. After she re-wet Gulliver, she unfolded the paper.

Fs injet jnts. lk in bag. stand on sore.

It must be from Charley. She would figure it out later.

She dropped some ice cubes in Gully's water bowl and in a glass of water for herself, smoothed the paper on the tabletop, and read it again. And again, struggling with the contracted words, trying to make sense of them.

At last, she thought she had the first sentence. "Flat shod inject joints." She said it aloud a couple of times. It made sense with the super small gauge needles she had found. They were the right size for injecting joints. Small as a hair. Almost painless.

But why would someone inject these horses? Maybe for the same reason other hardworking breeds get joint injections— to ease pain from stress or arthritis or injuries.

"'Lk in bag' . . . Like in bag, Gully? What do you think? Oh, maybe it's 'Look in bag.' Which bag? And what does 'Stand on sore' mean?"

She rummaged through her grooming bag: brushes, curries, combs, detanglers, and sprays. She checked the old backpack where she kept wraps and bandaging materials. Not there, either. She was about to give up when she decided to look in the yellow rubberized satchel where she stored her tools. In among the wrenches, hammers, WD-40, and duct tape, she found something she had never seen before—a stiff plastic pad shaped like the bottom of a horse's hoof. At its center, a sharp metal spike stuck out.

So that's what *stand on sore* meant. Nail this to the bottom of the hoof. Hours, days of torment as it dug in. The horse's feet would be covered in hematomas, punctured. Forced to move, he'd snap them up, try to keep them off the ground. Because it hurt too much to put them down.

Gulliver whimpered. He looked miserable, lying beside his water bowl, eyes squinted in pain. Billie knelt beside him. "What's up, boy?"

When she felt him, his temperature seemed normal. But he lay there, whining. In the seven years he'd been her dog, she had never heard him whine like that. It scared her.

Doc's phone rang a long time. When he answered, he was in the middle of a sentence to someone else. Billie heard him say something indistinct and another voice, female, reply.

At last he said, "Doc here."

"It's Billie. Again."

"How's Hashtag?"

She had to think for a minute. "Getting better, Doc. The cuts are healing, but it always takes longer than I think it should."

"Well, you know what I prescribe, Billie. Essence of patience, tincture of time."

"Doc, I'm calling about my little dog Gulliver. There's something wrong with him. He's lying here on the floor, crying."

She was certain he wouldn't be able—or maybe willing—to come out for a dog. He was strictly a large animal vet with a practice so busy he had no time left over for sleep, let alone add-on patients. But he would tell her the right thing to do.

"Well, m'dear, it so happens that I'm not far from you. In fact, I'm just down the road a bit. I have to finish up here then I'll stop by."

Billie hung up, slumped to the floor, and gathered Gulliver onto her lap. "Thank you," she said to the hot shed walls. "Thank you."

Doc still had his arm in a sling, soiled now and with a tear halfway up. It had been scribbled on all over, signed and drawn on. Moons, stars, horse heads in profile, a crude outline of a bull with a cartoon balloon over its head, saying, "I'm sorry, Doc!" He seemed to be moving better and smoothly managed the drop off his truck's bench seat onto the ground. He slammed the truck door closed with his good shoulder.

"Be glad when I get this thing off." He eyed her for a moment, evaluating. "I'll take care of your dog, Billie. Don't worry, okay? I know you love him. After I see to him, let's look at the horse you took such good care of who got caught in the wire."

Billie nodded, helplessly close to crying again.

Inside the feed shed with Doc she was aware that she should have wiped down the counters, swept the floor. But he didn't seem to notice. He started to bend to pick up Gulliver when Billie realized he couldn't because of his arm. She pulled a chair out from under the table for him. He sat and she lifted Gulliver into his lap.

He murmured to him; Billie couldn't tell if it was words or sounds. He looked into the dog's eyes, then his mouth and checked his gums. He felt down his neck, his back, his hind legs, his front legs, checked each paw. At his right front—the last paw he looked at—he said, "I'll be darned."

Then he checked all the other paws again.

"Did you walk him on cement?" he asked. "Maybe in Tucson?"

Billie shook her head no.

"His pads are sore on this foot. He's got blisters."

As he spoke, Gulliver tried to lick the paw, stopped, and ran his tongue in and out of his mouth fast. Doc opened his mouth again and gently pried open his teeth. He yelped and struggled to get away. Doc let him jump down.

"Well, Billie," he said. "I think your dog here got into something. I thought at first he'd scorched his foot. I see it in the summer all the time. People think their dogs' feet are made of asbestos, if they think at all. They walk 'em on pavement until they're blistered. But I'm thinking this little dog got into something caustic, and then when he licked his paw, he burned his tongue and the inside of his mouth."

Billie asked the only question she could think of. "Will he be all right? Did he burn his throat?"

"I don't think so. This seems pretty localized. I'll give you some ointment and a little pain medicine for a couple of days. Should be right as rain by then." Doc rested his good hand on her shoulder and squeezed. "Let's look at the horse," he said.

"I wonder," Billie said after Doc had checked on Hashtag and pronounced her on the way to recovery, "if Gully got into something at the show here last night."

"You had a show here?"

"Walking horses."

He stopped and faced her. He didn't say anything, but in his face she saw the same hard disapproval she had seen in Josie's.

"Flat shod only," she assured him. "No soring. They promised me."

He looked past her, toward the mountains. "You don't know much do you, about people?"

She kept herself from snapping at him. He didn't know about her previous life, the people she had interviewed, what she had seen. She probably knew more about people than anyone, she wanted to say. But she didn't say anything.

Neither did he.

She couldn't stand his disapproval. She imagined arguments she could make to him: they had promised her no hurt horses and she had made money at last. *Hell, I made money so I could pay you, Doc, damn it.* It was so much fun to have them here, the barnyard full of trucks, trailers, food, horses, dogs, music, kids, and folks enjoying themselves. And there was no soring! Maybe there was a cheater or two. But there are cheaters in every sport, right?

As if reading her mind he said, "Cheaters are cheaters, Billie. Crooks are crooks. Liars lie. Burners burn."

"We don't know that Gully got hurt at the show."

He stepped away from her. "You are defending them. What do these people do to their horses, Billie? They burn them. They are burners, and they burn their horses. At home. At shows. Use your eyes, Billie. And for God's sake use some common sense. You had a barnyard full of burners, and your dog got burned. Not just his paw but his tongue, from licking his paw. A caustic did that to him. These people use caustics on their horses' legs, don't they? No matter what they promised you, they are the same people who were at that show when you called me a while back. The same people who hurt that filly you . . . bought."

He wiped his mouth with the back of his hand, crevassed and stained. "Horse stealing's a hanging offense out here, m'dear. I'm glad you . . . bought . . . her. You did the right thing, then, by her. But now you're off that track, and you're messing up."

He climbed cautiously into the truck, protecting his hurt arm. "Your horse's cuts are healing fine. Your dog will be okay. But you I worry about. Take care, m'dear. Be careful who and what you invite into your life."

CHAPTER 16

BILLIE TURNED ON the laptop and plugged the flash drive she had gotten from Charley into the USB port. The first seconds were disorienting, fuzzy black-and-white footage of movement too blurry to discern. She realized the sound was off on her computer and turned it on. Southern voices. Indistinct words. A yell. A whinny.

She was looking at the inside of a barn. A man walked in front of the camera, toward a horse, pulled back his arm and punched the animal in the face. Billie flinched and pulled back as if it had happened in front of her. The man turned toward the camera, and Billie recognized Dale. He said something she couldn't understand, stepped to the next horse, and did it again. And again. Down a long row of horses standing in cross ties, watching him approach, unable to escape. He slugged each in turn, hitting with detachment and force.

Billie paused the video. It didn't make any sense. Why batter these horses, already tied in their stalls, helpless and immobile? She couldn't watch anymore. Tears ran onto her lips.

When she worked for Frank, reporting on the horrors of child abuse and rape, she had learned when she got overwhelmed to take a minute to anchor herself. She had done that so often and for so many years, it had become second nature. *My laptop,* she told herself. *These are my notebooks. My hands. My ranch. My home.*

She wiped her face with her palms, rewound and pressed play, her hand hovering over the stop button, poking at it to slow down the action so she could actually see what was happening. She missed it on her first pass, rewound and looked again. This time she saw that a groom knelt beside each horse, palpating its front legs the way an inspector would at a show. The instant a horse flinched, Dale punched it.

"He's stewarding the horse, teaching it not to react to the exam," she whispered.

The camera aimed at the horses' legs, following Dale. He bent down, lifted a front hoof, and squirted something from a bottle on its leg. The horse reared back then collapsed to its knees.

"Get up, you sorry son of a bitch!" Dale kicked it in the gut.

Billie watched the rest of the footage. Dale poking a horse with an electric cattle prod. Dale standing by while two grooms tried to drag a prostrate horse by its head. Dale burning a horse on the lips with a cigarette. Charley must have been the videographer, she realized. He had told her he was going to turn in more abusers than just Dale for the reward, and there were two grooms in this footage.

She pressed play again. This time she waited through more snow and smudges until, at last, there were new images, new voices. A woman talking, a man's mumbled answer. The woman's voice again. Eudora stepped in front of the camera, walking ahead of Charley down the barn aisle at the farm where Billie had worked. Eudora gave instructions, pointing to stalls and telling him what to do to each horse inside. They stopped, and she pulled open a stall door. A wild-eyed mare tied to the wall at the back of the stall tried to turn toward them.

Eudora said, "Get her done today, okay? She can cook overnight, and we'll see if she can move in the morning. If she's good and paralyzed with pain, he'll ride her. Otherwise, you can do more then. Got it?"

The camera swept up and down nauseatingly as Charley nodded. His hand rose toward his head, and the video went dark. When it flicked on again, Billie was looking straight at Sylvie, standing backlit in the stall door. Charley was inside the stall, looking out at her. She pointed, and he turned to see at what. The camera picked up the mare Eudora had been talking about. She lay on the floor of her stall. Sylvie knelt beside her, snapped a lead to her halter, and pulled. The mare didn't even lift her head. Sylvie kicked her, but she still wouldn't get up. She lit a cigarette and held it against the mare's rump.

Eudora's voice laughed. "This'll do. Go get Dale."

The video turned again into undecipherable smudges, but Billie heard the horse moan.

The mare was up when Billie could next decipher what was going on, crouching, shifting her weight from side to side, her front feet barely touching the floor. She tried to sit, but Sylvie prodded her with a pitchfork. Blood trickled from the punctures.

"If she does okay for Dale," Eudora said, "I'll break her tail this afternoon, and we can get her into the tail set in time for the Big Show."

The last thing Billie heard Eudora say was "Get the chains, Charley."

The last thing Billie saw was Sylvie, turned away from the horse, looking directly at the old man with the camera in his cap.

Billie pulled Gulliver onto her lap.

Was this why Charley had given her the flash drive? These last few minutes of evidence? This would give the government Dale, Eudora, and—oh, God—Sylvie. What was the punishment for a minor who abused horses in this way? Was seventeen a minor or an adult? What did this mean for Richard? For the other kids?

Did Richard know the extent of Sylvie's involvement? It was bad enough to ride a sored horse. But to participate in soring itself? If Richard didn't know about it, should Billie tell him?

The phone rang, startling her. The pain meds Doc prescribed for Gulliver had made him so groggy he didn't even flick his ears at the sound. Billie answered without checking and realized for an airless moment that the bank was on the line. When she got off the phone after reasoning and pleading, she felt strangled. Bills and debtors. Horses who needed to be fed. Clients who mustn't know what a hard time she was having in case they took their horses away and cut her tiny income. She was afraid of her own telephone. It was too early to drink. A bath would feel good.

She started to run the water then stopped and went back to her computer. She watched Charley's footage again. She knew how to make money. The way she always had before she ran away, came here, and started her life over on this ranch.

She pulled a notepad onto her lap and started to write.

Later, she took a break to feed the horses, returned to the casita, and finished writing around eleven. She poured herself a glass of wine then and filled the tub. What she had written was good. She could tell. The words had come with a rhythm that had transported her as she wrote. That was how she always knew she was on target. Tomorrow she would type it into the computer, editing as she went. She would send it as an attachment to Frank. She didn't want to be a writer anymore. She just wanted to ride Starship and live on her ranch with Gulliver and take care of other people's horses.

She lay back, closed her eyes, and with her toes, turned on the hot water.

CHAPTER 17

O N FRIDAY EVENING the phone rang after Billie had finished feeding and gotten back to the casita. She had an open beer can in one hand and a slice of cantaloupe in the other and didn't want to put either down. Gulliver, feeling better, was busy with an old rawhide he had dug up. It was too late for bill collectors. Billie answered without looking.

"Billie."

"Frank." She could hear the smile in her voice, and she knew that he could too.

"Billie."

"Frank."

"Billie?"

"Yes?"

"What were you thinking?"

"What do you mean?"

He sighed loudly. "We need to talk. In person."

"Are you still coming to Tucson?"

"I just got in. Meet me at Señor Roco's in an hour."

"It'll take me more than that to get there."

"Well, hurry up. I'll be in the bar."

She'd taken off the door to her closet because it protruded too far into the tiny living space when it was open, and she never closed it anyway. So she'd made it into the table where she worked and ate, when she wasn't working or eating off her lap on the futon. She'd hung an old serape she found at a thrift shop in its place as a make-do door. This she now held back with her forearm as she searched for something to wear to Tucson to meet Frank.

Nothing. There was not a single thing in there she could wear on a date. Which of course this wasn't. This was even worse, a late-night business meeting with her ex-husband— exponentially more important than a date. She riffled through a pile of semi-folded T-shirts and tank tops. No. The closet bar held a couple of hangers with Western wear shirts, their pointed collars and lapels with rhinestone snaps eliminated them. She could imagine Frank's disapproval if she dressed like that. The bureau drawers were stuffed with sports bras, cotton jockey briefs, sweatpants eroded by miles of horseback riding until they were almost rags. Sweatshirts. Boot socks.

She backed out of the closet, desperately looking under piles and into corners, then glanced up at a suitcase she'd stored up on the highest shelf when she first moved here. A suitcase she'd brought from New York. She slid a wooden side chair over, stood on it, and pulled down the bag. She hefted it onto the futon, and after a struggle, got the zipper to open. Everything inside was black. Black wool skirt, black slacks, black shoes, black jacket with black jet buttons, black pantyhose.

Tucked into a side pocket, she found a black lace bra and lacy thong and tossed them onto the kitchen counter. The microwave's clock told her she'd already spent a quarter hour just looking for underwear. She dove back into the suitcase and this time found a silk T-shirt in a brown so deep it was almost black, simple and softly elegant. She remembered spending three hundred and seventy-nine dollars for it in a Lexington Avenue boutique. She had paid cash, hid the receipt from Frank, and never wore it in case he asked about it.

She washed fast, running a soapy washcloth all over herself at the kitchen sink, then rinsing with a soaked hand towel. Not yet dry, she dove into the bra and thong, slipped on the silk blouse, and pulled on the first pair of jeans on the pile. Hopping, she shoved her feet into a pair of scuffed fat baby boots and ran to the truck. Before she got in, she rubbed the top of each boot on the back of her blue-jeaned calf and hoped that at least they'd look clean.

Parking in downtown Tucson was always tough. There weren't enough spaces for the compact cars and SUVs owned by townspeople and rented by tourists. Billie's long bed Silverado struggled to make the sharp turn into a rare open space, failed, and when she backed up to correct the angle of her approach, what seemed like a crowd of other drivers honked.

She twisted around to look over her shoulder. The driver behind her was trying to back up to give her space, and the one behind that was leaning on the horn. She turned forward and wrenched the steering wheel. The front of the truck made it into the space, but her tire bumped up onto the curb. She turned off the ignition and got out to see how badly she'd parked. Probably not bad enough for a ticket, and anyway, she didn't have time to look for another spot. She locked the door and jaywalked across Congress Street, jogging.

Billie wiggled through the small crowd that milled in front of the restaurant, pulled open the old wooden doors, and entered. It was crowded and noisy with talking and bursts of music that sounded like a band setting up. She paused for a second to take in the antique wall sconces and Saltillo floor tiles. She used to come here as a teen on dates. Twenty some years later, the place looked the same. Two old wooden phone booths huddled side by side near the entry. Wagon wheels hung on the walls. Spurs sat on tabletops, holding menus. The tables' edges were wrapped in lariats, the seat cushions covered in bandana cloth.

Billie squinted at the stage at the far end of the room to see if she knew what band was setting up. A banner on the wall advertised KXCI, the local independent music station, but she didn't see anything with the band's name on it, and she didn't recognize any of the bushy men clutching mandolins and guitars as they milled around in the blue spotlight.

She spotted Frank seated toward the middle of the bar, staring at bottles lined up on mirrored shelves. He hadn't seen her enter, and she paused to look at him for a minute. The years hadn't changed him much. Now fifty-three, he looked a little thinner than when she'd last seen him. Or maybe not. His jawline was sharp enough to see under his beard, his cheekbones more pronounced. Maybe he'd just aged a bit. He needed a haircut, unless he now wore his hair longer. He used to like it cropped so short his curls didn't show. Now the curls fell into his eyes and softened the edge of his collar. His hair and beard were still dark. She had always liked his beard, the feel of it, the professorial look of it, the way it accentuated his almost black eyes. She watched as he picked up his pen and held it between his second and third fingers, jiggling it in a gesture of impatience she had hated when they were married.

He glanced down at his wristwatch then turned and looked right at her as if he'd known she was watching him. He looked her up and down then reached over and pulled back the seat next to him.

"What do you want to drink?" he asked. "The same as before?"

"White wine. The house white is fine. Whatever."

He gave her a quick look before hailing the bartender.

"You nervous, Billie?"

"Nope. Why would I be? It's just you and me in a bar, again."

He took a long drag on his beer, watching her in the mirror. Billie expected him to toss back the bourbon chaser in front of him, but he turned and stared silently at her.

"So?" she watched her mirror-self ask. Above the neckline of her brown silk blouse, her skin was tanned almost butterscotch.

"You look . . . rugged, kiddo. I like the short hair." He reached for her hand. When she gave it to him, he turned it over, opened her fingers with his own and, holding them back, looked at her palm. He turned her hand sideways and examined the callous along the outside of her index finger and the one along the outside of her pinkie. Then he looked up.

"Will you have dinner with me while we talk?"

"Sure," she said, sounding casual, as if her future didn't rest on it.

He picked up the ballpoint again and resumed jiggling it between his fingers. He looked up toward the corner of the room, then to another corner. He whistled tunelessly, just an exhale, drumming the bar top with his pen. Bad signs, all of them. She sat silently, watching herself in the mirror. She should have worn a necklace, something bright at her neck. Otherwise, she looked good, hard and soft at the same time. Chic enough to suit him. Add the right jacket and she'd be good to go anywhere. She looked ready.

Finally he asked, "What were you thinking sending me that query?"

"What do you mean?"

"You know what I mean, Billie. That was a joke, right?"

She hadn't forgotten the way he could slice her to shreds with a few words, but she hadn't expected it.

"You know we don't do pieces on animals. For God's sake, Billie! Horses in Tennessee! Who wants to read about Tennessee? This isn't *Reader's* fucking *Digest!* You were kidding, right? Please, please tell me you were."

Recoiling from his sarcasm, she gulped the rest of her wine then looked for the bartender. When she spotted him, she held up her glass and mouthed, "White."

"How are the margaritas here?" Frank hailed the waiter when he brought Billie's wine then ordered one without waiting for an answer. He stood up. "Let's move to a table."

He moved them to a small table without consulting a waiter, pulled out her chair, and sat across from her. "Now," he said. "Explain."

"It's a good idea for a piece."

"You've been out in that Arizona sun too long," he frowned.

"You'd have had more chance at this magazine with a UFO story. And a UFO story has zero chance here. We're slick, Billie. Cutting edge. This is a National Magazine Awards publication—you know that—not a rag for the Humane Society. Why am I having to tell you this?"

Billie leaned forward. "Listen to me, Frank. This piece has everything you want. Money. Politics. Corruption."

She pitched it. When she finished he said, "Let's order."

Unsure if he was buying, she scanned the menu for something cheap.

"On me," he said. "This is business."

The twinge of disappointment she felt irritated her. Of course it *was* business. At least it was business. Long married and longer divorced, what the hell else did she want? She'd asked for an assignment, and when she'd asked she had thought that was all there was to it. Really.

When their food came—tamales for him and seafood enchiladas for her—they ate, not talking. She wondered what else she could say to persuade him.

"Billie?" He was looking at her empty plate, and she realized she had inhaled the food without even noticing that she was eating.

"Do you want something else?"

She had no idea.

"You always ate slower than I did," Frank said. "You were always the last one at the table when we went out." He said it as if he were proud of her for that.

Memories threatened to sabotage her. Memories of the parts of their lives together that she never allowed herself to think of. Restaurants with lines out the door, lines they bypassed when the owner recognized them and waved them in. First-class seats on airplanes, front row seats at fights and ball games, backstage passes to Broadway shows and the ballet.

"You gobble like that and you'll get fat," Frank blew out his cheeks at her.

"Not your business."

"It is my business if you want to work for me again. You have to be competitive if you work in New York. You have to write and look better than anyone."

"Give me this assignment, and I'll eat like a fucking bird the rest of my life, okay? If that's what you care about."

"I want you writing for me. But no horses. I like the danger angle you've got going, but it needs to be attached to something important."

"Trust me, Frank. This is important."

"I am not publishing a Pet Partners blog, Billie. I need chic. I need ecstatic readers. I need . . . Hell, you know what I need."

"Listen, Frank, you won't be out anything. I'll tell you what. Give me the job, and if you don't like it, I'll waive my kill fee. You won't have to take the article, and you won't have to pay me anything except my expenses if you don't run it." She had said it without thinking, had given away everything in an all-or-nothing gamble that she could make the article work.

"You do know that was a stupid offer, don't you?" he said. "I'll give you thirty seconds to change your mind." He unstrapped his Rolex—it was a new one, she saw, not the one she'd given him—and laid it on the table. "Starting now."

Billie didn't move, didn't blink. "Ten. Fifteen. Twenty," Frank looked at her. "Twenty-five." He strapped on the watch at thirty. "All right then, baby. I'll email you a contract early next week."

"You pay expenses," she said. "With an advance on them, so I can get started."

He nodded then signaled the waiter. "Dessert, Billie?"

She started to shake her head no but felt his leg press against hers, from ankle to knee. She closed her eyes. When he took her chin in his hand and turned her face to him, she kept them closed. After he kissed her, he said, "Order something sweet while I get us a room at the hotel across the street."

"I thought you were staying there."

He shook his head. "We're at the Arizona Inn for the conference. I figured you and I could talk better here."

"Where you wouldn't be seen with me?"

"Something along those lines."

Billie pinched a chip from the bowl in front of Frank and cracked it into pieces. "Who's we?"

"The conference attendees."

The awkward sound of *attendees* bothered her. "Who are *you* with?"

"You left me, if you remember."

"You've been coming on to me."

He laughed. "Look who's talking, kiddo. You got what you wanted. You can write the damn article. I'll pay your expenses, and if I like the piece, I'll buy it. And if I buy it, I might even run it. If I don't take it, you can try to sell it to some animal rights rag. And if you want to go upstairs, we can do that too, right now. But no strings. Not even the thinnest, weakest filament between us."

What she saw in his eyes surprised her, a pure sweet yearning for her. She realized that she had won. She'd gotten what she'd asked for not because he believed in her idea or cared about her cause, but because he still loved her.

"I'm going home, Frank," she said.

He nodded.

"But write me a check before I leave."

He wrote the expense check and handed it to her, but when she tried to take it from him, he held onto it until she looked up into his eyes. "Do me a favor, kid. Don't get yourself killed."

CHAPTER 18

TOO FIRED UP to go to bed when she got home, Billie changed into a T-shirt and made herself a mug of iced coffee. She sipped it standing at the window, looking out at the Milky Way while she listened to a new bunch of messages on the answering machine.

Visa had called wondering when her payment would arrive. There were three hang-ups. When she looked at caller ID, she found only toll-free numbers. Then Kristine had called.

"Billie? This is Kris. How's Hashtag doing? Are her cuts healing okay? Call me back."

Billie promised herself that she would call her back later in the morning after she checked on the mare's wounds.

The last message was from Richard.

"Hey there, Billie Snow. I've got you on my mind. So, call me back, okay?"

He'd called around nine. It was now almost three in the morning. She stretched out on the futon in her clothes, intending to sleep until dawn, but bounded up again. At the table, she shuffled through the clutter of papers, books, and handwork projects, dividing stacks and re-stacking them. She found a strand of rope she'd been tying into a halter then abandoned, and tossed it aside, maybe to work on later. She found notes from an essay she once thought she'd write, about moving to Arizona and starting a horse business. She found some knitting patterns she'd misplaced, for felted slippers and a ribbed watch cap. She stared at the cap pattern a minute, trying to remember if she'd planned to make it for Frank or someone else. There had been other men but none she had knit for. The cap looked like something she could have made for Frank when they were together. Maybe the pattern dated from her time in Manhattan. She slipped it onto the top of a shelf of books in case she decided to make it for him now.

Grabbing a Sharpie, she scribbled a list of things she wanted to be sure she had in place before she left for Tennessee. Should she bring Gulliver with her or leave him? She'd need someone to take care of the place while she was gone. She'd have to let Kristine know she'd be away and make special arrangements for Hashtag if the mare still needed extra care.

She fell asleep at the table with her head on her folded arms. Gulliver woke her, pawing to go out. She looked at her watch. She'd slept until nearly eight o'clock. When she opened the door, Starship bellowed and banged his feeder. She slipped into her flip-flops and followed her dog outside.

She scolded herself that she should have gotten up earlier, but she was barely awake as it was. After she fed the horses, she changed Hashtag's bandages, bent over, sweat making itchy prickly splotches on her face and neck that dried so fast they stung. The horse was healing. The lesser scratches had already almost vanished, and most of the deep ones were improving. There were two places, however, that worried her. One was a laceration close to the mare's left eye, swollen and oozing pus. Billie cleaned it with a gauze pad soaked in Betadine, a procedure Hashtag objected to by tossing her head every time Billie tried to touch it. It took almost a half hour of target practice to clean and disinfect the cut. Billie gathered up the used gauze pads from the ground, squeezed them into a wad, and stuffed them into the hip pocket of her shorts so Gulliver wouldn't get them.

The other spot that worried her was in Hashtag's right front armpit, where several strands of barbed wire had tangled, creating a mess of intersecting gashes with islands of flesh between them. She wasn't sure what to do. She'd like to get Doc out. But Kristine had told her she didn't want any more vet bills and that the accident had been Billie's fault. Billie could have referred her to the part of the boarding contract that said the horse's owner was responsible for any sickness or injuries, but she was afraid Kris would take her horse away if they argued.

Billie sighed and filled her cupped palm with Betadine, turning her skin the color of dried blood. She pressed it up against the mess of flesh. Hashtag squealed and raised a hind foot, kicked the air, then set her hoof down. Billie followed that with a splash of peroxide.

"I'm sorry, girl, but we've got to get you better, okay?"

The climb back up the hill to the casita in the late morning left her winded and Gulliver panting. His paws seemed to be feeling better, although she could still see bright pink skin when she looked past his scraggly hair. She opened the fridge and took out two ice cubes, dropped one into his water bowl, and sucked on the other then ran it around her neck, over her brow, and up the insides of her forearms. She put more ice into a glass, added water and drank, refilled it, and drank again until the glass was almost empty. She set it on the counter and went to call Kristine to report her mare's progress.

Fifteen minutes later, she hung up, relieved that Kristine wasn't going to take her horse away. She'd agreed to leave her with Billie if Billie agreed to care for her injuries without charging extra. It meant more work with no more pay, but if Hashtag left, so would her board fee.

Billie stood in the tub, reaching to turn on the shower, when her cell phone buzzed against the sink where she'd left it. She leaned over, saw it was Richard, and let it go to voice mail. She'd call him later, when she was feeling cleaner and clearer about what she wanted.

Billie watched through the window of DT's Bar and Grill as Richard parked his super shiny Dodge dually and got out. The window beside her booth was open about six inches to allow airflow so the bar's evaporative cooler could do its job. The air inside was so chilled she wished she'd worn jeans instead of shorts, and brought a jacket. Outside, she heard the squeal of Richard's electronic beeper locking the truck. Her own truck, parked beside his, canted a bit to one side like a resting horse. One of the leaf springs had quit a few years back and she'd never replaced it. Its windows were open, the doors unlocked.

While she watched, Richard patted his hip pocket, checking for his wallet or cell phone then, apparently satisfied that he had what he needed, he turned toward DT's. When he spotted her through the window, he grinned. On the seat beside her, Gulliver wagged his tail.

Richard entered in a blast of late afternoon sunlight and heat then slipped into the seat opposite her. "Hi, little dog. You sure must rate to be allowed in here." He reached across the table and offered his palm to Gulliver.

Billie smiled. "He's not allowed in, but DT said it was okay as long as no one complains."

She nodded at a couple of wranglers with handlebar mustaches and sunburned hands wrapped around platters of huevos rancheros and glasses of icy *horchata*. Beneath the wranglers' table lay a couple of blue heelers. And at the other side of the room, a half dozen bikers with fat tattooed arms sticking out of leather vests, their white hair in ponytails, fed bits of bacon to a fluffy Pomeranian the size of a soap bar.

"I guess you're safe for now," Richard said with a sigh.

They ordered burgers and curly fries, side salads, and sodas. As they sat talking she found herself imagining a life with him. Breakfasts, dinners. Maybe not for long, but for a while. He had money, kids, and calluses on his palms from his life with horses. It might not work out with him, but for a while it might be good. He did have a wife, Billie knew, but he had said she was on her way out of the picture, living in Tennessee. The kids divided their time between their parents. It was a work in progress, he had said.

"I was married once." She enjoyed Richard's small flinch when she said it. "My ex is in Tucson now on business. We met to discuss an article I'll be writing for his magazine."

"He works for a magazine?"

"It's his magazine. *Frankly*. He's Frank."

"Wow, really? I see that magazine everywhere. You still work for him?"

"No. I quit writing when I left him. But I hired back on last night."

When their food arrived, Richard ordered another Coke, ate some salad, then asked, "What's your article about?"

"Walking horses."

"I don't think I knew you were a writer."

"Like I said, I took a break from it for a few years. Now I'm back on this new assignment." She waited, watching him look out the window. When he looked back at her, she said, "I'm hoping you can help me."

"Always have a native host," Frank had said when she first worked for him. The weird phrase stuck in her mind. That was what she needed now, someone who lived, literally or figuratively, where she was going. Someone who knew everything she needed to know. Someone who could bail her out or who knew someone who could.

"I want to describe how the breed evolved, who owns these horses, and how they're trained."

Richard shifted in his seat, cocked himself away from her, and crossed his legs. Billie sensed that he was a door about to slam shut. "You want me to help you how?"

"Just with some background," she said. "And maybe some contacts. People I could talk to who would explain things to me."

"I don't know . . ."

Billie reached across the table and touched him, her fingers on his forearm, the same touch she would use to ask a horse to settle. She left her fingers on his arm until he covered them with his other hand, pressed briefly, and let go.

"Let's go to my house," he said.

"Let's."

CHAPTER 19

THEY SAT OUTSIDE Richard's log house in the starry dark on deck chairs, a bowl of popcorn on the ground between them, a goblet of Zapara Viognier in Billie's hand, and a bottle of Dragoon IPA in his. They watched the first of the monsoon storms gathering in the southwest. Lightning played across the sky, each bolt separated from its thunder by several seconds. Gulliver, curled up on Billie's stomach, trembled with each crash. Richard stood up from his chair and disappeared into the house. She felt herself relax, a small easing of the muscles at the corner of her mouth, as if she'd been holding onto a little smile she could now release. She closed her eyes.

Whatever he'd done in the past, at least he was easy to be with. He didn't constantly try to impress her, didn't talk too much or make goofy jokes like most of the men she'd dated since leaving Frank. In spite of the tension that had nearly swamped them earlier in the day, he had invited her to dinner, then to stay on after they had eaten, stretched out on the chairs, watching the first big storm of the summer play out a few miles to the west.

Lightning flared behind her eyelids. Her hand tightened on Gulliver's back, holding him closer before the bang. Still, he yelped and shivered.

Richard touched her shoulder. She opened her eyes.

"Try this." He handed her something folded inside a plastic baggie. She unzipped the bag and pulled it out.

"What is it?"

"It's a ThunderShirt," he said. "We used to have a cat who was terrified of storms. He died a couple of years ago. It might help Gully."

She pulled it on him, and he stopped shaking almost instantly. She settled back with her now dozing dog on her belly, her wine in her hand. Richard sat back down beside her.

"How would you describe Eudora?" Billie asked.

"Well, I'm not sure. You know, she raised me."

Billie turned her head to look at him.

"My mother was away a lot, and when she was home, well, let's say parenting wasn't her greatest skill. I practically lived at Eudora and Dale's barn in Bell Buckle, hanging out with their kids, training the horses, playing with their dogs. I ate and often slept at their house. Their son was my best friend, even though he was a few years younger. We fished the cricks and played ball together. We went to the same school in different grades and took the same bus. So Eudora was pretty much my mom."

He lapsed into a long silence watching the sky, stretched and crossed his legs at the ankle.

The time between the next flash—two bolts that flew at right angles from each other, one into the ground, the other across the sky—and its thunder was noticeably less. "It's getting closer," Richard said. "Did Gully react to it?"

"Nothing," Billie said. "I'll get him one of these shirts in Tucson when I go in."

"You can keep this one," Richard said.

He folded his hands behind his head. She was aware of him watching her. The kids were in their rooms, their windows shut to keep the cooled air inside, their curtains closed. In the storm's flashes, she saw his profile, the fringe of his eyelashes, his lips.

When he reached out and rested his hand against her cheek, she turned toward him and slipped her arms around his neck.

"The kids," he whispered. "We can't go inside. Come with me to the barn?"

She nodded her head against his chest. Standing, he pulled her to her feet.

"Do we need to tell them?" she asked.

"No. They know that's where I'll be if I'm not here."

He led her past the pool and down the dirt path toward the barn, Gulliver in his ThunderShirt trotting at their heels.

"Be careful!" she said. "Snakes! This is when they're out at night."

But he had already reached the barn door. He opened it and half pulled her through, down the aisle past Morning Glory's stall and into the office where he kissed her again. "There's a cot," he said. "I can open it for us."

"Chair!" She pushed him into the dusty recliner in the corner, slid her hands upward under his shirt then down to his belt. She undid his zipper, straddled him.

He pushed against her. "Take your shorts off. I want to be inside you. God, Billie," he groaned.

She stripped then hovered above him, hardly moving. She heard a horse shuffle around in its stall, another horse snort, and Richard's sharp intake of breath as he entered her.

She wanted to look at him as he moved inside her, but in the dark barn office, she could barely see him, only feel his hands on her hips, her breasts, then on the sides of her face, his fingers in her hair.

Afterward, he stroked her back as they listened to the storm. Thunder crashed closer and closer, and lightning sailed through the night sky. Gulliver whimpered.

Billie felt Richard's fingertips exploring.

"What's this?" he asked

She pulled away from him. "Nothing."

"I want to see."

He reached over and flicked on the overhead light. She watched him discover the network of thin, straight scars intermingled with a Morse code of small round bumps covering her hips, lower belly, and upper thighs.

"What *is* this?"

"It was a long time ago, Richard. No big deal."

"You did this to yourself?"

"Some of it. I had some pretty hard years as a kid."

"*Some* of it?"

She shrugged, stood, and reached for her shorts. She zipped the fly, gave each leg a downward tug, and almost unconsciously ran her fingertips around the hem, checking her flesh for the telltale ridges of her scars. Finding one, she tugged the fabric again to cover it. When she pulled her tank top over her head, she sensed Richard staring at the filigree of white lines on the tender skin of her inner arms.

"You really did a number on yourself," he said.

She shrugged. "Ancient history."

He reached for his own clothes and slowly pulled his T-shirt over his head. "What about the scars you *didn't* put there?"

She turned to him, palms up in a STOP gesture. "Like I said. I had some rough times, okay? No more questions."

The wind picked up. Branches shrieked along the sides of the barn. Sand and pebbles struck the rattling windows. Looking out, Billie saw lights come on in the kitchen windows of the house. The kids were in there, looking for their father.

"I have to get back," Richard said beside her. "But someday I want you to tell me what happened."

She stiffened. "Maybe there should be a scar rule for people, like you have for your horses. A limit on what's allowed to show."

Wind blew open the barn door and pelted the floor with blown dirt and pebbles.

"Let's get back to the house before this storm gets any worse."

Richard grabbed her hand and half-dragged her to the open door. Together they leaned against it to force it closed. Billie scooped up Gulliver, then chased Richard through stiletto rain that soaked their hair and clothes, turned the ground to slippery mud, and formed itself into hail that pelted them as they reached the kitchen door.

Billie rubbed her hair dry with the towel Richard tossed her from a folded pile of laundry stacked on the kitchen counter. She pulled her shirt away from her skin and slipped the towel underneath, using the same towel on Gulliver when she was done. Richard handed her a blue polo shirt from the laundry pile. She ducked into the pantry closet, closed the door, and changed among cans of beans, tomatoes, and bags of hamburger and hot dog buns.

When she opened the door, Sylvie was facing her father across the kitchen island. Alice Dean sat on the floor, a toy horse in her pudgy hand. The toy horse trailer lay on its side in front of her. Sylvie and Richard were obviously arguing, but Billie could barely hear them over the pounding hail.

"That's Bo's shirt," Sylvie snapped.

"We got soaked," Richard explained. Sylvie glared at him, but he ignored it. "You and I will finish this discussion later, all right?"

Another thunder crash muted whatever Sylvie said in return. She stalked to the refrigerator, opened the freezer door, and pulled out a gallon of rocky road ice cream.

"Isn't this a great storm, Alice Dean?" Richard asked.

"Daddy, I don't feel good." She coughed and stretched her arms up toward him.

He lifted her and set her on his hip.

"What's the matter, baby? You have a tummy ache?"

Billie felt a pang of loss that she would never have a child of her own to cradle and comfort.

Alice Dean coughed again. "No. My throat hurts." She pronounced it *froat*.

Richard felt her forehead. "You're kind of warm, sweetheart. Sylvie, get the thermometer from my bathroom, okay?"

Sylvie pressed her palm to her little sister's brow then offered her a spoonful of ice cream. Alice Dean turned away.

Sylvie set the ice cream on the counter and left—to look for the thermometer, Billie figured.

"I don't suppose you know a pediatrician?" Richard asked Billie.

"Josie might know one. Josie and Sam, my neighbors? Want me to ask them?"

"Please. Just in case."

Alice Dean rested her head against his shoulder and closed her eyes as he carried her up to her room.

Billie reached for her phone.

By the time she hung up with Josie, she had a list of three pediatricians with practices nearby, and the phone numbers for a half dozen urgent care clinics as well as for most, if not all, of Tucson's major hospitals. She handed it to Richard when he came back.

"That's great. Thanks, and to your neighbors. I hope we won't need these, but they're good to have."

"Josie raised her own kids," Billie told him, gathering her things to leave. "She and Sam were outfitters up north, and they had foster kids. So she's pretty organized about things like this."

"I see that. You don't have to go, you know." He pulled another bottle of wine from the fridge. "I remember meeting Josie, but I don't know her. Tell me about her."

Billie hesitated then hopped up to sit on the counter as he filled her glass. "Great neighbors. She's maybe a little critical of what I do and how I do it. She's got a lot of her own experiences and a lot of opinions."

Richard chuckled, setting out some little cakes on a plate and sitting opposite her. "But you do like her."

"I do. I wish she'd been my foster mother." It slipped out, and she was sorry the minute she said it.

"You were a foster kid?"

"It's in the past," Billie snapped. "I said no more questions. How about you, Richard? Tell me all the rough things from your childhood. Tell me the really, really bad stuff, the stuff that left you with scars."

She saw that he was taken aback by her edginess, and she regretted it. Not so much because she'd made him uncomfortable, but because she had accidentally revealed too much about herself with her outburst.

"There isn't any," he said. "Really not. Just what I told you about my mother. That was one of the great things about living where we did. The walking horse world is pretty tight-knit. It's a big family."

"Of perverts."

"What? No!" Richard said. "Listen to me. We looked out for each other and each other's kids. We went to school together and to each other's houses during the week. On weekends we all went to the Saturday night horse show and rode together. Sunday we went to the same churches, then to each other's houses for a barbecue."

"Sounds ideal," Billie said. "Except for the part about what you all were doing to the horses you rode. And you do know that people who abuse animals tend to abuse children?"

That was a dirty shot, deliberately misrepresenting studies by flipping them to say that adults who hurt animals hurt children, when she knew it was abused children who were likely to hurt animals.

"When my mom got sick, Eudora and Dale took over for

her so I was always taken care of. One of the big weekend shows got turned into a charity event to raise money for Mom's care. That's the way it is there."

Billie rolled her glass between her palms, struggling with herself. Carefully, she exhaled. "I need to go," she said.

"I wish you'd stay a while longer."

"Believe me," she snapped, "you don't want that."

"Billie, I don't understand what this is about. I thought we were having a good time, but you seem furious about something. What aren't I getting?"

"You really want to know?"

Richard nodded.

Billie emptied her glass. "Okay. This might not make sense to you, but here it goes. You and your friends had everything good . . . that's what you're telling me, right?"

"Pretty much," he agreed.

"You had—have—money and land and horses and each other. And all the good things that go with that. Right?"

"Pretty much right."

"So, what have you done with all this good shit? You've tortured animals. What fucking sense does that make?"

"I know," he said.

"You don't know, Richard. But I know. To answer your earlier questions, yes, I was a foster kid. I was beaten and raped, and when I ran away I was brought back for more. But before all that happened to me, my father was a trainer. He despised other trainers who mistreated their animals. My parents were killed in a car crash . . ."

"Jesus, Billie." He reached toward her, but she pulled away.

"Jesus yourself, Richard."

"Is that why you cut yourself?"

She pushed her wine glass at him for a refill. She should just shut up. The wine was fueling her outburst, as it had that night at DT's after the fire that killed her filly, but it felt so good to be angry. She felt clear and strong and right.

"Why I did that is my own business," she said. "For now, you just need to know that I am going to do the best job I can writing about these horses of yours." She set her glass on the counter and stood up, stumbled and caught herself. "Your friends have to be stopped. Someone has to speak up for the horses. Introduce me to people I can interview back in Tennessee. I'm asking for a guide through the whole mess there. Think about it. I'm going home."

She took a staggering step, and he was at her elbow, supporting her. "Stay," he said.

Suddenly she was exhausted and depressed. She didn't want to drive home. She felt exposed by her self-revelations, stupidly, glaringly ugly. As if she'd covered herself with glow-in-the-dark paint and turned out the lights.

"You've had too much to drink. I have a guest room. No one will bother you, and you can drive home later. Whenever. Make yourself comfortable. I need to see to Alice Dean."

She didn't want to stay at Richard's but it seemed the right thing to do. She nodded. "Fine. Where's your guest room?"

He showed her to a small, tidy room off the kitchen with exposed log walls, a log bed, and its own bath. "You can lock the door if you want," he told her. "I get up at six and make coffee, if you'd like it."

As Billie murmured a thank you, they heard Alice Dean start to cry upstairs. Richard looked up, as if he could see through the ceiling. Sylvie's voice joined her little sister's, inquiring, then Bo's, but Alice Dean's sobs continued, rising to piercing shrieks.

"Dad!" Bo called. "Dad, hurry!"

He spun and bolted toward their voices. Billie followed.

Alice Dean stood in the hallway in a pink sleeveless nightie, her body rigid, her arms and hands held stiffly out from her sides. Her eyes and mouth were open, the screams coming from her blended into an unbearable siren. Her plastic horse lay at her feet, its legs wrapped in white ribbons or tissues. Beside it, on its side, spilling onto the floor, Billie saw a jar like ones she had seen in trailers at the show at her place and in the barn where she'd worked at Angel Hair Walkers, and in the stall of the filly she stole from the show.

"Mommy," Alice Dean wailed. "I want Mommy!"

"Call 9-1-1!" Richard shouted. "NOW!"

Bo and Sylvie opened their phones as one, but Richard wrenched Sylvie's from her hand and hurled it against the wall. "Where did she get it, Sylvie? There isn't any in the barn, so where did she get it?"

As Bo started to give directions to the operator, Billie thought Richard was going to strike Sylvie. But he unclenched his fists and softened his tone. "Sylvie. I need to know so we can help her. Tell me!"

"My closet."

Sirens sounded outside. Billie opened the door for the ambulance crew. Red emergency lights strobed the night. Voices, polite but insistent, seemed to be soft and shouting at the same time. She pressed her back against the wall while the response team clustered around Alice Dean and her father, questioning him, trying to soothe the shrieking child.

One of the EMTs called for a chopper to airlift Alice Dean to the hospital in Tucson.

"I want to go too, Dad," Sylvie cried.

Richard grabbed her arm and dug his fingers in so hard Billie saw the skin turn white. "If you do come," he said, "you will keep your mouth shut. We have to let them see what did this, but we will not say what it's used for, understand? It's just something that was around the house that she got into, okay?"

Sylvie nodded.

"I'll stay here," Billie offered, "and feed the horses in the morning before I go home."

"Good," Richard said. "Thanks."

And they were gone.

Alone in the house with Gulliver, Billie washed the dishes she found in the sink. Any feeling of being drunk had left her. She thought of having another glass but decided not to. She turned the television on then off. She stood in the door to Alice Dean's room, its whitewashed log walls covered in win photos of champion walking horses. Billie stepped closer to look at the legends beneath the photos and saw that each bore the name of Richard's family—his parents, his wife, Sylvie or Bo, or Richard himself. The biggest, matted in pink and framed in silver was of Alice Dean on a walking horse in a leadline class. Billie couldn't tell if she had won the class or not, but she could see that the horses in the background were up on stacks and wore chains.

Billie went next to Sylvie's room, its floor littered with Alice Dean's toy horses. Billie looked into Sylvie's closet, a girlish mess of shorts, riding pants, and T-shirts dumped on the floor, the poles laden with frilly bling things.

Behind a rack of shoes and riding boots, Billie found a jumbo baggie lying on its side, spilling bottles, jars, and rags. Fumes stung her eyes and made her throat hurt. She backed away and closed the closet door after her.

She found black plastic trash bags on a shelf in the pantry and rubber gloves under the sink. As she approached the opened jars in the closet, her eyes began to water and she coughed. She pulled on the gloves and checked each bottle and jar, replacing and tightening the lids. Then she stacked them inside one of the trash bags, double bagged it, and tied off the top.

She didn't know what to do with it. Leave it in the room? Put it back in the closet. Take it outside? Then what? She carried it outside and tossed it into her truck bed then went back inside; she didn't know what for. Billie stood with her back pressed against the steel refrigerator door. The house was silent. Outside, an owl hooted, hooted again.

Her hands were sweaty inside the gloves. She peeled them off, careful not to touch the outside with her bare skin, using one to remove the other, and dropped them in the sink.

The house phone rang. The machine picked up. She heard a woman ask, "Richard? Sylvie? Bo? Where are y'all? Someone pick up, please?" Then she hung up.

A moment later, Billie heard the lively jingle of Richard's iPhone coming from somewhere. She found it lying on the bureau in Alice Dean's bedroom. He must have left it there when he carried her upstairs. It stopped ringing. In a minute, she heard the beep that indicated a voice mail.

She looked at the phone, her mind thick as sludge. Alice Dean's screams still exploded in her head.

He would need his phone.

She drove to the hospital, parked her truck, and waited in the lobby beside the double glass front doors until she saw Richard approach. He stopped several feet away from her.

"What, Billie?"

"I have your phone." She held it toward him. "You left it behind. Someone called."

He took it from her and looked at the screen. "The kids' mother. I have to tell her."

"How's Alice Dean?"

"She burned her face and hands. Chemical burns. She got the juice in her eyes. They don't know yet."

"Know what?"

He grabbed her arm and moved her to an alcove beside the restroom. "Stop asking questions! You have no right! If you hadn't been there . . . If we hadn't been . . . I can't talk to you. We were out in the barn . . . I shouldn't have left her alone."

PART II

CHAPTER 20

A FTER A THREE-HOUR delay in Dallas caused by thunderstorms, Billie's plane landed at the Nashville airport just after midnight. She picked up her rental car—a black Ford Focus—at the Nashville airport and drove the hour to Shelbyville. She took a room at the first motel she came to and fell asleep the instant she lay down, oblivious to the scratchy brown bedspread beneath her cheek and the sucking gasp and belch of the window air conditioner.

She woke shivering, her eyes burning with exhaustion. She rolled herself up in the bedspread and tried to drift off again, but there was too much to do. Closing her eyes brought visions of the day ahead, lists of where she wanted to go and who she might meet to interview for the article.

Sitting in bed, she called home. She'd hired Josie and Sam to care for the horses, and paid extra for them to keep Gulliver while she was away.

"All's good," Josie told her. "Your little dog's snuggled up beside Sam in bed. They're both asleep."

"Oh, God, I'm sorry! I forgot the time difference."

"I'm up anyway," Josie said. "I never sleep through a whole night. Old age. Just wait. You'll have to get up to pee then you can't get back to sleep. Add a snoring geezer . . ."

Billie laughed.

"Your horses are fine. I fed them at seven last night, and I'll feed them at seven this morning. If you don't hear from me, all is well."

Billie thanked her, got up, and showered. She did her best with the package of instant coffee in its cheap wicker basket, the skinny packets of sugar and powdered creamer, and the fragile wooden stirrers. The result was weak and cold, as familiar and evocative to her as Proust's madeleines. She had drunk coffee like this as a child with her parents, in other motels, and the weak flavor took her back to then. She didn't want to remember now. She wanted to get going, hop into the rental with its new car smell, its odometer hovering around seven hundred miles, its power everything, and the screen that showed what was behind her when she backed up.

The dawn moon hung over the tips of the pines at the far side of the parking lot, and the early Tennessee morning felt thick and sweet as custard. Predawn bird songs melted into each other as Billie stepped out of her motel room onto the sidewalk beneath the second-floor balcony.

She checked her cell phone to see if Richard had called. She knew he hadn't, but she kept checking. *He'll call later,* she told herself. *It's too early for him to visit Alice Dean in the hospital—if that's where she still is. He's busy with his horses.* She blocked an image of him with his wife. Mother of his children. She was a resident of this very town, Shelbyville, as was Richard, whom she'd grown up with and married, who had now returned after leaving her. So they could take care of Alice Dean. Together.

An image of his ranch, the gate locked, the house and barns empty, flashed in her mind. She had gone back there once after Alice Dean got hurt. There was no one there, not even the horses. When Richard finally called her, it was to say that he was flying to Tennessee with his kids.

"How is Alice Dean?" Billie had asked.

"In pain."

"Will she be all right?"

"We don't know yet."

"I'm so sorry." It sounded trite, inadequate, but she didn't know what else to say. She dropped her head into her hands, pressing the phone harder to her ear to catch his every breath. "I'm sorry, Richard."

"Not your fault, really. I mean really, it's mine. But we have to stop. I have to be at the hospital."

"Can we be friends?" she asked. *And you'll still help me with my article?* she didn't ask.

After a pause, he said, "Sure."

Hot air blasted from the room's air conditioner behind her, and a steady stream of water spilled down the wall from the unit onto the pavement. She walked away from the building, out into the parking lot edged with magnolias and spongy wood mulch. The still un-risen sun had turned the tarmac and its puddles an oily pink. She heard sparse traffic on the two-lane highway that ran in front of the motel—wheels slipping past, indistinct voices far away, indecipherable words. Somewhere nearby a cow lowed, a horse whinnied, another answered.

In the lobby, a gaggle of teenage girls who each reminded her of Richard's daughter Sylvie was lined up at the breakfast buffet, loading paper plates with fruit salad, scrambled eggs, bacon, and donuts.

"Excuse me," Billie said. "Can I get to the coffee, please?"

The line of long smooth legs and shiny hair parted for her. She took her cup to an empty table and sat looking out the picture window at a vast green stretch of lawn.

The girls were talking about a vampire movie they watched last night after they swam in the motel pool, comparing boyfriends to the movie's lead teen actor, and each other to the heroine. Billie noticed a newspaper discarded on the table behind her and reached for it.

Local trainer expected to plead guilty to multiple counts of animal cruelty, read the headline. A grainy mug shot of Dale bore the caption: *Dale Thornton, 71, accused of Horse Protection Act violations just days before the Walking Horse Big Show gets underway.*

If Dale or Eudora would talk to her, grant her an interview, this could be a break for her. It was worth a try.

"He didn't have a choice," one of the girls said to her friend.

Billie glanced over and saw that they had another copy of the newspaper and were looking at the same headline.

"My daddy says Mr. Thornton was told that if he didn't say he was guilty he'd be carted off to the pen and left there to rot."

"Or get raped!" her friend exclaimed. "That's what happens in jail!"

"Ewww! He's too old for that!"

"My daddy says no way can the government tell us what

we can and can't do with our horses."

Billie wondered who the girl's daddy was but decided not to ask.

"They're our property and we have rights!" the friend said. "We own them."

"Anyway, they don't feel pain. Not like we do. Animals don't have the same kind of nervous system as us. They're an-i-mals. Gee-duh, get it?"

The conversation veered to country music and musicians, and one of the girls sang a few bars of a current hit in an astonishingly lovely voice.

"You've got to audition for *American Idol*," her friend said as Billie's phone buzzed. "Or *The Voice*."

"Hey, Billie, you up?" Richard asked. He sounded relaxed and friendly, as if they hadn't had their previous conversation assigning blame for Alice Dean's injury.

"I am." She heard the grin in her voice.

"I saw that you called."

So this wasn't anything more than that.

"Can you help me out with some names of people to talk to for the article? I'm here in Shelbyville."

"I'll text you."

"Is everything okay?"

"Read the paper."

"I have."

"Well then," he said. "We'll catch up later, okay?"

She tried to keep disappointment and anger from her voice.

"No problem." She had hoped he would guide her to the right people to interview, people who were knowledgeable about soring, involved with it, whistle-blowers who might give her an insider's view. If nothing else, at least he could tell her what farms to visit. But he was gone, the connection ended. He acted as if Dale's problems were his own. Or was that just an excuse to distance himself from her? Maybe he was back with his wife.

She laid the phone on the table and glanced around. The girls had left without her noticing. She sat with her cold coffee and wrinkled newspaper, the day stretched sourly ahead of her.

Back in her motel room, sprawled on the bed, goose-bumped from the chilled air, Billie reached into her bag for her knitting. Just a few minutes, she promised herself, some stitches to soothe her, a few rows. The counting always helped, so did the repetition with her hands, the little stabs of the needles, the deft looping of yarn, the way the fabric grew into her lap like a cat.

It wasn't until she'd sorted out the body of the sock from the ball of yarn that she remembered her metal needles had been confiscated by airport security back in Tucson. The stitches lay unanchored and in danger of unraveling without the needle to hold them in place. Carefully, she folded the sock over and returned it to her bag. She Googled *knitting Shelbyville* and found just one shop. When she went out today, she'd find it and buy another set of needles.

Then she typed in *walking horse barns Shelbyville* and made a list, checking each farm against the Google map in her iPhone, selecting first those closest to the motel, then the ones that were farther away. Frank always wanted the elite, the rulers of every underworld. Billie looked up each farm's website and Googled the owners' names. Some she found. Many she didn't. It was as if they didn't exist.

CHAPTER 21

BILLIE PARKED IN the first space she found in the town square and peered out the windshield, searching for the yarn shop where she could replace her knitting needles. An ice cream parlor with *LUCILLE'S* stenciled in blue and pink paint occupied the address she was looking for. She decided to get an ice cream cone at Lucille's and ask for directions.

She locked the rental car then noticed that she'd left her unfinished sock lying on the front passenger seat. She unlocked the door and retrieved it.

On the sidewalk in front of each business, identical folding signs featured the silhouette of a Big Lick horse on a bright green background:

PROUD SUPPORTER OF THE
TENNESSEE WALKING HORSE BIG SHOW
We love our breed!

The sign in front of the ice cream parlor had been set down haphazardly, so it practically blocked the entrance. Billie sidled past it and pulled open the screen door. A bell jangled overhead as she stepped inside. She glanced at herself in a mirror that covered the entire wall—trying to double the width of the narrow room, she figured—and wished she had combed her hair and chosen something to wear other than a faded blue and red University of Arizona Wildcats T-shirt.

"Can I help you?"

The voice of the woman who appeared through swinging saloon doors at the back of the shop was soft, Southern, welcoming. Her hair was mounded on top of her head like the burl of a gnarled oak tree, and Billie wondered how much hair spray it took to keep it there. The woman wore turquoise eye shadow, thick black liner, and pink lipstick. She smoothed a pink and white striped apron over her dress, *Lucille* embroidered on its breast.

"Get for you?" Lucille asked.

Billie sat at the counter. "Decaf, please. No! Wait! Regular."

Lucille slid a cup and saucer into place in front of her, followed by a pink china bowl stacked with creamers. "You take sugar, honey?"

Billie shook her head as the older woman poured her coffee. "But I am hungry. I don't suppose you've got any breakfast ice cream?"

Lucille laughed. "Now that's a first. Scrambled eggs in a waffle cone. I should add it to the menu. I do serve food besides ice cream. Specials are there." She pointed behind her to a whiteboard leaning against the mirror, the menu written in blue cursive handwriting.

Billie looked at the list. "Macaroni and cheese, please, with sweet potato fries. Ranch on the side."

"You sure *are* hungry." Lucille smiled, tucked her order pad into the apron's frilly pocket, and disappeared through the swinging doors.

While Billie waited, she looked around at dolls in ruffled *Gone with the Wind* style dresses, teacups, butter dishes shaped like cows, patchwork squares salvaged from antique quilts that had been remade into pillows, placemats, and stuffed animals—all with tiny white paper price tags. Along the back wall, to one side of the swinging door, she spotted shelves of yarn for sale. She got up and went over to look, feeling squeezed between the shelves. She fingered the hanks, daydreaming about what she'd make with them.

Lucille returned with Billie's meal and set it on the counter. "Ketchup?"

"Please."

Billie squeezed her way back through the cluttered shelves and took her seat. She poured a puddle of ketchup beside her mac and cheese then reached into her bag for her knitting and laid it on the counter beside her plate. "I was looking for the yarn store when I found you."

"One and the same," Lucille said.

"My needles got confiscated at Tucson International. I forgot and brought metal, but I've never had a problem like that before. They didn't take anything else, not even my little scissors. Do you have any circular bamboo size 2s, so I can get them home when I return?"

Lucille rummaged in a bin until she found what Billie wanted, placing it beside the knitting.

"I couldn't help noticing the sign outside," Billie said.

"Ah-huh," Lucille replied.

"You a fan?"

"Of the Big Lick? Hell, no."

"But the sign?"

"Forced to display it."

Instinctively, Billie glanced around, looking for whoever might have forced Lucille to display a sign against her will.

"Aw you won't see anything," Lucille told her. "There's no one hiding behind the counter with a baseball bat or a torch. Those sons of bitches know what I think, and they know I won't shut up about it. But I had to listen to their threat, so I put out the damned sign."

"What was the threat?"

Lucille moved Billie's cup down the counter and refilled it. "You a fed?"

"I'm a writer, working on a piece."

"About?"

"Walking horses."

Lucille pulled up a stool and sat down. In the mirror, Billie watched the back of her lacquered head, the towering brown hair bobbing as she poured herself a mug of coffee. "You interviewing me?"

"I'd like to."

"You walk around this town and ask everyone what they think, you'll get a bunch of different answers. Some of them'll be true, others lies, on both sides of the issue. You'll find people who might talk to you. Some of them are against soring, like me. Some of them are for it. Of course they don't say it like that. You'll hear them moan about the threat to our industry, our way of life. But those are all euphemisms for soring."

Abruptly she stood up as the bell jingled and the door opened. Three men in business suits, jackets slung over their shoulders and ties pulled loose, leaned against the counter. Lucille greeted them as friends and regulars, joking with them as she poured Cokes and made up cones. She collected their money and wished them a good day.

When they left, Billie said, "I met Richard Collier at a horse show in Arizona near where I live."

Lucille pulled a stool over and perched on it, stretched out her legs, and crossed her ankles. She wore thick white support hose and yellow pumps with little flowers on the toes.

"Richard gave me the names of some people to talk to here," Billie said, which was almost true. That had been the plan anyway.

"He tell you to talk to Vern Stockard?"

"That sounds familiar," Billie lied.

"Winning trainer over on the dark side. You should talk to his mother."

Billie nearly groaned. Talking to someone's mother was a brush-off, a dead-end, hopeless and useless. She made herself nod.

"But will you talk to me too, Lucille? You're right here. You're outspoken. How do you feel about what's going on?"

"What *is* going on?"

"Soring," Billie said. "How do you feel about that?"

Lucille placed the backs of her fingers under her chin and batted her eyelashes. "Why, sugar-child, that is a thing of our evil misguided past. It's gone the way of tarring and feathering and Saturday night lynchings. We good Confederate Christians won't abide it anymore. Mind you, there are always a few bad apples in every barrel, in every sport. I am thinking now of reports about the use of performance-enhancing drugs by some major sports figures. But except for them . . . Can I sell you a bridge?"

Billie grinned. "Do you have any tips for me?"

"I sure do. Go home."

"Anything else?"

Lucille twisted her fingers in and out of the mug handle. "If I were writing a piece?" she asked.

Billie nodded, encouraging her.

"Vern's mother, Addie, works for our local papers. She's covered everything that's got to do with walking horses and horse shows for decades. Then you should go to some local shows, and the Big Show here, of course."

"That's why I'm here."

"And I'd go to the barns too if I was you."

"I heard the barns used to be open to the public but that they're closed now so you can't get in. Too many animal rights activists nosing around making trouble."

"That's true. A lot of trainers are just plain sick of being criticized. But all trainers want to make sales. They've got to win ribbons and sell horses. That's their job."

"My father trained reining horses."

"So you know then."

"Yeah. I do."

Lucille leaned across the counter, close to Billie.

"I'd hang out. There's one more local show nearby, then the Big Show. Buy a soda and a program at the shows and look interested."

"I am interested."

Again Lucille rose to take care of customers, this time a harried mother with screaming twin boys in a stroller. Lucille silenced them with cones dipped in jimmies, and got the mother a chocolate shake to go. When they left, she fished her cell phone from her apron pocket.

"Adeline. Lucille here. Get yourself on over, I've got someone for you to meet." Then she returned to Billie. "Like I said, I'd go to the barns. I'd go when no one's there. That's what I'd do. But I'm advising you against all that. I'm telling you to go on home and write about something else." She ducked back through the door and returned with a fresh pot of coffee.

"Mind if I ask how you got that?" Billie gestured toward a puckery scar on the back of Lucille's hand.

Lucille sat back down. "Here in the South, we deal with dissension by burning and lynching. I haven't been hanged, yet."

"Someone burned you? Why?"

"You mean, why me? Well, I own this place and others. I have some clout around here, by which I mean I've got some money. I own walkers, I don't let anyone hurt them, and I speak out about what's done to other folks' horses. I called the *Times-Gazetteer* and spoke with their reporter, Adeline. Told her what was what, used names. Blew the whistle. Next thing I know, there's a bottle of acid that just shows up on this shelf here in my sweet little store and just happens to not have its lid on tight, and when I take a hold of it to see what it is, it slips and splashes on me. Could have been worse. Could have been my face, could have been one of my horses."

"Did you report it to the police? Was there a trial?"

"Have you ever heard of Apple Hollow Farms?"

Billie remembered the name from the list of farms she had gathered on the internet. Judging by its website it was huge, with barns and outbuildings, a massive Tara-like home, three trainers, and an on-premises veterinarian.

"Well, our present chief of police owns it," Lucille pronounced it *po-lice* and gave the word a contemptuous ring. "His daddy owned it before him, and *he* was chief of po-lice too. You getting my drift?"

"So that's why you didn't report it."

"What would have been the point? Everyone knew what had happened and who had done it. I'd have been asking for a second helping of trouble."

Lucille cut a huge slice of peach pie, slid it into the microwave, then topped it with a double scoop of vanilla ice cream. "You want some sauce on this? Caramel butterscotch?"

Frank's disapproving face flashed in front of her. "You'll get fat," he'd said, as if it was any of his business.

"Sure," Billie grinned. "Why not?"

The sauce Lucille ladled on cascaded into puddles around the pie and hardened to candy where it touched the ice cream. She handed Billie a spoon and another couple of napkins then fixed a plate for herself.

"How did they force you to display the sign out front?" Billie asked.

"Threats against my animals. I take them seriously, as you can imagine. A lot of barns around here catch fire after people make accusations. Horses burn to death."

"Mine did," Billie said. "In Arizona."

"You met Richard out there?"

"Yes."

"I'm betting you made some trouble in the walking horse world that brought attention to you."

"I took a filly that a groom was hurting from their barn to my place, middle of the night."

"Whoa! You got a set of nuts the size of Texas, girl!"

"My barn burned with the filly in it."

"They were being kind to you. Could have been your house with you in it. Do not underestimate who's playing on the other side in this game."

Lucille ripped Billie's check from her receipt book and tucked it under her coffee cup. "No hurry. When these signs first showed up the big guns in the industry offered them to us, the businesses in town, to display. They wanted us to put a sign outside that says we approve of horse abuse. If we objected, we got threatened."

Billie was about to ask if she could take notes when the bell jingled, the door opened, and a Miss Marple-ish woman entered. She and Lucille were of a similar age and size, women thickening throughout their late fifties.

"Lucille, honey, how you spelling stupid these days?"

"This here's Adeline. She's the writer I told you about. Plus that, she's the mother of one of our top trainers, right, Addie? Listen, Addie, this gal here's writing a book."

Billie didn't correct her.

"Didn't get your name," Addie said.

"Billie Snow. Arabella Snow."

The woman frowned. "You're Arabella Snow? Why didn't you tell me, Lucille?"

"Tell you what?"

Adeline plopped onto a stool and ordered fries.

"I've read your work," Addie said to Billie. "In *Frankly*."

"I work for them." It was a stretch—she used to work for

them; she might work for them again if Frank approved the article—but not an outright lie.

"What brings you here?" Addie asked.

"The magazine wants a piece on the walking horse industry, who's behind it."

"I told her you'd help out," Lucille offered.

"Lucille, girlfriend, you are just begging trouble for me. I love my son and his pals as much as the next mother loves hers, but I don't want to cross them, especially right before the Big Show. It'd be like dropping our new friend here into a pit of massasaugas. And by the way, you're asking for a lawsuit unless you move that sign outside your door before someone trips over it and gets killed. You forgot you didn't finish setting it up, right?"

"I didn't forget."

"What you want to know?" Addie asked Billie.

"Horses are sored so they'll walk big and fast and win ribbons, and become champions and make money for their owners."

"That'd be about it," Addie said.

"Why don't people who hate torturing animals rise up and shut them down?" Billie reached into her bag for her phone and held it up. "Mind if I record?"

"If someone comes in, you'd better hide that thing or turn it off or whatever you do," Lucille said.

"I will."

A passing truck caught Billie's eye, a one-ton silver dually like Richard's. She felt flooded with missing him and, like a schoolgirl with a crush, wished the truck were his. It pulled into the parking space at the corner of the block.

"Dang that girl! She's doing it again!" Lucille said.

"You going to call the cops this time?" Addie asked. "That's a handicapped slot," she told Billie. "And she's not one bit handicapped, physically."

The truck door opened and Sylvie got out, slung her pink, fringed handbag across her shoulders, and headed across the green away from them.

"That one's a right piece of work," Addie said.

"Amen," said Lucille. "Now let's get back to what we were talking about. You wanted to know how soring's allowed to continue?"

"Yes."

"It's allowed to continue because the people with power want it to. Simple as that."

"And as complicated," Addie said. "My son, for example. I didn't raise him to be cruel to animals. But it's all around here. You want to make a living with walking horses—with any breed of horse—you got to win. And to win with walkers, you've got to sore them."

Billie nodded. "Who's in charge?"

"What do you mean?"

"If I follow the money all the way up to the top, who will I find?"

"Honey, you won't find anyone."

"When I looked for the owners of the big farms around here, I couldn't find them. Is that what you mean?"

Lucille nodded. "Corporations. Stuff like that. Syndicates."

"But who's in charge of them?"

"Hush. It's a secret."

"Really?"

Lucille cleared Billie's plates, setting them down with a clatter out of sight behind the swinging doors, then she wiped down the counter with a sponge. "No, not really. Old boy's network doesn't begin to describe this," she said. "You got to understand our society to get how this all works. If you're not born into it, you won't understand it."

"Help me," Billie said. "I've got to or I won't do you, or this topic, justice."

"Now there's a word!" Addie said.

"What do you mean?"

Lucille said, "Your justice, mine, your friend Richard's . . . they're not the same."

She hopped up to deal with a couple more customers, preteens in shorts and T-shirts, carrying backpacks and iPads. The kids seated themselves at the counter near the front of the store. Lucille slapped down menus, scribbled their orders, and barked, "Gotcha!" before ducking through the doors and disappearing for several minutes.

Addie's eyes followed her, as she talked softly to Billie. "This you do need to know. I'll try to explain. Take my son. Please. Sorry! Old joke."

"Rodney Dangerfield."

"Dangerfield is right. My son's a good man, like most folk in this industry. He did well in school, went to college, served in the marines. He's done four tours of duty and has two Purple Hearts. He married his college sweetheart, and they are raising a fine family—four good kids so far, another due at Thanksgiving. Everything's just right. Except for the horses."

The door to the shop opened again, and a crowd pressed into the narrow space.

"Lunchtime," Lucille said.

Addie looked at Billie. "Tell you what, why don't you follow me back to my place and we can go on talking there?"

"I'd like that."

She paid Lucille and thanked her then followed Addie outside.

Addie pointed to a black Subaru Forester. "That's me. If we get separated, I'll wait for you at the next stop sign."

Addie drove fast. Billie followed her out of the town square, south on a twisty tree-shrouded lane, feeling that at any second she would lose her and be lost. But good to her word, Addie waited at every stop sign until Billie had caught up.

Addie's house sat up on a hill that fronted onto a lane, making it look taller than it really was, just a normal-size two-story farmhouse, painted white with black shutters, surrounded by sumac and azaleas and dogwood and some dark green shrub with rubbery leaves that Billie couldn't identify.

She parked beside Addie, and together they climbed three wide wooden steps to the porch. Billie smelled honeysuckle and wood chips. Heat made sweat pour down her sides. Behind the house, a red barn stood with its doors wide open. Billie saw light from the doors at the far end falling on the wide aisle floor.

"Lemonade sound good to you?" Addie asked.

It sounded perfect.

The kitchen had a speckled linoleum floor, old white appliances, red and white cafe curtains at the windows, and a big standing fan instead of air conditioning. Billie sat at the claw-footed table, placing her glass on the square of paper towel

Addie tore off for her. She admired the kitchen's crisp white walls. Through an open door, she noticed a smaller room with walls hung with horse show ribbons.

"My son's office," Addie said. "Have a look if you want."

Billie saw a rolltop desk, computer, printer, and bookcase. It was the walls that drew her inside. Framed photographs of Big Lick horses standing beside a bald stocky man in his late thirties hung beside rows of championship rosettes.

"My boy's done well for himself," Addie said at her shoulder.

"Do you ever talk to him about it?"

"Not anymore," she said as she turned back into the kitchen.

Addie set a blue and white plate of cookies in the center of the table and sat opposite Billie.

"I'm going to spell things out for you because you don't have time to figure them out for yourself. It'd take you years to catch on, if you ever did." She put a cookie in her mouth then took a sip of lemonade. She got up and came back with a bowl of sugar.

She offered it to Billie, who added a spoonful to her drink. "What you need to know," Addie said, as if it were the title of an essay, "is that everything and everyone here's connected to everything and everyone else."

"May I record?"

Addie nodded and waited for Billie to get ready. "Okay? Things are connected here, as I was saying. Not in just the regular way that all people in all small towns are. It's special here."

"I don't understand."

"No, you don't. Since you know Richard, let's start with him."

Billie nodded and pushed the recorder a little closer to Addie.

"Richard is married to Mary Lou Collier, nee Simons, whose family owns car dealerships here and most of the rest of the state, all the major American makes. They also own a tractor company—I forget their name. Those tractors and the trucks from their dealerships are used on most of the farms around here. Now this family also owns a meat business and raises hogs and sheep for pork and lamb. They process their own animals, so they have huge barns like Hormel does. They have slaughter plants and rendering plants, and out behind them, they've got anaerobics and whatever else they need to clean up the mess. So this family employs a lot of people. Those people want to keep their jobs, right?"

"Right."

"The meat is served in our restaurants, owned outright or in partnership with other local families. Just drive down Main Street here in town, or anywhere around here, and you'll find family-owned restaurants and chain restaurants—Flippy-Flapjacks, for example—where the animals are served. Your eggs. Your bacon. Your ribs and broilers. Sausages and roasts and stews. All raised right here. Also in the supermarkets. You getting some idea of the scope of this one family? Okay. Now let's start to link them up, say to Dale and Eudora Thornton since Dale was in the news today.

"Those folks own the mortuaries. We have a dozen in this township, all with different family names—Addison's, Howard and Pyke, Forever Beloved—so it looks diversified, but they're all owned by Eudora's family. The churches belong to Dale's in the sense that his family donates more money than any other. They've funded the construction of a half dozen or more churches and Christian schools. Different denominations, all beholden to the same people. People who also own our correctional facility, and some might say our courts.

"Did I mention that the mayor is Richard's brother-in-law?"

Billie stared at her. "No."

"And the mayor's father-in-law is our US senator."

"Which one?"

"Springer."

"And they all sore horses?"

"Nope. Not all of them. But they won't cross those who do. Soring didn't get going until the 1950s. I was just starting to work for the paper then. I covered the little horse shows around here. Not the big shows, not the championships. I wasn't trusted to write about those yet. I saw trainers start burning the horse's legs and hurting their feet a few years after I came to work. By the '70s it was so bad, you'd see blood running down their legs in the show ring."

"What started it?"

"Just some dumbass guy riding a hurting horse in a show. The judges liked the way it pranced when its feet hurt, gave it a blue ribbon, and here we are, what, sixty, seventy years later."

"What keeps it going?"

"Senator Springer needs those votes, that money, his friends. Now, I happen to think that piece of shit doesn't care what's done to anything but himself, but even if he did, he'd have a devil of a time opposing the Big Lick. By supporting it, he gets everything he needs or wants."

Billie took a long draught of her lemonade. The sugar hadn't sweetened it enough and she shuddered.

Addie smiled. "I enjoy a good shiver in the summer," she said. "And I like sweating in the winter. That's the best time for chores if you ask me. In a snowstorm. Can I pour you some more?"

Billie shook her head no. "What effect is the current scrutiny of the walking horse industry having on people here, on the industry itself? And what about the case against Dale?"

"It's a damper, for sure. Trainers are pulling out of shows. A lot of them are selling their farms. It looks pretty bleak for the walking horse world."

"And your son?"

"Bleak for him too. Like everyone else here. A way of life ending, yadda, yadda . . ." She filled her own glass. "But . . ."

"But?"

"The good old boys are being called names in the press, trashed on the internet, exposed for the slime they are. All very unpleasant. But really, is this any reason for them to stop?"

"What do you mean? I thought that everything was falling off—attendance and sales. I thought the big shows were closing or going to close."

"And so they are. The walking horse world is letting the media, the outraged public—get what it wants. The walking horse world is shutting down and, in quotes, going away."

"But that's not what's really happening?"

"Bingo, my friend. The Big Lick world is a chain of linked interests going all the way from the stable hand to our man in Washington."

"Your man in Washington?"

"Really, there's more than one. Senators. Congressmen. But for now, let's stick with Senator Springer."

Billie recalled the senator's round face and aggressive manner from TV appearances. He was popular with certain conservatives for his positions on gun control—he was against it, and abortion—also against it, and war—in favor, it seemed to her, of every conflict the administration considered.

As if reading her mind, Addie said, "It's not just the right wing. Liberals like Dickinson are on the wrong side of this too."

Dickinson was a favorite of Billie's. She had long admired his compassion for children in the courts, and for those in foster care. Kids like herself. "Why?"

"Money," Addie said. "The lickers pay off a lot of politicians. They make donations to their causes and their campaigns. Sixty thousand and more."

Billie whistled.

"The scrutiny now on soring isn't enough to stop it, but it's enough to be making people uncomfortable. For example, you're here. And other reporters covering protests and issues. In years past, there'd be a spurt of interest, outraged articles. Then it'd die back."

"Now?" Billie asked

"Social media. This won't fade out the way it used to. There's a brighter light shining on it. Twitter. Facebook."

"That's why Dale and Eudora went to Arizona?"

Addie nodded. "They went there to get horses ready for the shows where they won't be hassled. Where they can do whatever they want to get ready for the Big Show, somewhere no one knows them or cares about them. Listen, when you get to the show, find me. I have seats above the fried chicken stand. Same seats every year. Stop by."

CHAPTER 22

ILLIE PULLED OUT of Addie's driveway, wondering about the trainers like Dale and Eudora who were looking for places to continue to abuse their horses, out of sight of people like her, journalists who fed outrage to activists. A few yards down the road, she pulled off onto the shoulder, turned on her hazard lights and scribbled into her notebook. "What will happen if soring gets driven out of Tennessee? It's tolerated here, championed even, but at least it's visible. If the trainers and owners seem to comply, pretend to quit, but really just relocate for most of the year . . . The pressure to end it will ease up. Face it, not enough people care enough. Why fight over this when there are seals being clubbed, thoroughbreds being drugged, dog fighting?"

Her pen skidded across the page when a semi-truck blasted its air horn at her as it passed. The Ford rocked in the slipstream and her heart thudded in her throat. She slipped the notebook back into her bag and pulled back onto the narrow road.

It was lined with farms. Barns set back in fields lush with summer grass. As Billie passed, she saw horses grazing, flocks of goats and sheep, and ducks and geese drifting on ponds. Wherever the roads intersected, antique shops alternated with diners and gas stations on the corners. Farm stands, laden with produce, hand-lettered signs advertising ridiculously low prices begged her to stop. But she drove on by until she found the narrow road leading to Bell Buckle. When she'd mapped the walking horse farms, she had found a concentration down this road. Her plan was to start here, just drive up to barns, get out and say hey.

By the end of the day, she'd have a list of places scoped out, maybe even a few interviews to report on to Frank. Preliminary for sure, but she'd be oriented at least. He'd always liked her to check in with him when she was on staff at the magazine, let him know what she had found out, who she'd spoken to, and what she had planned. He was one of those editors who liked to be involved. She'd known writers who hated Frank's style. They wanted independence and lots of space to work in. But she liked his involvement. Conversations about their work that started early in the day continued in the taxi on the way home, through dinner, and went to bed with them. She loved it.

"Saves me a shit load of time if I keep my writers on track as they work," Frank said. "Otherwise I've got to fix copy later and redirect them."

She wanted to be sure that things were going to work the same now.

Trees, thickly covered in kudzu vines, grew close to the road. Their branches arched overhead, throwing deep shade. Ahead, she spotted a farm sign and slowed until she could make out the logo—white letters inside a gold oval: *Angel*

Hair Walkers. Home of the Best Ever Walking Horses. Dale and Eudora's farm. She squinted down a long drive toward neat rows of barns in a wide field. A wooded hill rose behind the barns, creating a scene of bucolic peace.

A half dozen media vans were parked on the side of the road. Billie pulled over and sat with the engine idling. She'd planned to interview the Thorntons last, but here she was at their farm, along with local reporters and even media vans from Nashville and Knoxville. She could back up to the gate, ring the buzzer, and see if they let her in. Now that Dale was in trouble, they could make her life difficult by letting everyone know who she was and what she was doing. There'd be no sneaking into barns for clandestine interviews under false pretenses. On the other hand, if they were helpful, they'd make everything so much easier for her. Dale might talk to her about the charges against him. That would be a coup. Dale and Eudora were exactly the kind of people Frank would want her to interview and use to get her to the highest levels within the industry.

While she debated what to do, another heavy livestock trailer stuffed full of hogs passed her, its slipstream rocking her car, trying to pull her along. She steered onto the road and followed it for a mile or so until it turned into the driveway of an agrifarm like those she'd seen earlier. She wondered if it was bringing animals to the farm, and from where, and for what.

She decided not to risk an early meeting with the Thorntons and drove on until she came upon another farm. Its weathered barn stood close to the road, a large *Simeon Wilkerson's Walking Horses for Sale* sign teetered at the foot of the drive. She turned in and parked in front of the open double doors. A pregnant calico cat licked her belly on a pile of manure speckled straw. Pigeons fluttered in and out of the barn doors, and a one-legged rooster hopped up onto a bench that tilted against the barn wall.

Billie lowered her window. "Hello?" she called. When no one answered, she got out of the car and slammed the door to draw attention, but no one came. She knocked on the open barn door and shouted, "Hi?" Then she stepped into the barn, allowed her eyes to adjust, and called, "Anyone here?"

She heard a door at the far end of the barn open then close, and a man lumbered toward her. The barn reeked so badly her eyes watered, but the tools had been picked up and leaned against the walls. A manure cart was heaped with soiled bedding and parked in the middle of the aisle, but she saw rake marks in the aisle dirt, and the stall fronts had been swept clean.

"Help ya?" The man was sloppy fat, his face whiskery, head bald. Pouches under his eyes spoke of ill health.

"This your place?" she asked. "Are you Mr. Wilkerson?"

"Simeon," he said. "And you?"

"Billie Snow." She extended her hand.

He gasped and coughed. He took her hand in his and squeezed, fleshy and moist. "Can I do for you?"

"I think I might want a walking horse to show. I'm driving around to see what I can find for myself. Your door was open, so I just came on in. I hope that's okay?"

"Sure, sure. Nothing to hide. Not like some others around here. Nothing to hide, me. You might say that's 'cause I got nothing. Lost it all. Losing it all. First the economy, now the damned inspections at the shows and all the bad publicity.

Really hurting business. You can't imagine."

"Guess not," Billie agreed.

"What kind of horse you want, Miz Snow?"

"Call me Billie."

"Billie. I got horses. Some of 'em are nice. Were nice. But I'm selling out." He waved his hand at the barn aisle. "I can show you what I've got. Of course they're not really ready to show just yet. Well, one of 'em is. If you tell me what you'd like to see, I could fix it up, and you come back later to see it."

"Show me now," Billie said. "If I see something I like, we can decide what to do about it."

"What kind of riding you want to do? You looking for flat shod? Plantation shod? Trail? Big Lick?"

"Big Lick," she said. "I mean, I think that's it. I want to go to horse shows and do well in the big classes."

"Performance horse, then. Big Lick. I've got a horse for you." He led her to a stall with a black horse standing in it, his halter tied to the wall. He had been recently groomed; she could still see brush marks on his hide. He wore stacked shoes, and his forelegs were wrapped in fleece bandages. "This here's a two-year-old stud colt," the man said. "He should be the champion this year. He'll be top two-year-old in the country. I've got to sell him, though. Darn shame. I'll get him out for you, and you can try him right now. Royal!" he hollered.

"Is that his name?" Billie asked.

"Royal," he yelled again. "My boy," he said to her. "ROYAL!"

The man who appeared from the murk was a younger version of his father, maybe in his forties. Fat festooned his belly and puddled just above his knees. "Whatcha want?"

"Lady wants to ride Jazz. Help me git him ready."

Billie felt panicky. "Isn't he too young? Just two?"

"He's not even two yet, coming two's more like it. But he knows his job. Don't he, Royal? Royal this is Miz Billie Snow. She's horse shopping. Miz Billie, this here is my son."

Royal nodded toward her. She tried to smile back at him. He looked as soft as a glob of tapioca, but he moved almost gracefully, as if his weight were nothing to him. He slid his eyes over her, leaving prickles between her shoulders, but after he'd glanced, he turned away to his work and didn't look back.

Royal swung open the stall door and stepped inside. He grabbed the colt's halter, clipped a lead shank to it, and turned him toward the door.

"You sure I should ride him now?" Billie asked. "I could come back."

Both men stared at her, but Royal brought the colt out into the barn aisle.

"You're not a goddamned tire kicker are you?" Royal asked. "We get a lot of them, people faking an interest for one reason or another. You're not one of them, right?"

Simeon disappeared into a room and returned with a flat, slick-looking saddle over his arm, which he set atop a tack box. He went back and returned with a bridle with a wicked-looking shanked bit and hung it on a hook by the saddle.

Royal handed Billie the lead rope and briskly went over the horse with a brush. Dust flew out from beneath his strokes. He ran a rag over the young stallion, set a saddle pad onto its back, then the saddle. Within what seemed to Billie like mere seconds, the colt was saddled. The father took the lead rope from her and bridled the horse while she tried to think of a way out of riding. She could not ride a hurt horse, and this youngster was obviously being sored.

"I haven't ridden in ages," she lied. "And I've never been on a stallion."

Royal guffawed. "Just don't sit on his balls."

Simeon lumbered back into the tack room and emerged with a handful of chains that he dumped in a clatter on a metal chair. Grunting, he undid the fleece wraps on the colt's legs, balling them expertly into rolls as he tossed each from hand to hand. He straightened up to toss them onto the tack box then, gasping, he bent and unwrapped the cellophane that had been beneath them. He handled it with his fingertips, and when he was done, wadded it and threw it in a wastebasket then wiped his hands on a rag.

"You going to get on now I've got him ready for you?" he asked Billie.

She looked at Simeon and Royal, about to refuse. But in their faces, she saw pride in this horse they had trained. Both men were watching her, ready for something. She felt their eyes judging her, ready to dismiss her, to get mad, to throw her out. She could just leave, plead fear or allergies or something, but if Frank found out she'd had a chance to ride one of these horses and hadn't, he'd outright sack her.

Silently she apologized to the horse then put her foot in the stirrup and swung aboard. The stirrups were too long, and the horse quivered with power. It was power, she decided. Not pain.

"I say this is the horse for you," Simeon assured her. "Royal, put his bracelets on him so he steps out sweet for her."

Royal grabbed chains from the pile on the chair. Billie heard him grunt as he bent and wrapped them around the horse's pasterns. He stood up by pulling himself up the stallion's leg, hand over hand.

"I've never ridden a walking horse," Billie said.

"Like fallin' off a log," Royal chuckled.

"What should I do?"

She saw that Royal was about to crack another one, probably say something like "Keep one leg on each side of your horse," when Simeon stepped up close and laid one hand on her knee, the other on the reins she held.

"Hold them up high, like this," he said. "It's different than you're used to. Pull back on them reins more than you think you should, keep a steady pull. At the same time, put your leg on him and squeeze him up. You're telling him with your legs to go forward and with your hands to go high. The more leg and hand you use, the bigger the lick. Start easy, now."

The saddle felt slick, and there was nothing to hold on to if Jazz spooked. Billie wrapped her forefinger into his mane to steady herself. The good thing about grabbing the mane instead of the saddle, her father had taught her, was that the mane stayed in the center of the horse, while the saddle could slip. Everything felt new and wobbly to her. She prayed the horse wouldn't bolt. The barn aisle stretched ahead of them, a couple of hundred feet long and maybe forty feet wide. Cluttered tools and piles of manure lay mounded into a center median jumbled together with wooden planks, wheelbarrows, pitchforks, and a small green tractor.

Jazz stepped off as soon as she asked him, and when she asked for more at the man's urging, he gave it to her. She had water skied as a child, and this felt the same—like she was being lifted right off the earth and into the air. His front legs rose high with each stride, his hind legs reached farther and farther under him until he was moving forward in a smooth, steady crouch. They seemed to fly down the aisle, the chains clinking as they hit his legs. She knew they were landing on burned flesh, making him snap up his feet to get away from the torment.

"Hey there, sister, you can ride," Simeon said when she pulled up after several laps. "You should buy this horse. You can win big with him."

Billie slid off and patted the horse's lathered neck. She felt sickened from having ridden a sored horse but thrilled by the power she felt when he moved. And he was just a baby, barely developed. What must one of the mature horses feel like? Ashamed, now she understood why someone would do this, what was in it for the rider besides money.

"He's lovely," she said. "Beautiful and so well trained. But I'm not going to buy the first horse I ride. I have to look at more before I decide."

"'Course," he slumped. "'Course you do." He pulled off the saddle. "There's no market anymore. Everyone's hurting. All these investigations and new rules are shutting us down." He unhooked the chains and crammed them into his pockets. He led the horse to its stall and took off the bridle. "Get in there you piece of shit," he said, but his hand slid over the horse's back as it entered the stall, lingering appreciatively. He latched the door. "I'm heading back to Minnesota soon as I can get out of this." He gestured at the horses.

"Minnesota?"

"I first saw these horses at a show near Saint Paul. Thought I could train some. The good ones bring a lot of money. So I moved here. Did okay for a while. But I don't like what I have to do to get the wins. I didn't know I'd *have* to do it. I thought I could train without it. But if I didn't do it, I lost. Now the government's all over us too, checking up and testing and disqualifying even sound horses. They don't know what they're doing half of the time. Most of the time. But it's shutting down the industry. I can't make a living. I can't even hire help, can't afford it anymore. It's just me here, and Royal."

Billie flashed on herself, doing all the work on her ranch.

"Haven't got it in me. I saved some of these horses from other trainers who went bust. Now it's my turn. Nothing I can do about it."

"What do you want for the horse I just rode?"

"Fifteen thousand. And that's a steal. A year ago, he was worth a hundred grand."

Not a single horse on her ranch, not even Starship, was worth more than fifteen hundred.

She got Simeon's phone number and promised to call. He said sure like he knew she wouldn't, and she didn't try to convince him otherwise. As she drove away, she wondered what lay ahead for the horses living in filth in his barn and for the two-year-old she had just ridden. She imagined saving him, driving all the way from home to this ramshackle farm to get him and bring him to her ranch.

CHAPTER 23

A s BILLIE RETRACED her way back toward Shelbyville, the dozens of sleepy walking horse farms she'd passed in the early morning were now bustling. Trucks had been hitched to trailers, their doors open and piles of tack boxes stacked beside them. Men and women bustled in and out of the barns, some leading horses, everyone seeming to have a purpose. But when she tried to turn into the driveways, she found them blocked. Gates had been shut and bolted on some. Other driveways were obstructed by tractors or flatbed trailers that prevented her from driving in. At the fourth barricaded farm, she parked the rental car beside the road, got out, and hiked toward the barn, skirting a Polaris ATV with a dump cart hitched to it, filled with hay bales.

A gangly boy loped down the driveway toward her. "Closed!" he shouted.

"I just . . . Bo?"

He looked younger somehow, appearing so unexpectedly. He stopped then continued toward her, his hand raised in a stop gesture.

"Bo, it's me, Billie. From Arizona."

"We're closed." He scowled. "What are you doing *here?*"

"Here? What do you mean? Where am I?"

"This is our place," he said then added, "Mom's."

She took a step backward, looking around for something that would have told her. She realized she had never once asked the name of Richard's almost-ex's farm.

"It's good to see you, Bo. How's Alice Dean?"

He glanced away from her, back toward the barn and the people there, who were turning to look at him. "She's better," he said. "You should go."

"Bo!" a woman called. "You need help?"

"I'm fine, Ma!" he yelled back. To Billie he said, "There's a horse show tonight everyone's going to. We're getting ready. I've got to go, Billie. Please."

Billie squinted over the boy's shoulder, trying to see his mother, Richard's wife. The sun was behind her, making it impossible to see well, but she seemed slender and possibly tall, the same body type as Sylvie. Billie felt a wave of jealousy. "Where's the show?"

"At Adam's farm. Jesus, Billie . . ." He turned away.

Billie wanted a longer look but did as he asked and headed back to her car. Before she got there though, she turned. "Thanks!" she called. "I'll find it!"

He had already returned to his mother at the end of the long driveway and was helping her hoist a hay bale into the back of a truck. He paused to look at her for a second then turned back to his work.

After an hour's drive on crisscrossing country roads, Billie found herself at last on a narrow, tree-shrouded lane that dipped and rose and dipped again before settling down into a long, shaded straightaway that sloped toward the distant sparkle of a river. Small, exhausted-looking houses with peeling paint and missing shingles hung close to the little road. Between the houses sprawled farms, many clearly struggling, but three or four were opulent, manicured, with paved driveways, whitewashed fences, and barns that dwarfed the homes.

She was singing along with the radio when she rounded a sharp curve and slammed on her brakes, nearly ramming into a faded red pickup truck. She realized it was the last of a long line of vehicles creeping toward a sandwich board sign with letters spelling *ADAM'S FARM/SHOW TONITE* and an arrow pointing to the right. She followed the pickup off the road and into a field. A man took five dollars from her and gave her a program. She found a spot to park in a ragged row of cars and trucks disgorging couples and families with folding chairs, picnic baskets, and coolers. She slipped her cell phone into one hip pocket of her shorts and a wad of cash into the other pocket.

Even though it was past six in the evening, the humid Tennessee heat struck her like a blow when she got out of the car. Grass tickled her ankles. The scent of rich earth, vegetation from the nearby forest, horses, and bug repellant transported her to horse shows from her childhood, to state fairs and carnivals.

A rectangular white fence created a riding arena. People set up their chairs nearby, spreading blankets on the grass and unpacking their coolers. Billie spied a snack stand by the arena in-gate. By the time she reached it, she was sticky with sweat. A sign under a blue shade offered lemonade and sodas. She chose lemonade, and with her first gulp, felt her core temperature plummet. She looked around.

Behind the arena, dozens of horse trailers and RVs were parked haphazardly. Horses were being unloaded and tied to the trailers. A shimmering scrim of insects hovered every-where. Gnats and mosquitoes zoomed at her ears and bit the backs of her arms. And, although she couldn't see them, she knew that ticks clung to blades of grass and leaves, poised to latch onto her. Flies pestered the horses, landing on their legs and bellies, their noses and ears.

She was tempted to wander over to the trailers. Instead, she leaned against a sapling and sipped her drink, swatting at the mosquitoes and shivering with each bitter swallow.

By the time she'd finished, she had a sense of the move-ment around the arena and in the trailer area. Most of it was what she'd expected—owners, trainers, and riders prepar-ing their horses and themselves to enter the ring when their class was called. But gradually she became aware of other factions. Workmen erected portable lights for the arena. Two men moved from trailer to trailer, stopping to shake hands at each vehicle as if they were running for office, a welcoming committee. As she watched, she noticed that with each hand-shake, they glanced over their shoulders, expecting trouble.

A half dozen horse inspection officers were stationed at the arena in- and out-gates. They had established an area for the horses to be examined, using police tape and traffic cones.

A van with a government logo on its side that Billie couldn't make out bounced across the field and stopped beside the inspection area. Five men and one woman wearing identical khaki slacks and bright blue polo shirts got out and set up a card table near the other inspectors. They unloaded ice chests, draped stethoscopes around their necks, and loaded clipboards with papers.

Billie spotted Lucille and Addie seated in folding lawn chairs beside the arena.

"Well, hey," Lucille greeted her. "Come set. Grab her a chair, Addie. Addie's boy's got hisself about a hundred of 'em."

"I'll get it," Billie interrupted. "Just tell me where." Addie pointed to a stack of chairs folded and leaning against a rusted two-horse trailer parked a ways off.

"He won't mind?" Billie asked.

"Won't even notice."

"We're done for now," Addie said when Billie returned. "Now the feds are here, everyone will pack up and go home."

"Maybe not," Billie opened the chair and sat in it, grateful for its comfort. "No one's leaving yet."

"You're right," Addie said. "I wonder what's up?"

"Do you have a horse in this show?" Billie asked her. "Does your son?"

"Not today. We heard the government might be coming, so we decided not to bring a horse. The inspections are bogus, completely subjective and unfair. You can have a horse who's passed every inspection of his life and still have the feds turn him down. Then what? Then you've got a mess for nothing. I'm just here tonight to watch. Like you."

Addie's lament reminded her of what Simeon had said earlier, the complaint about unfair inspections. She unfolded a chair and set it beside Addie, who offered her an orange from the ice chest and crossed her ankles to wait for the show's classes to start. Billie wondered how people who picnicked beside a spectacle of tortured horses could think of themselves as innocents.

She wanted to ask those questions in the article, so she retrieved her notebook from her bag and scribbled them down. As she slipped her pen back into the notebook's spiral binding, a movement in the trees at the far side of the field caught her eye. A person? she wondered, peering. She couldn't see anything. Most likely a deer or a cow.

Addie still talked beside her about the horses she used to own. She'd be a good source about the breed's history, Billie realized, as Addie reminisced about showing in the 1950s and 1960s.

Billie saw movement in the woods again. Then, again, it stopped. She kept her eyes on the area where she'd seen it, and when she'd finished scrawling her notes on what Addie had told her, she excused herself and headed around the far side of the arena, and from there to the woods.

The loamy smell of damp soil rose from the ground. She heard a bird's song. But she didn't find anything there, just some trampled leaves that could have been a spot where deer or wild pigs slept. Deeper in the woods, she saw a flock of startled birds rise. Shiny vines twisted around the tree trunks. Poison ivy? Poison oak? Poison sumac? She tucked her arms in close to her body and sidled back out toward the show. Maybe she'd imagined something to get away from Addie's lecture and the stress of waiting to become a spectator again at another Big Lick show.

Over the sound of a woman on the PA system announcing the sponsors for the horse show—truck dealerships, a restaurant chain, a mortuary, and a meatpacking company—Billie tried to listen for sounds in the forest. She strained to hear footsteps or voices, but a splatter of applause gave way to a man's voice reading the Lord's Prayer, children reciting the Pledge of Allegiance, then a live organ played "The Star-Spangled Banner," which ended in cheers.

Billie saw Charley standing beside a black horse with white legs, brushing it with long sweeps. She walked over. "Hey."

He looked at her without pausing but glanced around.

"This is the first time I've seen a show where the feds showing up didn't send everyone scurrying." He pulled a comb from his pocket and ran it through the horse's mane, carefully straightening knots. "I've been wondering if what I heard was true—that there is a new way to fix a horse, a way that doesn't show up during inspection." He coughed.

"Wouldn't you know about that?" Billie asked.

"Once I would have. Not so much now. The boss is keeping an eye on me, I'm pretty sure. I don't get told the things I used to. But no one knows which shows get the federal inspectors coming in. Mostly they don't appear anywhere—too little funding, too few inspectors, too many shows." He attached a ribbon to the browband on the horse's bridle, fluttering it with his fingers. "There's so much hostility toward them that even in their righteousness, they hate their job. You see them when they came in?"

"I did."

"You see how they stick together like gum on the sole of a boot?"

"That doesn't really work," Billie said. "As an image."

Charley ignored her. "They're scared to death. Walk like guns are trained on them."

"Are there? Guns?"

"There is everything, Billie Snow. Mostly though, shit happens behind the scenes. The good folks of Shelbyville don't want an OK Corral shootout and forever fame. They pick their targets pretty carefully." He stuck the comb back into his overalls pocket then slipped it out again to tap himself on the chest. "You see this?"

"What?"

"This is a bullseye right here. Maybe you can't see it, but I sure can feel it."

A string of riders passed by, calling hellos to Charley who answered each with a cheerful "Good luck!"

When they had passed, he flipped a saddle pad onto the horse's back and followed it with a saddle.

"I saw you chatting with old Addie Stockard. Her son Vern has been showing sore horses all his adult life, starting with the horses he trained for her. There was a time when she'd say he'd never sore a horse. I have heard that bullshit ever since I started to work in stables as a little bitty boy. *'Oh no, ma'am, your horse is so talented. I'd never have to resort to that!'* All these trainers say that to their clients if the clients bother to ask. Most owners know damned well what's going on in the barns and don't give a shit. Long as their horsie comes home with rosettes and a trophy, it don't make an anthill of difference how that happened. But some are natural-born worriers, like Addie. Don't hurt my horse. Just make sure it wins."

She should be writing this down, but she didn't want to interrupt him, slow him, or call attention to herself. She'd just have to remember.

Charley bent double wheezing. "Damned asthma. Maybe I caught some damned bug from the kids at Dale's barn. When school's out, the place crawls with kids. Their parents pay for them to have lessons and the character-building experience of cleaning stalls and brushing horse hides. And the folks get a few hours each day to work or fuck."

"Did you babysit Richard's kids?"

Billie watched Sylvie, several trailers away, prepare Dale's blue roan stallion for this evening's show. She had him tied to the side of the top-of-the-line Sundowner four-horse, aluminum, gooseneck trailer. She knelt beside him with a long-handled screwdriver in her hand, tightening the bands that held on his heavy shoes until he pulled back from pain.

Behind them, seated on the fender of a small aluminum trailer that was parked askew, Billie glimpsed Royal talking on his cell phone, an infant in a pouch on his chest, and a toddler sitting on top of his feet.

"I will turn in the last evidence I gathered to the feds next week," Charley whispered. "I could still be adding to it, but I got a bad feeling."

"What kind of bad feeling?" she asked.

But Charley stepped away from her and the horse he'd tacked up, and waved to someone. Richard, Billie saw, getting Sylvie mounted and spiffed up for a trip around the ring on her horse. The girl was a beauty, Billie thought, tight-bodied and slender. Like her mother.

"I've known her since she was an infant," Charley said. "I taught her how to show horses and how to sore them. She was a natural, the most talented kid I ever worked with. Good at everything, and a great little chemist. Loved to burn a horse's legs then see what that did to its gait. She listened to everything I told her about how to win. She made it all her own. Then she improved on it."

He stared over Billie's head, tears on his cheeks.

CHAPTER 24

ILLIE WOKE EARLY and lay on her back, looking at the motel room. She'd been here long enough that it felt familiar, almost homey. The Formica bureau was covered with her open suitcase and mounds of laundry. The bathroom door had a towel hanging from the knob. She'd kicked off her sandals after sitting on the bed last night. One had landed on the floor, the other lay upside down on the bedspread.

She got up, brushed her teeth, ran her hands through her cropped hair, and washed her face. She pulled on no-wrinkle brown slacks and a tan blouse, draped her linen jacket over her shoulders—her reporter-on-the-job work clothes—and headed to the courthouse for Dale's trial.

The courthouse stood at the outskirts of town, rising from the middle of a black asphalt parking lot. She parked, got out, locked the car, and strolled across a strip of lawn and up the steps of the granite building.

She hadn't expected the lobby to be crowded. A mass of young people gathered in front of a trio of girl *a cappella* vocalists singing the University of Tennessee fight song "Rocky Top" in precise harmony.

"Part 4. Downstairs on your right," she was told when she went to the information desk. She descended the stairs, stepping in time to the music, aware of the superb acoustics in the building, aware that this had nothing to do with her job but loving it.

Downstairs, away from the filtered sunlight in the lobby, fluorescent light soured the narrow bench-lined hallways. Billie glimpsed Dale at the far end of the hall, talking to a small cluster of men she guessed were his lawyers. He wore a yellow plaid short-sleeved shirt, carried a tan jacket over his shoulder, and looked sweaty in spite of frigid air-conditioning. She edged over toward them. Snatches of bluegrass drifted down, and she noticed people hushing up to listen, but not Dale's group. They spoke somberly, so softly she couldn't make out their words, mumbling to each other. One of the lawyers reached up and squeezed Dale's shoulder, which brought his gaze to her.

"What's she doing here?" he asked clearly so a half dozen people in addition to his attorneys turned to stare.

"Looks like media," the lead lawyer said. "Ma'am?"

Billie extended her press pass.

The heavy wooden door to Part 4 opened, and Billie followed Dale and his team inside. The air was icy, the room empty except for the court stenographer in a cardigan fussing with her table in front of the witness chair.

Billie sat in the back row, watching. There was no question that Dale was tense, possibly scared. He mopped his face several times, and she saw that his hands trembled. When

Eudora arrived and came to sit beside him, he leaned over to give her an awkward kiss but missed her cheek. Billie heard his lips smack air. Eudora touched his cheek with her fingertips. The judge entered along with a smattering of people Billie didn't recognize, who scattered themselves in seats near the front. Richard leaned against the wall in the rear, beside the door, looking ready to bolt. Someone slipped into the chair beside her and tapped her arm.

"Addie!"

"I couldn't miss it," she said. "Thought I might be useful to you too. I know who most of these folk are. I'm a human scorecard, you could say."

"Thanks! I was feeling pretty lost."

Addie dropped her purse on the floor between them, fished inside, and brought out a package of Black Jack chewing gum. She offered it to Billie, who declined with a shake of her head, then unwrapped two pieces and folded them into her mouth.

Addie reached back into her handbag and brought out her knitting. She settled it into her lap, twisted the yarn around her finger, and set to work, needles making soft clicks. Envious, Billie wished she'd brought her own so she could sit alert but relaxed beside Addie as the hearing unfolded.

"Ma'am! Ma'am!" Billie wondered what she'd done wrong before she realized the judge was pointing at Addie. "There is no gum chewing my courtroom. Please dispose of it. Now."

Addie pulled the wad from her mouth, reached into her handbag, and emerged with the empty wrappers. Slowly, she selected one, folded the other, and replaced it in her bag. She removed the gum from her mouth with her fingers and rolled it into the wrapper, using theatrical gestures.

"Okay?" she asked.

The judge resumed his seat, nodded to her, and called the attorneys to the bench.

"Pompous ass," Addie said, just loudly enough to prompt the judge to glance over at her. "I had him in third grade, and he was already a stuffy little brat. Now he's a stuffy middle-aged man. But you know, I'm actually proud of him. He turned out okay."

"Does he know who you are?" Billie asked.

"'Course he does! These tiny towns back here in the hills, we know each other all our lives. A lot of sorry folk back here, that's for damn sure. He came out okay though."

The judge rapped his gavel once and glared at her. She shrugged and blew a discrete little kiss that made the lawyers laugh.

"Is he a good judge?"

Addie slipped the yarn along her needles and turned it to knit the next row. "Now I didn't say that."

"For this case, I mean? Is he impartial?"

"I didn't say that either."

The room was packed when the hearing started with witnesses being called to testify about Dale and his business. Where he'd grown up, what his connections were, how far he'd risen in the walking horse world. Billie was aware that at some point the courtroom door opened for a latecomer. She turned to look and saw a man in a seersucker suit—his tie open at the neck, a black briefcase in his hand—enter and sit in front of Addie.

"Who's that?" Billie asked her.

"No idea."

Witness followed witness, first detailing Dale's alleged crime, establishing where it occurred, how it was discovered, what was discovered, alluding to an expert witness who would testify even more damningly about the condition of the horses in Dale's barn.

Eventually, the judge asked the bailiff to bring in the expert witness.

"I'm already here, your honor." The man seated in front of Addie rose.

"Are you Dr. Michael Spearman, of National Chemical Forensics?"

"I am."

"Dr. Spearman, you're not allowed to be here."

"But sir—"

"Before we began, I informed the attorneys that witnesses would not be permitted in this courtroom before they gave their testimony. That is to keep anyone from hearing someone else's testimony and adjusting his or her own to match. Were you not aware of this rule?"

"I wasn't."

Addie stopped knitting, her attention fixed on the judge. "Ah, shit," she murmured.

"What's going on?" Billie asked.

Addie didn't answer her.

"Ladies and gentleman," the judge addressed the room, "I regret that we have a mistrial. Mr. Thornton, you are free to go."

"What happened?" Billie asked as Addie rose.

"Trial's over."

"But why?"

"You heard the judge."

"But why didn't the witness know? Why didn't someone tell him? The attorneys knew, right?"

"Exactly." Addie stuffed her knitting into her bag and headed for the door. "That's the sixty-four-dollar question."

Billie jogged to keep up with her, brushing past Richard at the doorway. Briefly, she felt his hand on the small of her back. If anyone saw it, it wouldn't look like anything, just two people passing in a close space. But it lit her up with memories of their lovemaking.

The performers were gone from the lobby.

Billie saw a reporter grab Richard's arm. "Comment on the verdict? What do you think of what happened, Mr. Collier?"

Richard pulled away and shoved through the throng, Billie in his wake.

Where had they all come from? When she'd entered the courthouse ninety minutes ago, there had only been a few reporters. Now there were five times as many people pressing forward with microphones, iPads, and cell phones. Most of them obviously didn't recognize him, but they shouted random questions at him anyway. Once he reached the far side, he turned and looked back. Billie's eyes found his and he paused. Then he moved on.

Reporters also mobbed Dale, who stood with his back to a wall, head held high, Eudora at his side.

"Because I am innocent!" Billie heard him say.

Outside, thunder cracked overhead, and rain battered the pavement. Billie looked around for Richard but couldn't see him. Somewhere in the crowd, in the rain, she thought she glimpsed

Charley's grizzled head. When she looked again to make sure, he wasn't there. She stepped off the sidewalk into a puddle. Water sloshed over the tops of her shoes, soaking her feet.

She spotted Richard ducking into his truck and ran to him. Rivulets streamed down her forehead into her eyes. "Can we talk?"

"Sure," he said, as if he knew it was the wrong answer.

She waited for him to offer her a dry spot in the truck. When he didn't, she asked, "Where?"

"Your motel?"

Her pause was infinitesimal, trying to hide her relief. She told him which one.

"Nine tonight okay for you?" he asked.

"Sure," she said.

As suddenly as it had started, the downpour became a sprinkle, then stopped. A mosquito landed on her elbow. Another whined around her ear. She should have brought bug spray to the press conference. She had some in the car. She wondered if she had time to go get it. Something bit her on the back of her neck, and she swatted at it. Steam rose off puddles left from the downpour, puddles that reflected a huge sign advertising the horse show, and insects of all sizes and appetites zoomed through the sodden air.

Just as she was about to return to her car to look for repellant, news vans pulled up. Most were from local stations and Nashville and Knoxville, followed by a trio sporting logos from ABC, CBS, and NBC. They were followed by a swarm of sedans and SUVs that parked among them, nosed in toward the curb. Reporters and video crews waded through the standing water to set up. There must be at least a couple dozen media types, she realized. She felt like a wallflower, standing alone to the side.

"That's him!" She recognized Dan Tiger, who anchored the 11 PM news.

Richard got out of his truck and extended his hand. "Hey, Tiger!"

There was a tense pause before Tiger took the proffered hand for a quick squeeze. "Surprised to see you here, Richard."

A young woman grabbed Richard by the elbow and moved him so he stood under the Big Show sign.

"This is good," she said. "Stay right here."

Billie moved in closer.

"What the fuck are you doing?" she heard Tiger say.

Richard gawked at him then a look of outrage overtook his surprise.

"Don't I remember your riding in this same arena a decade ago, Tiger? On that bay mare your father-in-law bred and raised, and that you trained. If I recall, you sored that horse all the way to a championship."

"You want to put us all out of business?" Tiger leaned in close, pulling on Richard's shirt as if searching for a place to clip on a microphone. "You should keep your mouth shut or it might get shut for good."

He turned away before Richard could say anything, nearly bumping into Billie.

"Get out of here!" he demanded.

She flashed her press pass at him, and he shoved past her.

Another woman, her face covered in a thick layer of make-up, stepped past Billie to Richard.

"You ready?" she asked him. "Look at the camera. Just be

natural. Three. Two. One . . ."

The reporter positioned herself in front of him, faced into the camera, and said, "This is Sally Ann Wagner, here at the home of the upcoming Tennessee walking horse Big Show in Shelbyville, Tennessee to hear what a long-time trainer and owner of these beautiful animals has to say about the controversy over the means used to train them. As we speak, there is a group of horsemen walking—no riding!—on the Capitol in Washington, DC to bring attention to what is often referred to as 'the plight of the walking horse.'"

Billie caught a quick, subtle flinch in Richard's eyes. She had resolved to change the title for her article when she learned how much he hated that phrase, clichéd from years of overuse.

Unaware, Sally Ann continued. "The case against Hall of Fame trainer Dale Thornton has just been thrown out. Here, outside the courthouse, protesters have gathered. Animal rights activists and others claim that these horses are tortured to make them step high.

"Today, we are here to talk to Richard Collier, whose family has been active in the walking horse industry for three genera-tions. Mr. Collier and his family own, train, and show walking horses. In fact, Sylvie Collier, Mr. Collier's daughter, is being touted as perhaps the next—and youngest ever—winner of the coveted world grand championship class."

The reporter stepped aside and turned to face Richard. "People within the walking horse industry claim that these complaints will ruin them and destroy their livelihood. They say there is no abuse involved, and the horses are loved and well cared for. Please tell us, Mr. Collier, your opinion of this controversy."

She held the microphone a few inches in front of his lips. He cleared his throat and took it away from her. She looked startled, but he ignored her and faced the camera.

"My family has raised walking horses for generations," he said. "I have been privileged to work with these gentle animals all my life. I have ridden, trained, and shown them to the highest championships in the land."

Billie looked out at the faces in the crowd before him. The media vans had attracted passers-by, and there was quite a crowd. She spotted Richard's daughter Sylvie flirting with a cute tech guy.

She was aware that Richard's pause had gone on too long. People were worried, restless. Wondering if he was finished, if he had frozen from stage fright. He licked his lips, swallowed.

"Every horse I showed, every horse I won on was sore. Every single one." He paused to let it sink in and heard a rustle, then a rumble from the crowd. He interrupted it. "You cannot make a horse move like that—can't make a horse do the Big Lick—can't make a horse pick up its front feet so high and fast and step under so deeply behind unless you sore it."

Reporters stepped toward him, shouting questions.

He raised his hand. "Hear me out!"

They subsided enough for him to continue.

"I am a God-fearing man!"

They fell silent at this. Billie had never heard him use this come-to-meeting voice before. He sounded like a politician.

"Raised among you and with you. I have already said that I have come to believe that soring is wrong. But more than that, I have come to believe that soring is a sin. So I am here to tell you that I have sinned against God's creatures. I have sinned but I repent. I am here to speak the truth. I have done that. There is not a single Big Lick horse who is not sore. There is no horse going into the ring at the Big Show who has not been sored. There is no trainer, no owner, no show rider, no exercise rider, no groom, no stable hand who does not know this. We are all guilty of this sin. We must all stop it now. What we do is wrong. I never thought I'd side with PETA or the Humane Society or any other animal rights group. But I'm telling you, in this instance if in no other, they are right. What they say we do, we do. We must stop. We must."

Over the cacophony of shouted questions, Billie heard applause. And booing. She stepped in and extended her iPhone. She saw wariness in his eyes, uncertainty.

"Mr. Collier," she said, "why have you said this? Aren't you worried about your safety?"

"I said it because it's true. It needs to be said." He raised his hand in a silencing gesture. "No questions. Thank you," he said then turned away.

The crowd followed him to the truck, honking questions. He ignored them, his walk faster than theirs. But when he arrived at the truck, Billie was already there.

"Thank you for your time." She wanted to put her arms around him, tell him she was proud of him.

"I'll call." He closed the door.

She wondered if he would.

When she turned to look back at the crowd, she spotted the witness whose presence in the courtroom had gotten the case thrown out, talking with a couple of reporters.

"Dr. Spearman!" she approached him. "Arabella Snow. *Frankly* magazine. Can I talk to you?"

CHAPTER 25

ILLIE SAT CROSS-LEGGED on the motel bed, pillows behind her, a slice of take-out pizza from the greasy box on the bureau balanced on her knee. She had tidied the room and balled her laundry into a plastic bag then stuffed it into a corner of her suitcase. She hadn't been able to eat any of the pizza. Her stomach kept dropping as if she were on a roller coaster. A note lay on the bureau beside the TV, printed in a computer font that looked like an old typewriter. *Go home now or you'll never see home again.*

Claps of thunder shook the motel and lights flickered. The TV spewed news of the foul weather, viewer photos of thick gray skies, rain against buildings, and trees bent over onto a road. If Gulliver were with her, he'd be shivering in fear. She'd bundle him in his Thundershirt and cuddle him until he slept. Her chest constricted with longing for places she knew, for Richard.

"Another summer storm has dropped an inch and a half of moisture onto our already soaked countryside," the announcer said. "High winds downed tree limbs and power lines in Marshall County, and parts of the city of Lewisburg are without electricity. But that has not put a damper on Shelbyville's preparations for the horse show. Let's go over to station meteorologist Sue Ellen Rosemont at the main arena. Sue Ellen?"

The screen cut to a shot of a young woman with streaming wet bangs, cradling her mike inside the flaps of a yellow slicker.

Billie turned off the TV and set the unfinished pizza slice on the bed. She got up and checked the door to be sure it was really locked, the chain securely in place. She brushed aside the curtain and checked the window, which was locked but leaking. She took one of the thin towels from the bathroom, rolled it, and stuffed it against the sill. When she closed the curtain, she made certain it covered the window. She wanted a shower, the comfort of hot water, but didn't want to be naked, didn't want to be behind the closed bathroom door with the water running.

This wasn't the first threat she'd ever received. They'd been a pretty regular fact of her earlier life when she worked for *Frankly*, digging into the filth of child prostitution and urban sex clubs with powerful members. Threats were just part of the landscape. She routinely turned them over to legal to take care of. But this sodden note, slipped under the flimsy door to her room for her to find, terrified her.

Her cell phone buzzed. By the time she'd searched the bed and found it under a snarl of sheets and T-shirts, it had gone to voice mail. Richard's name appeared in caller ID. "Billie, I can't make it tonight. I'm sorry. I'll try to reach you later." She called him back. When he didn't answer and she got his voice mail, she hung up.

Staring at her phone, she saw that she had missed a call from Frank.

"We need to talk," Frank's voice said. "And soon. I don't think much of this stuff you sent me yesterday. You know the kind of material I use and this isn't it. Call me."

She sat back on the bed, her spine hard against the headboard, pulling pillows into her lap. The air conditioner was so loud it would cover the sound of anyone approaching her room. But when she turned it off, the room became a sauna within minutes. So she turned it back on. If only Gulliver were here with her to greet her, curl onto her pillow wagging his tail and wiggling. He made her feel welcome, at home. She missed him, her horses, her ranch, her desert where the storms were intense and powerful then over. Minutes after a storm passed, the sun had baked cactus and humans, steam rose from the dirt, and flooded washes subsided.

She reached for her cell and called Josie.

"Wilde Adventures," Billie's neighbor answered.

"Hey, Josie."

"Hay is for horses, Billie. How's it going back there?"

Billie heard Josie's sucking inhale on a cigarette, the pop of her lips when she held the smoke inside. "Thought I'd call and see how everything is out where you are. How're the horses? How's Gulliver?"

"That little hooligan's doing alright," Josie said. "He's sitting on my lap right now. We've got a big old storm coming, but he don't seem one bit bothered."

"And the horses?"

"Mostly okay."

Billie waited a beat for the bad news she heard brewing.

"What's wrong?"

"It's all okay now, I guess. Your gray horse, Starship, colicked. I got Doc out for him. Figured that's what you'd want."

"How bad was it?"

"He was on the ground, thrashing. I couldn't tell if it was just a bad gas colic or if he'd got a twist or an impaction. Old Doc gave him a couple shots and tubed him with mineral oil, and he got back up in about a half an hour. Doc gave him some fluids too."

"Is he okay now?

"Seems just perfect. But Doc noticed he had a couple of summer sores from the flies laying eggs on his belly and nose, so he treated them and left some ointment for me to put on every day. Turned out two other horses had 'em too. Hashtag had one on her lip. "

"Should be easy to clear that up," Billie said.

"You won't need to. I told the owner about it, and she decided to take her home. Picked her up this morning."

Billie could have yowled. The vet bill for Starship alone could wipe her out, probably reaching over a thousand dollars. And she'd lost her only boarder. "Did she pay what she owed before she took him?"

"I didn't know what she owed, Billie, so I couldn't ask. Guess you'll have to settle up with her later." Billie heard Josie's husband Sam in the background. "Hold on, Billie. Sam's got something he wants to say."

"Hey there, Billie. I hate to add to things, but I checked on your house, and you've got a big old leak in the roof right over that couch thing you sleep on. I'm afraid it's ruined, and you're going to have to get the roof repaired."

She could scream, but what good would that do? This time of year, everything went wrong in the desert. Stuff you weren't even aware of in the dry months broke, leaked, shorted, and washed away. She'd grown up in it, but every damned year something caught her by surprise. The roof shouldn't have, as it had leaked each of the five years she'd lived there. But those other years she'd been home and had moved the futon and set out a big stew pot to catch the drips. She'd forgotten about it, and now her bed was wrecked and the house needed repairs. "You want to fix it, Sam?"

"Heck no. My roof days are long over. You want I should call Ty for you? He could come out after he loads up the last order at the feed store today, stop by your place on his way here for dinner."

She should have thought of Ty herself. He'd get the job done fine for her. She had no idea how she'd pay him unless Frank accepted the article.

"Thanks, Sam. Maybe I should get an estimate for the work."

"No point. No one'll do it cheaper, and you need it done. And fast, before we get more rain. You get mold in that old adobe, and you're going to be in a world of sorry."

She hung up and pressed her phone to her forehead.

It felt like every creature on earth depended on her. She couldn't get fired. She covered her eyes with her palms and exhaled, breathed in, then slowly forced the air out. And again. What had Frank taught her when she first worked for him? Put yourself into your work, he'd said.

She opened her eyes and looked across the room at the note she'd found when she got back.

She pulled her laptop onto her knees.

Tonight, she wrote, *I found a death threat in my motel room when I got back from interviewing owners of Tennessee walking horses. A note slipped under my door. I am huddled on my bed, shaking . . .*

She stopped at about five hundred words and sent what she'd written to Frank with one word typed on the subject line at the top: *Better?*

It was an hour later in New York than in Tennessee. She pictured him working in his office in the apartment they'd shared, a pool of light on the papers on his desk, light thrown by the Tiffany lamp she'd bought at auction and given him for their fourth anniversary. When she left him, she had almost taken it with her, but decided instead to leave everything except a carry-on suitcase and her computer. Maybe he'd already gone to bed.

She lay back on the pillow, holding her phone in her hand to be certain she'd get the call. If it came. After a while, her eyes closed. Just for a second, she told herself. Just to rest. The ping of the mail program woke her.

You've got the job.

CHAPTER 26

ACEMENT SIDEWALK CUT across the lawn outside the stadium where the Big Show was held. Hundreds of fans lined up waiting for the gates to open so they could get their seats. Vendors pushing carts with grilled corn, fried chicken, tamales, and ice cream sold out early. Children catapulted from excited to cranky to weepy. Their parents lay raincoats and picnic blankets on the lawn for them, and they slept or played with blades of grass and fat black ants. The parking lot filled then overflowed. Cars and vans and SUVs parked on the street, wheels up on the curb. The police didn't bother to write tickets.

Billie felt awkward, almost shy about approaching strangers with her questions. Her reticence was useless and didn't even make sense. In her experience, there was always someone willing to answer any question she might pose.

She stepped up to the line and caught the eye of a man standing near her. "Excuse me," she said. "I'm working on a story about the horse show. Do you mind if I ask you a few questions?"

The man gave a who-me? shrug, looking past her as if hoping someone would intercede.

She forged ahead. "How do you feel about the negative publicity about the Big Lick gait?"

"What? Who are you? Beat it!" he said. "Leave me alone."

The response, even though unfriendly, relieved her of her shyness. She was simply working. She stepped onto the lawn and pulled out her iPhone.

"The town of Shelbyville is putting on a party," Billie dictated. "Come one and all. This is the culmination of a year of preparations, training, grooming, and showing the most magnificent Tennessee walking horses in the country, in the world." What she'd said was awkward, but she'd fix it later. "Tonight in this very arena is the ultimate competition, when the best of the breed meets the best of the breed. But what makes a great walking horse?" She spoke loudly enough for her phone to hear her, softly enough so, she hoped, few others did.

"Pardon me." She extended the phone toward a woman with four small kids hanging on her arms and legs like sloths on a tree. The mother seemed to constantly pluck children off some part of herself only to have them reattach. The oldest boy leaned against her, jabbing at a tablet. Peeking, Billie saw that he was playing *Angry Birds*. His mother was pregnant with what was at least her fifth child, and Billie wondered how many more there were at home.

"What would you say makes a great walking horse?" Billie asked her.

The woman stared at her with exhausted eyes.

Billie tried again. "Is there a horse you're rooting for tonight?"

The woman pried a toddler's fingers from the waistband of her shorts and handed him a PayDay candy bar. "I don't know," she sighed.

The older boy spoke up. "I want last year's world grand champion to become this year's world grand champion. I want him to win."

"How old are you?" Billie asked.

"Nine."

"Do you think the Big Show is a good horse show?" she asked. "Do you think it's fair?"

He looked at her as if she had serpents exiting her ears. "You asked about winning."

Billie turned back to see if his mother agreed but saw that she had grabbed another child by its wrist and was shaking it loose from one of its siblings.

"Where's your father?" the woman asked no one.

Billie's phone pinged. Frank's name appeared in bold type, followed by his message: *Getting anything good?*

Local color, she tapped into the phone.

Just got a bribe offer, Frank wrote. *Good one. To trade you for a senator.*

She didn't understand what he meant.

I call you off, kill the article, and get everything I ever wanted to know about the senator. Haven't decided if I should take it.

Out at the end of the professional gangplank, she felt him slice through the rope behind her. It had happened before. She'd be drowning in a second.

LOL, he texted.

She typed, *Very funny.*

He didn't reply.

She separated from the line of customers waiting to go inside the arena and found a quiet spot under a vast maple tree. Leaning against it, she tried to breathe, to think. How should she play this? If she let Frank know that she was terrified, he might call her off the piece. She'd lose the job. She didn't want to revisit the chain of catastrophes that would befall her and everything she loved if she got fired. She needed the payment, in full, and soon.

But if she acted flippant, too casual, he might not realize how dangerous this assignment was. And she needed him to know, to admire her for what she was doing. The greater the danger to her, the better her chances of selling the piece that grew out of the danger. He'd said the job was hers, but that didn't mean he couldn't change his mind.

Her phone rang. Frank had called instead of continuing to text.

"You scared, Billie?"

Of course she was scared.

"No."

"Good. Tell me what you're looking at."

"People lined up to see horses tortured."

"Is this different from bullfighting?"

"How the fuck would I know?"

"Okay. *That's* the Billie I hired. Now go get me what I need."

She stared at the screen for a moment, wondering if she could get her fingers to let go of the phone. Keeping it in her fist, she stuffed her hand into her pocket and hung on.

Billie worked her way toward the front of the line, excusing herself, saying she was looking for someone while reporters worked the edges of the line like grass tickling a snake.

A couple of Patterdale terriers chased each other between her legs and across the lawn—small, dark, wiry dogs who were used to hunt opossum and boar. They were featured on some walking horse websites that advertised them with multiple fonts in varying sizes and colors. The dogs were displayed with their slaughtered victims on one page, their darling puppies on the next. These two barreled through the crowd, making kids shriek and adults laugh.

The line finally moved. People poured through the gates into the arena. Billie found a seat behind two overdressed women and a whip-thin man all in black. She tapped his shoulder. "Do you think we'll have to wait much longer?"

"For what?" the man asked.

"For the show to start?" she answered.

"Naw," he said. "Soon."

Billie sat back and looked around. She sat in a football field ringed with bleachers. Huge screens at either end overlooked the venue, already flashing advertisements for local businesses. She realized that riding here in this arena was the dream of every walking horse owner and rider who entered their horse in shows. To get here, they had to win competitions all year then compete against each other until the final twenty or so horses and riders—polished, lacquered, groomed, sored— swept through the in-gate into the lights, slamming against a wall of cheers from the audience.

The stands filled steadily. Capacity, she guessed, would be about twenty-five thousand people, but she should check to be sure. People arrived carrying folding stadium seats because they knew the bleachers didn't have backs. She hadn't known and hadn't brought anything to lean or sit on.

"What time's the first class?" she asked her neighbor.

"Seven-thirty."

"I thought you said it was about to start," she said.

"Time's relative," he replied. "I've waited all year for this. An hour is nothing."

So there was plenty of time to explore. She stood and sidestepped to the stairs then descended until she spotted an EXIT sign. She left the arena and passed a little park where a group of musicians performed country music. Their audience clapped and swayed, stamped, and at the end of each song, shouted "more!"

Billie headed over to the rows of barns. Dozens of identical buildings were tricked out in banners and decorated with flowers and fake lawns. The whole area teemed with trainers, riders, and grooms. Walking horses were being led, ridden, washed, brushed, tacked up, and untacked.

The phone in Billie's pocket buzzed. Without looking to see who was calling, she pressed decline, opened the camera app, and snapped a shot of the scene before her. She texted it to Frank then checked her missed calls.

Richard. She was redialing when the voice mail light flashed.

"Billie, are you here at the show? Call me."

She tapped call back. "I'm here," she said when he answered.

"Meet me at the fried pickles."

"The what?" but he'd hung up. For a moment she wondered if she should give up on Richard, just let him go. But he could probably guide her better than anyone, if he would.

When she found him, he handed her a Diet Coke and offered her a taste of his fried pickles. She declined, reading the menu board aloud. "Fried Snickers? Fried Oreos? Fried butter? Why did I think you were joking?"

"Best food in the South here. Did you see about Bo?"

"What about him?"

"Look up!" He pointed to the massive screen facing them at the far end of the arena displaying Bo's name.

"He's going to play the national anthem at the start tonight."

"Will he sing it?"

"Nope. Fiddle it."

"Seriously? I knew he played but I didn't know he was that good."

"Seriously good," Richard said. "He loves it."

While they talked, she took pictures. Of the menu. Of overweight people lined up for fried butter. Of people in souvenir hats. Of hardworking hands—calloused, wrinkled and stained—gripping programs. Of fathers with toddlers on their shoulders. Of corn on the cob. Of Richard.

"Hey!" he objected.

"Just for me," she promised. "Where's Sylvie?"

"With Dale. Getting her horse ready."

"How can you reconcile being against soring and having your daughter ride sore horses?"

"Is this an interview?"

"I guess."

"Well, I can't reconcile it. And I can't do anything about it. Sylvie is almost eighteen. I can't stop her. I may not agree with what she'd doing, but she's too grown up now for me to control. Doesn't mean I sanction it. She's my daughter and I love her."

"And the rest of your family?"

"I can't speak for them. We all grew up soring horses. I've quit and I'm speaking out against it. That makes me unpopular with my own kinfolk. But I'm doing what I think is right. And so are they."

"They think soring is right?"

"Let's say, they think it's *their* right. Billie, can we quit this interview and just be ourselves for a while? It seems I'm on stage all the time now. Press and media interviews and then all of it all over again. I'd like to just be with you, not your editor, not your iPhone, not your notebook. Can we?"

"Can you tell me how Alice Dean is?"

"She's home now. She'll be fine."

"I'm glad. Yes, we'll just be us."

"I'd kiss you if I could."

She watched his lips as he spoke, imagining them, remembering them and the shape of his earlobe, the taste of his neck.

"Stop it," he grinned at her.

"Can't."

He leaned forward to whisper, "I'm sorry I couldn't make it last night. Can I see you later?"

His breath fluttered the hair at the nape of her neck.

"I'm working," she said.

"You have to stop sometime. Call me later."

"Maybe," she said, aware of glances their way. "I'll be sure to watch Bo's performance."

Billie finished her Coke and tossed the paper cup into a trash bin. She descended a flight of metal stairs to the ground floor where the horses were prepared to enter the arena. She caught a glimpse of Sylvie leading her horse through the massive metal double doors into the enclosed inspection area. Billie tried to follow, but a guard told her it was closed to the public. She pulled out her press pass.

"Inside then," he told her. "But you have to go up to the landing. No one on the floor except competitors, their teams, and the inspectors."

She climbed the stairs to a balcony crowded with reporters. Bored by what seemed to be nothing going on below, they were chatting with each other, telling stories of other assignments. Billie apologized her way to the front, where she could see over the rail.

Below her a half dozen horses were being led in tight circles around traffic cones. The horses tripped and stumbled over their padded shoes. Each horse was attended by a handler or two and a trio of inspectors who palpated and swabbed their lower legs and hooves.

Dale stood beside Sylvie, holding her horse's reins. From where Billie stood overhead, the horse looked profoundly miserable. He squatted on his haunches and shifted his weight from one front foot to the other. As the inspector bent to examine the horse's legs, it pulled away. Dale extracted a cigarette from his pocket and lifted it toward the animal's eye. The horse froze and remained motionless during the rest of the inspection.

Billie expected someone to comment on what she'd seen, the horse intimidated into immobility, cued by the cigarette—just like in the video of Dale that Charley had given her.

The babble of reporters gossiping continued around her. A fan roared. The inspector said something Billie couldn't hear. No one was going to mention the cigarette.

"He's stewarding that horse with a cigarette," she yelled over the voices, into the fan's roar.

Dale's head swung toward her. Sylvie looked up. And so did the inspectors. And the other competitors. Immediately Dale started talking to the inspectors, making not-me gestures.

Billie spent the next half hour watching, marveling at what the inspectors seemed to ignore. Then she wandered off to find the restroom. As she left the toilet, she was startled when Eudora stepped quickly up to her. The older woman stuck out her hand, and as Billie reached to shake it, she grabbed Billie's hand and pressed something hard and round against her ribs.

"Stay close to me," Eudora said. "Or I *will* shoot you."

CHAPTER 27

THE GUN—BILLIE HAD no doubt that it was a gun—prodded her foreword, but if she moved too fast, Eudora tightened her grip and pulled her back. They left the arena and made their way outdoors through a drizzle past throngs of people to Dale's barn.

Eudora shoved Billie into a heavily draped stall where horses were taken for the final prep before going into the show ring. Someone slapped a thick wad of cotton over Billie's eyes, tied a rag over that to completely block any light, and dug her phone out of her pocket.

"You are a serious problem, my dear." She recognized Dale's voice. "I'd hoped we could manage you—for your own good as well as ours. But that's not working out."

He grabbed her wrists and yanked her hands behind her back. Pain sizzled through her shoulder as he wrenched her rotator cuff. She felt it tear, a growing agony filled her world, worse and worse. She screamed. He slapped his hand over her mouth then hit her on the side of her head, one sharp crack.

She awoke to the stench of urine and manure and pain that nearly overwhelmed her. Her head hurt, and her shoulder screeched. When she tried to move, she couldn't. The effort exploded in her rotator cuff, and her effort to suck in air to scream alerted her that she was gagged as well as bound and blindfolded. Claustrophobic panic made her struggle. She fought herself to stillness, made herself barely inhale, made herself still.

She didn't know where she was, if she was alone. What, besides horse waste, did she smell? What, besides pain, did she feel? If she made her breaths inaudible, she could hear a PA system in the distance, announcing something. She must still be at the show. She wondered how long she'd been unconscious. She heard voices coming closer. Terror washed through her. She heard a horse snort nearby. She smelled more manure, fresh. The horse was as terrified as she was. The handle of a door turned, the voices suddenly came very close to her. She forced herself to lie completely limp.

Footsteps approached, paused. Dale said, "She's still out."

She waited for the answer, but there wasn't one. He must have turned from her, because when he spoke again, his voice sounded farther away. "You want to buff those boots before you go," he said. "Just because they almost disqualified you in the last class doesn't mean—"

"I know! Where's the fucking rag?" Sylvie snapped.

"Behind you, on the shelf."

"What's he need?"

Billie didn't understand the question at first, but Dale replied, "Three drops left front, two on the right should get it done."

"Which bottle?

"That one." The horse started to scrabble, trying to get away.

"Quit!" Dale growled at him. "God damn you son of a bitch. Get in there, Sylvie, and get it done."

"No!" Billie tried to shout, but at most she made a soft grunt behind the gag. The restraint made her crazy, and she thrashed on the floor, desperate to stop them, desperate to get loose.

A boot landed on her neck, compressing her larynx and cutting off her air. She tried to twist her head away and heard Sylvie laugh.

"What's going on?" Richard's voice.

"We found your girlfriend, Dad."

"Get that horse ready," Dale said. "I'm not telling you again."

"Make *her* do it," Sylvie said. "I want to see her do that."

"We don't have time for this crap, Sylvie. You'll miss the class, and you're already in trouble."

Dale grabbed Billie by her sore arm and stood her up, unknowable agony buckling her legs. She swayed, and he shoved her backward until something hit her behind the knees, forcing her to sit down. She turned her head, trying to find the tiniest bit of light beneath the blindfold. Searing jabs shot from her head, bruised where Dale had punched her, and her neck where she had been stepped on. She tried to swallow but couldn't.

"Give me the juice," Richard said. "I like to use two drops on the right and three on the left. Suit you?"

Eudora's voice answered. "Put some of this on his pasterns and use those chains."

Billie realized that Richard was soring Sylvie's horse, dripping chemicals on its legs like the old pro he was. His protestations that he was out of this life, the interviews he'd given about seeing the light and changing his ways, his damnation of all things Big Lick—all lies. She had believed him, stupidly in love. The media had believed him. Still did. The light of righteous reformation shone on his head, but it was all false.

When they finished with the horse, Billie heard the thud of its padded hooves on the stall floor, approaching her, passing her by.

"You're on your way," Eudora said. "Dale'll be right behind you."

"We want to be there when Bo performs," Richard said.

"I'll try to get there too," Eudora replied. "And Dale. Don't want to miss him."

"What you going to do with her?" Richard asked.

"Put her there."

Billie wondered where there was.

"Make sure you lock it," Richard said.

Billie felt the last shred of hope leave. Then return. Maybe he'd come for her later when he could.

Without a word, Eudora lifted her from her seat on the tack box, opened its lid, and shoved her in, slamming it closed. Billie heard the hasp close, then the metallic fumble and click of a padlock. The space was smaller than the trunk of a car, and far from empty. She lay on something curved and hard that dug into her hip—a stirrup or some grooming implement. She was folded tightly, her knees to her chest, her hands tied behind her, and she lay directly on them. Everything hurt. There was no room to maneuver into a more comfortable position. The box stank of liniments and chemicals. She wondered how much oxygen was in there. The realization that she might smother made her force herself to breathe slowly, evenly, counting her in and out breaths. Doing that calmed her a little. Tiny breaths. Light tiny breaths. There was nothing she could do about the pain, not in her shoulder, her head, neck, or wrists. Her world was pain, but she concentrated on leaving it behind. *Not my pain,* she thought. Doesn't matter. She wasn't completely successful, but she was able to get the sensations to seem less important.

In her mind she made herself smaller, then smaller still, bringing herself toward a center she visualized, a place where she was all right, where she could move. Her fingers felt around the tiny area they could reach. Her T-shirt, the waistband of her jeans beneath it, the stitching on a hip pocket. She felt a small round rivet, softened a bit by the T-shirt.

Infinitesimally, she coaxed the shirt up. From the arena, she heard an announcement, cheers. A voice intoned the Lord's Prayer, followed by applause.

"Please, now," Billie heard, "all y'all rise and place your hands on your hearts for our national anthem played for us by Shelbyville's own rising country fiddler, Bo Collier!"

The single opening note of the anthem, achingly sweet on the violin, reached her as the tip of her middle finger slipped just past the rivet and barely inside her hip pocket.

She felt nothing but fabric. She didn't even know if there was anything in the pocket she could use. Her fingers were numb from loss of circulation, but she often carried things—not even really aware of them—a pen, some baling twine, a knife. If only she had a knife, she might, just might be able to . . . to what? She couldn't escape the locked box, but that didn't matter, any iota of relief she could manage, she would take. A looser twist of whatever bound her wrist, a slight wiggle to move herself off the sharp edge of whatever she lay upon. She forced herself to move her finger deeper into the pocket, ignoring the agony it caused her shoulder. *What the fuck?* The shoulder was ruined. She had nothing to protect.

The tip of her finger touched something hard and narrow. She tried to remember what was in there but couldn't. Might be a credit card. She flattened it against the outside of the pocket and tried to work it up. Her finger slipped. She wriggled it back down, pressed against the object, tried again to slide it up.

Bo was elaborating on the tune with riffs of fast notes. She wanted it to last, perhaps his playing was keeping Dale and Eudora and Sylvie away from her. When he stopped, they might return. With Richard.

She managed to get her index finger inside the pocket and to get a tentative grasp on whatever the thing was. She had it, lost it, got it again. Pressing the pad of her middle finger down and the nail of her index finger up, she held onto it long enough to get its top edge over the top seam of her pocket.

She had to stop. Just for a minute. She had no more strength and no more feeling in her hand. She wasn't even certain that she still held on.

Outside the barn, she could hear people talking, horse hooves passed by, the rev of an ATV engine.

The anthem ended to cheers. They'd be back soon. She had to get whatever it was out of her pocket. She heard herself grunt and thought she might have it in her hand. She felt tingles but nothing that told her for sure. As fast as she could, she raised her shoulder and removed her hand from her pocket, praying that she held whatever it was in her hand.

She explored the shape with her deadened thumb and despair flooded her. It was just a credit card. She remembered sliding it into her pocket when she paid for her ticket.

Her hands had moved a bit in their ties as she struggled to grasp the card. She didn't know what her bonds were made of, rope or baling twine or wire. She didn't hear Dale's voice until he was close by.

"Grab the other handle, okay? Let's take this out to the trailer."

There was no answer, but she felt her feet rise higher than her head. Whoever had grabbed that end wasn't strong enough, and dropped it. Somehow Billie managed not to make a sound when she hit the ground.

"Use two hands," Dale said.

Whoever they were lifted the tack box with her in it. She felt them half-stagger out the stall door then around to the side of the barn where the trailer was parked. The metal door banged open, and she was heaved inside. Someone grabbed a handle and dragged the box away from the door. Every bump sent jolts of pain through her, but she kept quiet, holding her moans inside.

"Give me the key!" Dale's breathless voice sounded annoyed. "Hurry."

She heard the gear bags that hung on the inside of the trailer's tack room door bump and their contents rattle. She heard the key turn the lock, and they were gone.

She had shifted position. Her hands lay atop a soft cloth lump. She wiggled her fingers into the material, searching for something, anything. Tears choked her, tears she halted as fast as she could. She didn't want to drown on her own damned snot.

The rags felt greasy, and she tried to imagine what they'd been used for. Then the burn started—slowly at first, then spreading and intensifying over her palms, between her fingers, onto the backs of her hands and up her wrists.

Pain made her want to scream but she couldn't. She had to think. Maybe there was something else nearby, something useful. She forced her hands deeper into the saturated fabric, intensifying the burn. Nothing. She dug deeper, feeling like she was sticking her arms into flames. She felt something hard and thin, didn't know what it was but pressed her wrists against it, harder and harder, trying to saw across it. With two short, stabbing jolts, her wrists separated. She wrenched at the blindfold then pulled the gag out of her mouth. In the dark of the tack box, she couldn't see anything. She patted around, her hand finally touching something hard and curved. She hoped for a hoof pick but quickly realized it was just a useless horseshoe. But maybe not useless.

She wedged it between the lid and body of the box and wiggled it to the lock. There she slammed it as hard as she could with her hand. The lock held, but the top edge of the box gave. She saw light and struck again, then again and again. Finally, she was able to wedge an arm into the space and force it open.

She crawled out and looked around. The door was locked, so she couldn't exit that way. But the divider between the tack room and the first stall didn't reach the floor. She dropped down and slid beneath it then crawled underneath the next one. She pushed on the main door to the trailer, the one the horses entered through. She heard the latch rattle. The door didn't budge. She looked around. Light poured into the space from narrow slats near the top of the trailer's sidewalls, spaced too closely together for her to get her hand through. But the slats at the top of the back door had a little more room. She crammed her hand between the bottom slat and the solid part of the door, squeezing her knuckles and scraping her skin. She pushed her forearm into the space as far as it would go and felt around. With the tips of her fingers, she felt the door handle but couldn't make her arm go in further, couldn't get the inches she needed to grab it. Knowing she might get stuck, she crammed her arm further, then further still. Her fingers wrapped around the metal handle and she tried to pull to lift it. Stuck! Her arm had swollen, and she couldn't get it out.

She spat onto her skin where it met the trailer slats, spat until she had no more spit. She pulled again. Her arm slipped, she pulled the lever, and the door swung open.

CHAPTER 28

DISORIENTED, BILLIE GLANCED around the alley behind Dale's barn. People in the distance led horses, rode, and strolled from barn to barn. An elderly couple in an electric golf cart rolled past her. She fought an impulse to duck and hide, an even stronger impulse to go find water—a drinking fountain would do—to try to rinse the burning chemicals off her arms. Instead, she smiled and raised her hand in what she prayed was a casual greeting. They waved back. She didn't see anyone else nearby and no one seemed to have noticed her. From the arena, she heard the announcer calling horses and riders into the ring. Dale and Eudora and Sylvie were probably there. She didn't know how long she'd been in the tack box, then in the trailer. If one of Sylvie's classes was going on now, that would give Billie time to get away while everyone was at the arena.

This is going to be one hell of a good article, she thought through the pain in her arms, through her fear. She forced her hand into her front pocket, feeling for her phone. Gone. Of course, they'd taken it from her. There were phone booths on the arena grounds, holdovers from a pre-cell phone age, but she wasn't about to stop to use one to call Frank. That time would be better spent searching for her own phone.

She found it in the barn tack room, discarded on the floor and partially covered with hay. It had been smashed beyond any hope of repair, but she returned it to her pocket anyway.

She took a deep breath and stepped out from the barn onto the walkway. A team of carriage horses decked out in the Big Lick boots trotted past her. She didn't see until they passed that Sylvie stood behind them, her back to Billie, surrounded by a bunch of teenagers. Spurs jangled off their heels, and the legs of their pants were turned up to keep them from dragging in the dirt. Sylvie was handing out an armload of sodas and cigarettes. The blue roan stallion stood beside her, its reins held by a stocky redheaded boy about her age. She leaned toward him for a lingering kiss, took the reins from his hand and turned to put her foot in the stirrup. And saw Billie. For the briefest moment, they stared at each other.

Billie bolted into a tight alley between buildings and pressed herself against the wall. She struggled against a panicky need to escape, run anywhere, hide. Her mind racing with images of the showgrounds, she took a deep breath and held it. She couldn't just flee. She had to get the story. For Frank. For herself. For the horses. Her legs felt weird and tingly from being cramped up in the tack box, but she had to keep moving or they'd catch her. Should she take time to try contacting the police? Dale had dodged an indictment, no problem. It would just be her word against his. Not much chance of success. A federal marshal? How long would that take? She'd have to find one then get a search going for evidence in the box she'd been locked in. If she could even find someone to believe her.

She decided to slip into the crowd, let the flow of people carry her to the in-gate and disappear into the turmoil there. She expelled the breath she'd been holding, drew in another, and stepped out of the alley.

A dense crowd surrounded her, people pushing in opposite directions. Some tried to reach the metal stairway that led up to the bleachers, while others shoved and dodged toward the inspection area and the vendors beyond. She remembered Addie saying that she had seats somewhere near food in the grandstand. Billie decided to head there. First, she had to cross a pathway, a sort of chute—designated for horses leaving the warm-up and inspection area to enter the arena. A class was announced as Billie approached. Shouts drew her attention down that pathway into a covered area where horses and riders milled about. Fluorescent lights shone down from the high ceiling, casting a greenish light.

"Look out!" A woman in riding clothes shoved her out of the way.

A cluster of people surrounded a Big Lick horse as it staggered into the chute. They shouted at each other and at the horse, goading it to frenetic excitement. Its ears pinned back, eyes ringed in white, saliva dripping from its mouth. The horse reeked of terror. Billie recognized Simeon, the man she had met in his derelict barn, the man whose horse she'd ridden. She realized that the black horse in front of her was that same one, Jazz, now led by his owner. Simeon saw her, recognition flickering briefly in his face before Royal shouted something that took his father's attention away from her.

Behind them, Sylvie sat astride Dale's blue roan. Eudora hung onto its shanked bit while Charley snapped a rag over the girl's boots. He rolled down her pants leg so the cuff settled across her instep and dipped below her heel, then reached up and tugged at her jacket until it lay smoothly. Dale wrestled the horse's broken tail into a waterfall of hair then lashed it into a metal tail set, slapping the horse each time it tried to kick him away. When it tried to sit down to escape the torment, Dale punched it in the belly.

Billie noticed that as he did this, he was also watching the inspectors at work behind him. At a moment when they became especially busy looking at other horses, she saw him mouth to Eudora, "Okay, now."

Eudora bent to adjust the chains around the horse's legs. Billie saw her slip a screwdriver from her pocket and use it to tighten the metal bands holding the stacked shoes onto the hooves. Almost instantly, the horse shifted its weight from foot to foot. Eudora looked up at Sylvie and nodded. Sylvie gathered the reins, sat tall, and set her spurs into the horse's flanks. It leaped forward, scattering handlers and inspectors.

Sylvie spotted Billie and pointed. Eudora darted at her like a snake striking. Billie ducked, tried to run, but the crowds blocked her.

"Coming through!" She slipped into the stream of spectators and allowed it to carry her deeper into the viewing areas around the arena then up a flight of metal stairs into the grandstand.

The bleachers were packed. She climbed over the benches below the walkway and sat down, looking toward the inspection area, then the food kiosks. Her heart banged in her throat, and she gasped for breath.

"You okay?" the elderly man seated in front of her had turned and was staring. Billie realized she was breathing quick, audible gasps.

She nodded. "It's hot!"

"Need a doctor?"

She shook her head no. "I'll be okay in a minute. Thanks."

She thought she felt her phone vibrate in her pocket and pulled it out to answer, but its screen was still blank, the glass a spiderweb of cracks.

"I think it's broken," the man in front of her said.

She nodded then turned back to look at the crowd. She didn't see anyone following her, but they'd come soon. They couldn't let her escape to charge them with kidnapping. And if they caught her, she was dead.

She tapped the old man's shoulder. "Can I borrow your phone? Just for a moment?"

He handed her an ancient flip phone and she thanked him.

She got Frank's voice mail. "I'm at the Big Show—the big horse show championship. I was kidnapped and locked up. I got free. I'm hurt but I'm going back. Dale Thornton did it to me. He's in the news for soring horses. Just telling you in case I don't get out. Start by looking at him."

She slapped the phone shut and handed it back to the old man, who was staring at her. "You need help?"

She tried to smile. "I'm okay."

"You don't sound it."

Quickly, she stood and thanked him again. She headed back down to the warm-up area.

"Ladies and gentlemen!" the announcer rejoiced. "Put your hands together and welcome the best of the best of the walking horse breed. Vying for this year's world grand champion title!"

A groom pushed past Billie as she made her way toward the in-gate. A brown and white spotted horse, rider up, surrounded by crew, loomed ahead of her. Behind them, a dozen or more horses milled around or stood tied or held by grooms in the final moments of preparation before going into the ring. She recognized Sylvie's golden ponytail at the back of the group in the warm-up area and ducked behind a pillar in case she turned.

". . . from Rocky Top, Tennessee riding, well, *Rocky Top!*"

Billie realized she'd only been half listening to the blaring announcer. At the name *Rocky Top,* the rider in front charged his brown and white stallion through the chute toward the arena. His crew ran alongside, whooping and whipping the horse's belly and flanks. Despite the pain in his feet and legs, the stallion moved faster and faster, spurred forward into a solid wall of hoots, cheers, stomping, and clapping from the audience.

A hand fell heavily onto Billie's shoulder. Would anyone hear her scream in the din? She spun, ready to fight for her life.

"Hey you!" Simeon still held the reins of the horse he'd tried to sell her. "If you'd bought him, you'd be on your way to glory tonight!"

She had to fight for his meaning, that he was talking not about her danger but about the shrieking audience, the brilliant lights, and the trembling horse he held.

"Get your fat ass over here, Royal," he shouted to his son. In full dress riding clothes, his shiny black pants legs folded up to stay clean, bowler hat crammed onto his head and sweat pouring from beneath its brim, Royal shuffled over. He nodded to Billie and, grunting, heaved himself into the saddle. Jazz sagged then recovered.

Stressed though she was, Billie noticed how well Royal sat the horse, as if he'd left a hundred pounds behind him.

"When do you go in?" she asked.

"He's next to last," his father answered for him.

"How are you feeling?"

"Like barfing." Royal answered for himself.

"You'll be fine," she told him. She glanced over toward Sylvie, who still seemed unaware of her.

"I know! But you asked how I feel and that's how I feel. Doesn't mean I will barf, just that I could."

She stepped back against the wall and wished she could call Frank again. If only she had a working phone. He might answer. He might even be calling her now . . .

She heard her name and turned. Richard embraced her.

"How great to see you!" His arms tightened around her, rigid as metal strapping. "I've got people I want you to meet after the show."

She tried to wrench away but he held her. "Come with me," he said loudly. "How's things in Arizona? I sure do miss it there."

His arm around her, he guided her toward the chute, held her in waiting behind the next horse to enter, then shoved her along behind. "Come sit with me while we watch Sylvie," he roared. "Won't be long now." He pushed her forward, up the stairs to the lowest tier of benches then to a stretch of empty seats. He shoved her into one and sat beside her, never letting go.

"What the fuck is going on?" she demanded.

"Hang on a minute!" he shouted into her ear as the audience around them exploded into applause and cheers when another horse entered the arena. "You're a dead woman if Dale gets you."

"What am I if he *doesn't* get me?"

She lost his answer in the blare of the announcer's call for yet another horse to enter.

"You're hurting me! My arms are burning from stuff I got on them!"

"Sorry," he said. "This'll help it for a few minutes." He pulled a small aerosol can from his back pocket and sprayed her arm. Instantly the pain stopped.

"What was that?"

"Lidocaine."

"That's the stuff the inspectors are looking for!"

"And aren't you glad I have some? I'm glad you're free, Billie. You saved me the risk of going back to get you."

"You asshole! You're part of this. I couldn't see you, but I heard you with Eudora and Dale. I heard you agree to sore Sylvie's horse. You told me you were through with all that. You goddamned lying—"

"Wait! You've got it wrong!"

Billie stood to leave. Richard pulled her back into her seat.

"Ow! My shoulder!"

He let go of her. "What happened?"

"You try being tied up and thrown into a tack box and see how you make out."

"I'm truly sorry Billie, but still—you've got this all wrong. Please just think a minute and imagine what I walked into," he said. "You tied up on the floor. Eudora with a gun. And my daughter there in the middle of it all, acting like this was some kind of lark! I had maybe two seconds to get her out of there before she became an accessory to kidnapping. She could have ended up in prison. You could have been shot. I'd sore a hundred horses if that's what it took to get the two most . . . to get you and Sylvie to safety."

The crowd exploded into cheers as Jazz entered the arena.

"What about the horse you sored, Richard?"

"It doesn't matter."

"It matters to the horse!"

"You matter more, Billie. Surely by now you realize that everything you're doing to expose the walking horse industry puts you in danger. Your barn was burned as a warning—"

"And to destroy evidence, Richard! That fire killed a filly your friends had nearly crippled."

"They're not my friends anymore Billie, and I told you before I'm doing what I can." He pointed toward Sylvie, just visible in the warm up area, poised and ready to perform. "That's my little girl same as Alice Dean. Alice Dean's getting help. Now it's time for Sylvie to get help."

Billie stood up. "Might be time for you and Mary Lou to get some too."

"Where are you going?" he asked.

"I'm getting to work."

"Please sit. You're safe here with me—"

"Dale and Eudora are busy watching Sylvie." She hoped that was true. "Goodbye, Richard."

The audience roared as Sylvie entered the arena. Grooms ran beside her horse, slapping its belly with a crop, shouting along with the crowd. Billie expected to see Charley running along too, but he didn't appear. Billie glanced at Richard, who was focused on his daughter's entrance. As best she could in the crowd, she ran, intent on circling the arena to find the fried chicken stand and Addie.

Before she reached the arena exit, Dale stepped out in front of her from behind a huge stack of hay bales. The last thing she remembered before blacking out was a knot of baling twine on the ground and the feel of his thumbs digging into her neck.

CHAPTER 29

BILLIE SMELLED HAY. Her hands were tied behind her back, and her knees and ankles were tied together. There was tape on her mouth. She tried to straighten her legs and bumped into what felt like a bale. When she pushed with her feet, her head contacted another bale. She tried to wriggle into a sitting position, but pain in her shoulder made her moan. On her second attempt she bumped into hay overhead and fell backward. She seemed to be sealed into the middle of a mow. How big it was, she couldn't guess. It might be just one bale in each direction, or a dozen.

She could hear the PA system but couldn't tell how far away it was. She didn't know how much the hay would dampen sound. Above the crowd's roar, the announcer bellowed Sylvie's name. Youngest rider ever, he said. Then he announced the horse's owner—Eudora Thornton—and trainer—Dale Thornton.

"In spite of meddling by our government!" she heard. "In spite of the war being waged against our sport and our breed! War against our very way of life!" he shouted. "We take PRIDE in this victory! PRIDE in our glorious breed! PRIDE in our trainers and owners and riders!"

With each shouted *PRIDE* the audience roared louder, screamed more shrilly, whistled.

"Victory lap!" the announcer bellowed to more roars.

She wrenched her body against the ties, beat her feet against the bale, trying to push it away. She hurt. She wanted to go home and forget she'd ever learned anything about walking horses. She'd write whatever Frank wanted her to write, never argue with him again. She missed Gulliver. What would become of him and her horses if she didn't make it out of this?

She heard Dale and Eudora nearby, their voices muffled by the arena's cacophony.

Then she heard Eudora ask, "What about our friends in the hay?"

"Unfortunate accident awaits. Spontaneous combustion. Nasty."

Friends? Billie wondered. Her arms burned, the pain increasing moment by moment. She shut her eyes and clenched her teeth. A bale thudded onto the pile above her, then another. Someone was out there, stacking them on her.

"*Please!*" she cried into the tape that covered her mouth. "*Help me!*"

In her mind she saw the filly Hope burned to death, limbs contracted, face contorted into a scream. Billie saw the empty eye sockets and smelled burned flesh.

"*No! Please!*" But no sound escaped her gag.

She felt the thuds of hoof beats approaching, slowing, stopping. Sylvie said something she couldn't make out either, but she heard the girl's excitement.

"We'll go to the inspectors," Dale said. "Now!" and the hooves retreated.

Billie pictured Sylvie and the horse waiting for their turn with the inspectors, Sylvie leading him in tight circles to the left and right around the traffic cones, leading him away then back toward the veterinarians. She imagined them bending to examine his legs, palpating for tenderness, flinches, pain. Looking for scars while Dale stood close by, cigarette dangling from his lips.

"Can you hear me?" Charley's voice. He coughed, ending in a long, gasping retch.

"Yes!" she shouted, silently.

"They got me in here with you," he said. "They put something in my inhaler. Rompun, I think. Can't breathe. I can't get out of this hay pile. Maybe you can. Don't you forget what I gave you. My last words. Remember."

She listened for more, but there wasn't any.

She tried to struggle loose, but they'd tied her tighter this time. This time she wasn't going anywhere.

"All okay with the inspector?" she heard Eudora ask.

"Close call," Dale answered. "But we got through."

"I smell gas." Sylvie's voice.

"I got some from maintenance for the ATV," said Eudora. "It's almost out. Let's go celebrate."

"Where's my dad?" Sylvie asked. "And Bo?"

"We're meeting them at the Road House," Dale said. "Charley's already loaded the horses, but the trailer's got a flat, so he's going to change it and catch up with us."

Billie didn't want to die like this. All the times in her life she'd cut and burned herself on purpose, the times she'd nearly killed herself working for Frank, or riding horses, or at home alone in drunken despair. Not like this, murdered in a fire in the type of place she loved most of all, a barn with horses, dying to the sound of her screams and theirs.

Dale, Eudora, and Sylvie left, their excited voices drifting away. A door closed. She was alone. Waiting. She didn't know for what. Someone to come back with a lighter, a match.

The door opened.

She stopped struggling to listen, waiting for the sound that would start the inferno.

Silence. Then a grunt. Another. And another. Someone was moving the bales. She tried to scream again, roaring into the tape that covered her mouth.

"Is someone there?" a male voice.

Light poured onto her. She shrank away, terrified that it was fire. Fingers probed her hair, her head, snagged her ear, grabbed at her shirt.

"Oh my God!"

Bo ripped the tape from her mouth and cut the baling twine that bound her.

"What happened?" he asked over and over. "What happened? I came back for my fiddle and smelled gasoline."

"Go," she said to Bo. "I won't tell them you were here."

"You sure?"

She nodded.

He backed away, eyes wide and wild. "I'm sorry. I'm so sorry!"

"You need to get out of here *now*, Bo. Run!"

He turned and darted for the door, slamming it behind him.

Billie reached for Charley between bales. She touched his

arm, fumbled for his wrist, and felt for a pulse. None. She changed her grip and tried again. Nothing.

Voices sounded outside. The door rattled. Billie crouched behind the stacked hay, hoping that whoever entered wouldn't notice it had been tampered with. The hay hook Bo had used to pull the bales off of her lay on the floor. She picked it up, ran her hand from the tip of the red metal hook to the wooden handle.

When the door opened, Eudora and Dale were arguing.

"He was turning us in," Eudora said.

"He wasn't the first bastard to try. This will take care of him—and her."

Billie prayed that one of them would leave. She didn't know how she'd manage to take them both on.

"I'm going to settle up with Dom," Eudora said.

As if in answer to her prayer, Billie heard the door close.

"So long," Dale said.

For an instant, she didn't realize he was talking to her, addressing her where he thought she lay trussed in the middle of the hay. He struck a match. She smelled it, heard the whoosh of flame as it caught. Fire raced along the bales as he lit them. The room became an instant inferno, the air vicious as venom. The hair on her face singed. Dale stood between her and the exit. His eyes widened with surprise when he saw her. She had to get out.

"MOVE!" She couldn't hear her own scream over the fire's roar.

Dale stepped backwards, toward the door. He would step out and close it with her inside, she knew. Ignoring the searing pain in her shoulder, Billie swung the hay hook with both hands, bringing it down as hard as she could, burying the point in his neck. He grabbed at it, fighting to pull it out, and slammed her into the wall. She braced her feet against it and pushed off, hurling herself into the flames, dragging him with her. With both hands, he clutched his neck, trying to pull the hook out. She let go and ran.

Outside, Billie collapsed retching, gasping clean night air. Eudora charged past on her way back into the barn, shrieking her husband's name. Fire wrapped around the door, crawled up the wall. The roof exploded in flames.

CHAPTER 30

BILLIE TURNED THE truck and trailer into the fair-grounds in Deming, New Mexico, parked beside an empty arena, and got out with Gulliver. They both stretched. She felt like she'd been sitting for days. Well, she had. Last week, she'd driven from Arizona to Tennessee in three days with her trailer empty. But the trip home with her new horse was taking a lot longer. Every three hours she'd pulled off the freeway to unload Jazz and lead him around to stretch his legs. She offered him water, timothy hay, and if there was grass, she let him graze. Every afternoon she stopped for the day, using Google to find fairgrounds with stalls and arenas where she could turn him out to roll and to run if he wanted to. So far he hadn't wanted to, but he had the opportunity.

She'd reach home by tomorrow afternoon, pull into the ranch, and settle Jazz into the corral she used to quarantine incoming horses. From there, he'd be able to see Starship in his corral, and the other horses in theirs. In a few weeks, she would move him so he'd be across a fence from Starship. A week or so after that, she'd turn them out together.

Billie's cell phone buzzed in her pocket. Richard. Again. She let the call go to voice mail. How many times was that? Ten? She wondered for the tenth time why she didn't just block his number.

She walked to the back of the trailer, wincing as she lifted and straightened her arms to open the door. Her rotator cuff still bothered her and she might need surgery to repair it. Most of the bandages were off her arms and hands but the skin felt hot, as if it were still burning. Scars had formed, but the doctors said they would lessen over time. She didn't know if they'd be permanent or if they'd fade to nothing. The ones on the insides of her elbows tugged and hurt when she tried to straighten her arms, but these too the doctors said would improve. She was sick of being told how lucky she was to have escaped the barn fire that claimed three human lives. No horses had died in it, but the owner, the trainer, and the head groom of Angel Hair Walkers had been incinerated.

Jazz stood tied in his trailer, his black rump to her, his face turned over his shoulder as far as the rope allowed, looking at her. Talking softly, she sidled in beside him until she could reach the rope's slipknot and undo it.

Carefully, she backed him out, letting his hind legs take the brunt of the descent onto the ground. He paused with his front feet still on the trailer floor then slowly lowered them outside, one at a time, easing his weight cautiously onto each in turn.

While Gulliver chased a prairie dog into its hole, Billie let the big horse graze some parched grass, offered him a drink from his bucket, then tied him to the outside of the trailer.

From the back of the truck, she got her kit with his

bandages and dressings and set it on the ground. Kneeling, she unwrapped his legs and examined the gauze beneath the wraps. It was still a seeping mess.

When she told Doc she was going back to Tennessee to buy Jazz and bring him home, he told her that horses who had been sored took a long time to clear the chemicals from their bodies. Now she knew what he meant. She wondered what he'd say when he came to examine his new patient tomorrow evening after she got home, what changes he'd make in the treatment. She could only hope that Jazz's prognosis would be better than the filly's had been.

With fresh gauze, she cleaned the wounds, re-treated, and re-wrapped them. She injected Jazz with his evening dose of pain medicine. Through it all, he stood immobile and trembling, still afraid he'd be battered, shocked, or burned if he moved. It was going to take a long time for him to trust her or anyone else. If he ever did.

She led him to the arena and turned him lose. Without his huge stacked shoes, she supposed he could run, but he never did. He stood rock-still, tolerating her while she petted his neck. When she backed away, he sighed his relief. She closed the gate, and he slowly walked toward a patch of weeds that looked like they might once have been grass, and nosed them.

Frank had called while she was driving and had left a message on her cell. She pulled a folding chair from the back seat of the truck and set it up in the cool wind where she could keep an eye on her horse and terrier, who was now chasing tumbleweeds. She grabbed the bag with her knitting in it, a shawl for herself this time, and told her new phone to dial *Frankly.*

Frank answered, "Where are you?"

"Deming."

"Where?"

"Southwestern New Mexico."

"Pretty?"

"Pretty flat. I'll be home at the ranch tomorrow."

"How's the horse?"

"Quiet."

"Is that good?"

"Not this kind of quiet. His legs are still weeping chemicals. He's still in pain."

"You can tell?"

She nodded.

"Billie?"

"I can tell. When will my piece run?"

"I have a proposition for you," he said.

Billie watched a dust devil form about a quarter mile away. The miniature tornado swooped and spun, ducking left then right. As it approached, it grew, lifting trash cans and wooden pallets into the air along with sand and dirt. It roared past Jazz, missing him by inches. He didn't seem to notice.

"Billie?"

"Sorry, I was watching a dust devil."

"Really? What's that?"

"What's your proposition, Frank?"

"I'll make you a contributing editor here at *Frankly*. You'll do four pieces a year for me, and I'll give you a raise. Three of the pieces I'll choose. You can choose one."

"I don't know, Frank."

"Think it over."

"I'm not coming back to New York."

"No one asked you to. Anyway, I'm getting married."

Vertigo made the chair tilt beneath her. She grabbed the truck's door handle and hung on.

"You'd be inconvenient," he said.

"Married?"

"I want you safely where you are."

He hadn't answered her about when the article would appear. Didn't he know? Of course he knew. She mustn't pressure him. He'd made her an offer. Could she say no? She had spent the money from the article within forty-eight hours of receiving the check. She'd paid Sam and Josie for watching the ranch and feeding the horses while she was gone. She'd paid Josie extra for taking care of Gulliver. She'd bought a load of hay and grain. There was enough money left over to repair the leaking roof. Instead, she had phoned Simeon. "Is that horse I rode still for sale?"

It was crazy, she knew. The horse was nearly two thousand miles away and probably crippled. It would cost a fortune to buy him, get him, treat him, care for him. But she was driven by guilt that she'd ridden him.

"I've about sold him already," Simeon told her. "Mary Lou Collier wants him."

"How much is she paying?"

"Aw, I'm headed back to Minnesota, Billie. Jazz didn't win his class so I'm practically giving him away. Hell, I am giving him away."

"Twenty-five hundred," Billie offered. "I'll trailer out and pick him up in a few days. Just have to arrange for help here then I'll come. Less than a week, okay? Deal?"

So the money was gone. She might get the reward for the information Charley left her. She had turned the thumb drive over to the Humane Society, copying it first. She didn't know if the reward would materialize, or if it did, when.

She'd spent her last dollars on another horse.

"I could use the work," she told Frank.

"Write up some ideas for me," he said.

Maybe when she got home she'd be able to think clearly. She'd ride out on Starship, across the mesa and up into the mountains, Gulliver at their heels. Maybe one day she'd be able to ride Jazz. She'd take him up into the foothills at dusk and turn him to face south so he could see the lights moving along the interstate. All her horses liked that. While Gulliver flopped down to pant, Jazz would stand watching traffic, his heart beating under her bare calves.

Ever since Dale and Eudora tried to kill her in the fire, she'd expected her sleep to erupt into nightmares about Dale's death, but so far it hadn't. She still felt the hook sink into him, felt her arm rip it through his flesh, saw his eyes when she shoved him into the fire. But she didn't feel regret or guilt or shame. Not anything except rage. Not yet anyway.

After she hung up with Frank, she used her phone to Google nearby yarn shops. She found one along her route that she might go to later in the morning. The brief stop would give Jazz a rest, and she could add to the yarn she'd collected on this trip—just a few hanks she picked up at local stores. At first they were more for souvenirs than for projects, but recently an idea for a saddle blanket for Jazz had formed in her head. So far she had one skein from Tennessee, and two from east Texas bought in a shop where she heard the new country music sensation Bo Collier on the radio.

The peaks of the Florida Mountains captured the final rays of the setting sun. A three-quarter moon rose in the darkening sky. Billie gathered Jazz's hay in her arms, stuffed it into his hay net, and carried it into the arena to give to him. He turned away from her. She left the hay on the ground and walked to the rail. Looking for Gulliver, she didn't notice Jazz come to stand beside her until his shoulder touched hers. She raised her hand and scratched his withers. Together they watched the dog and the tumbleweeds in the wind.

The End

Made in United States
Troutdale, OR
06/18/2023

10660168R00192